THE KALIS EXPERIMENTS

TIDES BOOK I

R. A. FISHER

ACKNOWLEDGMENTS

Thank you, Jennifer Wortman, John Scarboro, and Cary Wage for telling me what you thought.

Thank you, Jane Fisher. You know what you did.

Thanks most of all to Tomomi and Taiki, for believing in me long after you probably should have given up.

PROLOGUE
THE DEATH OF XEREKS LEES

THE SKY WAS RED ON THE LAST DAY OF XEREKS Lees's life.

Calveeni's dangled from the biggest mangrove tree at the western tip of Maresg, its wooden beams dappled russet by the sun squatting on the hills behind it. Whitecaps dotted the ocean and sighed up to blend their murmur with the hum of conversation. The emerald hills, like Calveeni's famed balcony, were the color of rust in the bloody light cast between the remnants of a storm that trundled out of sight to the east.

The restaurant was three stories tall and as shapeless as the rest of the buildings of Maresg, built at an angle in the fork where the trunk of the tree split into two great branches. The top floor leaned over the water, supported by more giant limbs, and the balcony jutted out even further, held aloft by a snarl of frayed ropes and wooden chains tied higher in the tree.

Xereks Lees, once one of the most powerful low merchants in Skalkaad, now one refugee among thousands who hid among the branches of the tree city, entered from the Walk with his five bodyguards trailing behind him, and pushed his way to the front of the queue. He was broad without being fat, and jowly. His silver-gray hair was pulled back in a taut, slick ponytail. His beard was a wiry dull gray, trimmed to a point and a little unkempt.

"My table, if you please," he said to the frowning host, in a pleasant voice that didn't reach his eyes.

The host, a gaunt clean-shaven man with a handsome middle-aged face, pressed his lips together and glanced at the grumbling queue behind Lees.

"It's fine today," Calveeni's tired voice called through the closed kitchen door, a moment before the proprietor himself appeared with a slight bow to Lees.

He was a lean, balding man with a black mustache that drooped to his chest, and he was a head taller than the host he stood behind. He wore a long white chef's coat, rumpled and stained with brown blotches.

"Please have a table brought up from the dining room for Mr. Lees." He turned toward the former merchant. "You prefer the south side of the balcony, do you not?"

Lees gave a little smile and nodded. "Indeed. Along the rail, if you please."

Calveeni tapped the host on the shoulder. "You heard the man. Don't keep him waiting." He gave Lees another bow. "Thank you for joining us again, Mr. Lees. I apologize for the delay. I hope you enjoy your meal." He smiled slightly behind his mustache and turned to walk back through the open door to the kitchen.

Lees pressed his lips together in an expression of thanks, and followed the host up the spiral stairs, to the upper dining room and the balcony beyond.

The balcony was always crowded, but a small table was rushed up and placed in Lees's preferred spot on the southern corner, with mumbled apologies to the patrons that needed to move their chairs to make space. The busboy set it down near the low railing and waited for Lees's curt nod of approval before scurrying back inside. When Lees looked out, it was as if he were suspended above nothing but a few stunted mangrove trees and the dark, ever-changing nothingness of the Expanse, seven hundred hands below. When Lees sat here, he was free of Maresg.

He moved his chair so that his back was to the sea, where he had the best view of the sunset without suffering its light in his eyes. Two of his bodyguards and his valet, Orvaan, took their places around him, careful not to block his view, while the other two stayed behind to hover by the door that led inside.

He stared into the horizon for a while, lost in his thoughts, letting them mingle with the shifting static sound of the distant water. He thought of his home—his real home, north in Eheene, and wondered for the thousandth time if he was a coward for hiding here. Maybe that's what they all called him now, and maybe they were right. That's the thing about being a fugitive. Too much time to think about everything he'd lost. Too much time to think about everything.

The breeze grew cool. As the sun dipped lower into the Upper Peninsula and the ruddy green of the mountains on the horizon deepened to a black silhouette, a pair of Calveeni's errand boys emerged from the kitchen and began lighting the oil lamps that ringed the balcony with long candles. Lees realized he'd been sitting there for a half an hour without being served so much as a glass of wine.

Several patrons in his immediate vicinity had cleared out, leaving him in the center of a ring of empty tables. There were probably still a dozen people downstairs seething to get a seat, but Calveeni had apparently learned when to give Lees his space. Too much space, for that matter. Lees was hungry, and more than that, he needed a drink.

He saw one of his usual serving girls—a tall, pretty, black-haired woman with a hint of the desert folk around her eyes—bring a round of cheap beer to a table of N'naradin merchant marines on the far side of the rail. Lees's scowl deepened. He was just about to tell Orvaan to get her attention when another girl he'd never seen before emerged from the swinging door and headed in his direction. She had a pitted complexion and a round, flat face. She was so short that she was only a head taller than him while he sat, and her body was lumpy and shapeless under the tight yellow and black dress Calveeni made all his girls wear. A portly, pocked-faced bee. He grimaced. Her left hand was a mangled claw, the index and middle finger torn away, the rest rutted and twisted with burns. She was altogether too grotesque to be working the balcony, except for maybe her eyes, which were large and slanted and brilliant green, and too sharp for Lees's liking. He would make a point to say something to the owner on his way out. Even in Maresg, there had to be standards.

"The usual," he spat before she had a chance to say anything.

He turned his attention back to the view. The sun was behind the Peninsula now, the sky above a blazing pink, easing first to red, then to violet overhead. To the east, a few stars began to twinkle.

She laughed a nervous laugh, which she probably thought was charming. "And what would that be?"

His scowl grew, and he turned back to her with an exaggerated sigh. "It would be what I've had the past twenty times I've come here. Exactly the same thing. If you're too incompetent to know what that is, I'm sure there's someone here who can help you."

She seemed unfazed and blinked down at him with a condescending smile. "Wouldn't it be easier for you to just tell me what you want, rather than going and being a pain in the ass about it?"

Lees's expression darkened. "I'm being patient because you're new," he said, in a low voice. "Everyone should be given a chance. You'll find I'm nothing if not fair-minded. However, I'm an important man who should be treated with respect, and I don't—"

"I know exactly what kind of *man* you are." Her voice dropped to match his, her tone etched with sarcasm.

Her blank smile had transformed into a sneer. The bodyguards grew tense.

"Yeah, I'm new at Calveeni's, but I've been in Maresg long enough to know your type. You were important, or at least you think you were. Skalkaad, if I know accents. Probably Eheene. You're the city sort. A real citizen. Some big-shot until you pissed someone off and you had to hide here. Think you're unique? You're not. Half the people in this city are hiding from someone else. People like you never learn. Here, you're nothing. And as long as you're here, that's all you'll ever be."

Lees made a last look around the balcony for Calveeni to reign in his girl, but it had cleared except for three or four tables on the north side and the drunk merchant marines along the opposite rail. Everyone avoided watching whatever was going on at his table, and in his anger, it didn't occur to him that the balcony was never this empty.

He sighed and inclined his head to the right. "Orvaan. Please."

The man on that side, balding and pear-shaped, moved more gracefully than it looked like his body would allow. He took one step forward and grabbed the girl by the wrist.

"Take this whore down to the bridge and educate her," Lees said.

The girl's eyes grew wide. She screamed and bent her knees, struggling to wrench her arm from the big man's grasp. Her panic made her stronger than Orvaan was expecting, and she almost slipped from his grasp. They grappled. An empty chair toppled. She spun around until her back was to Lees and she stood between him and his bodyguards. Lees stood, his chair clattering into the polished wood of the waist-high rail. His face was white with anger and painted pinkish-red by the evening twilight. His bodyguards by the door took their first step toward the scuffle.

The waitress finally managed to wrench her wrist free from Orvaan, and she staggered backward. Her flailing arms slammed into Lees's stomach. He doubled over with a grunted cough. She tried to straighten, holding her bruised wrist with tears in her eyes, but the back of her head collided with Lees's face. The girl cried out in pain and tripped over her own feet, lurching into Lees again, who was already off balance, now grasping his broken nose. Her fall knocked him further back, and he tumbled over the guardrail with a yelp. The girl screamed again and spun to peer over the edge of the railing, sobbing, rubbing the back of her head. Lees plummeted through the dim, pink light. He yelled something lost in the sound of the sea, then cut off as he smashed into a knot of mangrove roots exposed by the retreating tide. His body lay broken and motionless for a moment, then slid into the Expanse and vanished into the black water.

"Heaven forgive me, Heaven forgive me, Heaven forgive me," she muttered through choking sobs, backing away from the railing.

Orvaan and the other bodyguards tried to grab her, but they were slow with shock. She shrieked and darted toward the kitchen, dodging around the two who'd stood by the door, now halfway to the table.

The whole incident began and finished in a few seconds, and heads on the other side of the balcony were only now turning, curiosity overcoming empathetic embarrassment.

———

The Eye was up, almost full and filling the sky overhead, flooding the bridges of Maresg with reddish purple light. The rusty, angry oval of its pupil was wide tonight, looking off somewhere beyond the western horizon.

It wasn't late, but Calveeni had closed early. Too much excitement today, and he wanted to go to bed. He was latching up the cash box under the boards beneath his desk when there was a soft knock. He froze. He'd locked up everything before retreating to his office. Even the balcony. He stood, smoothed the small rug over the hatch in the floor, and went to the door.

It was the flat-faced serving girl, Nola, still wearing her black and yellow dress, now with a light leather jacket buttoned against the night breeze. Her green eyes were rimmed red, but she wasn't crying. Calveeni nodded and pushed the door open wider, and she ducked under his arm into the office.

He slid the bolt closed behind her. "I guess Lees's people didn't find you."

She smiled and produced a gray velvet bag. It was small enough to fit under her jacket but big enough that Calveeni was surprised it hadn't bulged more while hidden there.

She dropped it on the desk, where it settled with a metal clatter. "Thanks for the job."

He frowned at the sack, chewing on one end of his mustache, and shook his head. "Lees was a bastard, and in the month you were here you did a better job serving tables than half the girls that've worked here for years. Keep your tin."

Nola's shook her head. "It's not my tin."

He looked at the sack again and opened his mouth to protest further, but then nodded. "I guess I won't see you around here again."

"Nope." She turned and strode to the door, unlatched the lock, and softly closed the door behind her.

———

It was one of those jobs. The kind where the actual job was the easiest part. In fact, killing Xereks Lees might've been one of the easiest rubs she'd ever did, once she got around to it. Maybe the last easy rub, since these days the knot in her stomach twisted tighter, and the dreams grew darker with every job she finished.

With Lees, she got lucky, even for her. Calveeni had been one of Ormo's, even if the chef didn't know it. Nothing unusual about that. Lots of people from Skalkaad didn't know where their tin was coming from. It was safer that way, and the smart ones knew not to ask.

Of all the places Lees could've chosen to spend his time, he picked the one spot in Maresg where Ormo was going to find him without even trying. All Nola had needed to do was show up with a big sack of money and wait. Then again, someone could probably make a pretty good case for a lot of things working out that way.

Ironically, the most insignificant part of the killing Lees job was killing Lees. Weird looking back on how things work out sometimes. Weird that something as mundane as an accounting problem could turn her into whatever she'd become.

1

THE BEGINNING

IT WAS STRANGE THAT ORMO HAD ASKED SYRINA to meet him in his suite instead of his Hall, and it pricked at her thoughts as she crossed the broad court-yard toward the Palace, where the fifteen towers of the Syndicate crowded together like a bundle of blunt spears. The northern sky was thick with winter fire dancing against the glow of the Eye, whose purple and red gibbous loomed to the south and gobbled any starlight that might have competed with the flickering green and yellow in the north. The black ellipse of a private airship etched itself against the moon as it drifted toward the western dock tower.

Winter fire splashed against the high marble and obsidian walls, while the Eye drained the world of all detail, reducing the dry fountains and pacing guards to vague, two-dimensional shapes. The dull hum of the naphtha generators resonated beneath the flag-stones under her bare feet and combined with the groan of a steamship whistle rolling across Eheene from the harbor.

The cold was intense. The mercenaries manning the priceless iron gates and the tops of the walls were layered in hound skins and silk underclothes, but Syrina could still see them shivering in the dim conflagration of light. She was naked, the cold a faint nuisance in the back of her mind. No one was looking her way, and if they did, they wouldn't see more than a tick of motion across the marble flagstones their eyes wouldn't be able to follow.

She was covered with fine black tattoos. They seemed to move, coming together and branching again in infinite complexity, like a fingerprint, from the top of her bald head to the bottoms of her feet, over her lips and under her nails. Just her green eyes, guarded by black lashes, could be clearly seen. The same minute manipulation of her muscles that kept the cold at bay blended her tattoos into the surroundings until she was just a shadow, even to herself.

The Palace doors, like the larger gates to the compound behind her, were emblazoned with the Spiral of Skalkaad, but instead of etched steel, the doors were black burnished brass. The three white arms of the Spiral were opal. The three black ones set with tiny black pearls.

Syrina forced eye contact with the black and silver clad Seneschal posted at the doors until he noticed her and stepped aside with a hasty, nervous bow. The hallway stretched beyond the foyer, built from blocks of obsidian. Every twenty paces, there was a short stairway of white marble leading up to the next tier. The hall was lined with iron doors marked with spirals, but otherwise unlabeled. Above each portal was a large marble hand, palm upward, holding a hissing bluish flame. Syrina had no idea what lay behind any of the doors except for the second-to-last one on the left, and that's where she went.

Her knock against the heavy metal sounded dull, like banging on a stone wall. But a few seconds later it silently swung inward. The Seneschal who greeted her with a wordless bow didn't lead her into the study where she'd met Ormo the few other times he'd summoned her to his private quarters, though she could see the light from the fireplace glinting on the half-open bronze door that led there. Instead, the little man led her further into the chambers, to the spiral stair that led to the top of Ormo's tower.

The Seneschal left her there and disappeared back into the palace. The stairway was broad, the steps shallow. There was no guardrail. Each stair was again cut from alternating obsidian and white marble. In the center, a massive brass brazier was sunk into the floor, burning with blue flame fed by pipes that ran all the way to the naphtha cisterns buried below the city. There was no other source of light, but the brazier flickered and glowed against the polished walls all the way to the top, where Syrina could make out a mosaic of the Skalkaad Spiral set into the ceiling.

The cold didn't particularly bother her, but the warmth from the brazier was pleasant. She took her time mounting the stairs and hesitated a moment at the top to bask in the faint rising heat.

"Kalis Syrina," Ormo said when she stepped out onto the terrace.

He waved off her bow and opened his arms to fold her into his robes for a brief, warm embrace. She returned the hug, glad they were meeting in his private quarters, where Ormo preferred forgoing with the usual formality he upheld when seated on his dais.

She stepped back when he released her, taking in the details of her surroundings. Twenty years of training and nine more as one of Ormo's Kalis, but this was the first time she'd been here. A half-dome of marble arced over and behind her, robbing the view of the fourteen other palace towers and the winter fire in the north. The ubiquitous Eye loomed high over the southern horizon, rendering the steepled marble rooftops of Eheene faceless in its electric amethyst light. Beyond the city, she could make out the black plain of the Sea of Skalkaad. The bows of the ships gleamed where they anchored in the deep water beyond the harbor, slaves to the tides. The harsh glow of their beacons illuminated the thin frozen mist that had settled across the bay, but the water seemed to swallow their light. Wind came in icy gusts.

Ormo was wrapped in thick robes of blue and white, though the colors blended under the Eye into varying shades of violet. Beneath his hood, Syrina could make out the black and white geometry of his painted face. His breath froze when he exhaled, and the vapors fell like a dying bird and vanished in the shadows cast by his bulk. He was round, and the shortest of the Fifteen, but Syrina didn't quite come up to his chin.

"You have always served me well," he rumbled.

She tried to make out his expression, but it was impossible under the hood and the paint.

"I know there have been Kalis who have served their masters better than I have." She wondered why she felt uneasy.

"You're young yet. Your thirtieth year. I hope to have you for another hundred or more. That is, in fact, the reason I summoned you up here."

Syrina couldn't think of anything to say to that, so she waited. She thought she could discern a smile from the shadows under his hood. Anxiousness and excitement vied for control of her stomach.

Ormo put his thumb and little finger in his mouth and let out a high, warbling whistle. A second later, a white and silver owl with wings flecked in black swooped from behind the half-dome and floated down to perch on his shoulder. It settled and blinked at Syrina with round, curious eyes. It stood twice as large as Ormo's hooded head, and tufts of dark feathers stood from its crown, curving inward like horns or pointed black ears.

She couldn't think of anything to say to that either.

"His name is Triglav. A good name. A god ancient even to the ancestors. A god of war. Appropriate, maybe. Especially if you were to take him as your pet."

Syrina blinked. She'd never heard of a Kalis receiving a gift before, much less a pet, and she said as much. But even as she spoke, she felt a pang of something unfamiliar when she looked at the owl. She realized, inexplicably, that she liked it.

"That's true," Ormo replied.

Now she was sure she could hear a smile in his voice.

"Take him as an exception to tradition, then, in exchange for your future loyalty."

"You have my loyalty already, Ma'is, now and always."

But an alien sense of mistrust seeded her gut. Ormo didn't do anything without a reason.

He gave a slight shake of his arm, and Triglav

floated over to Syrina's shoulder and stayed there, gently grasping her naked skin with black, needle-sharp talons. She felt the tug of affection again, stronger this time, and it leaned over to press its head against hers. She guessed it liked her, too.

"Of that, I have no doubt," he said.

"And how do you think this bird is going to help me?"

Ormo let out a deep chuckle and reached out a gloved hand to pat her cheek. "It's a clever creature and well-trained. Just as you are. I have faith that you'll find many uses for him in the years to come."

"Of course," Syrina said, without hesitation, pushing aside a hundred questions buzzing around her head. "So what would you have me do, Ma'is?"

"Only what I would always have you do, Kalis. Now here is a name..."

2

THE ACCOUNTING PROBLEM

IT WASN'T LEES'S NAME THAT ORMO GAVE HER then. It was more than a year before his name came up. In the meantime, things returned to business as usual for Syrina, with the addition of Triglav. Watch him, steal that, kill her. Working with the owl became as natural for her as it had being alone. He seemed to know her thoughts, and he always did what she wanted.

When Lees's name came up, it came up like all the others had.

————

She met Ormo in his Hall. It was decorated like his private chambers, and for that matter, like most of Eheene. Walls built from obsidian and white marble blocks made a rectangular checkered pattern, otherwise unadorned. Naphtha braziers hissed bluish-white flames in the corners and left only the top of the dais in the center of the vast room in shadows. The onyx floor whispered and hummed when Syrina's bare feet padded over it, but she'd long ago stopped being disconcerted by the sound. Triglav circled somewhere outside. He'd find her within a few minutes of coming out and either land on her shoulder or follow above, depending on his mood.

"There's a delicate situation I'd like you to look into," Ormo said.

He began a lot of the jobs he gave her that way.

"Of course there is," she said. "As usual, I'd like nothing better."

"I know."

Once again, she could feel his smile through the paint and shadows, as sure as she could feel Triglav's presence somewhere outside.

"As I said, it's a delicate matter. Subtlety is of the essence."

"Isn't it always?"

He chuckled down at her. "There's a merchant—a low merchant—named Xereks Lees. For the past several years there have been growing discrepancies between his reported profits and costs. They're beginning to show troubling tendencies. I'd like you to investigate the matter."

Syrina couldn't hide her disappointment. "If it's an accounting issue, Ma'is, do you need a Kalis to deal with it? Surely—"

"Mr. Lees is a powerful man. About as powerful as someone can be without being invited to join the High Merchant's Syndicate. Powerful enough that perhaps one day he'll be asked to replace one of the Fifteen. His power, no doubt, comes in part from the backing of one of my colleagues. It's for this reason I have ignored his inconsistencies until now. However, they have begun to affect my own interests past the point where I can pretend they don't exist. If I'm going to pursue any action against Mr. Lees, legal or otherwise, I need to know what's happening so I can decide whether it's worth the risk. If it is, I need proof I can bring to the other High Merchants. Enough that the one backing him will have no recourse against me."

Syrina nodded and sighed. *Paperwork.* "Delicate. Fine. Where can I find this Xereks Lees?"

"He manufactures a wide range of ceramic and metal machine parts for local interests—naphtha refineries and the like—and for steam machines in N'-narad. His offices are adjacent to his warehouse near the commercial port in the Foreigner's District. Exporter Row."

"N'narad. So he has dealings with the Church?"

"I don't have details, but as difficult as it is to trade with N'narad without getting involved with the Church, it is likely."

"Okay, then. Delicate. I'll see what I can find. Anything else I should know?"

"He gets most of his raw components from Naasha Skaald."

"Who? The name sounds familiar."

"The materials merchant—copper mostly—who's been having trouble with Corsair raids on her coastal smelters."

"Ah, right."

"Lees's costs have been going up parallel to Skaald's security expenses, same as everyone else's."

"I see. All right. I think I can use that."

"I have faith, Kalis. Let me know if there's anything else you need. Until then."

———

Syrina spent the rest of the day hashing out her plan and getting some old documents from Ormo's archives that would be easy to alter. Then she stopped by the room that Ormo kept for her for a couple hours to put on the face and clothes of a young N'naradin merchant marine. She went with a male since women in N'narad who weren't Church officials tended toward less martial occupations. She preferred the faces of the poor for generic poking-around jobs. Merchants and other affluent types never did their own work if they could hire a lackey to do it for them, and foreign peasants were common and ignored where she was headed. It wasn't unusual for unscrupulous captains to abandon their hired help to the alleys of the Foreigner's District if they were going back empty and didn't need the extra hands. Contracts forged with fresh, illiterate sailors often included provisions about getting paid upon return to their home port. Abandoning rubes in distant lands was an easy loophole. The wait was months or even years to sign onto a ship going back to wherever they came from, and a lot of them wound up getting remedial work in the District in the meantime. A few might even apply for Skalkaad citizenship, and a small fraction of those might earn enough tin to get it and see the other side of the wall that separated the District from the rest of Eheene.

As she dressed, she prepared her mind, getting into character, and she thought about what Ormo had told her. If this Lees was dealing with the Church of N'narad, it could make things a lot more complicated.

———

It was well after dark when she reached the high, copper gates separating Eheene from the District. The wall was twenty hands of granite, topped with another twenty of vertical pine posts, polished on the city-side, which was unguarded. She had no problem scaling over it and slipping past the mercenaries that sat on the ground on the other side playing cards, even with her tattoos hidden under the false skin of a seventeen-year-old N'naradin boy. They were looking for people sneaking into the city, not out of it.

The contrast between the District and the rest of Eheene was stark. Wide cobbled streets and high marble houses were replaced with narrow, unpaved alleys and low wooden hovels. And there were no lacy bridges, no oily canals. The streets in the rest of the city were all but abandoned this late, but the District thrived at night. People staggered from the multitudes of bars and brothels, laughing, fighting, and shouting in a confluence of languages. Honest peddlers hawked on every corner, yodeling about everything from cups to locks to ceramic piping. Others whispered from the alleys, selling tiny leather pouches full of delezine and the glass pipes to smoke it in, or sex, or slaves, or all three. Once, a few years back when she'd been there on another job, Syrina had been offered a wailing infant.

The bronze pipes that fed Eheene's naphtha lamps were concealed by the elegant architecture on the citizen's side of the wall. In the Foreigner's District, aging copper tubes ran along rooftops from building to building, or led along the edges of the muddy streets, half-exposed and green with patina. In some sections, pipes had burst generations ago and never replaced. Now those streets were lit with

21

torches, and candles flickered behind crooked shutters.

The District might be alive in the middle of the night, but Lees's office wasn't going to be, so she made her way to an inn she'd used before. An ancient, sprawling, dilapidated mess universally known, for some reason, as the Cranky Maiden, even though the sign over the brilliant orange door showed only a bed and a spilled pewter mug. It was less than a span from Exporter Row.

Syrina swaggered in looking drunk enough to not get noticed, but not so drunk that someone might try to rob her and put down two N'naradin tin Three-Sides from Ormo's infinite coffers. Enough for a private room for a fortnight, plus another ten copper balls to be sure she got one where the locks worked.

The main floor of the Cranky Maiden was a high-ceilinged common room with a dozen long tables and a bar that ran the length of the back wall. Behind that, doors led to various private meeting rooms, the kitchens, and the cellar. Across the front of the room, filthy windows let in murky yellow light. Two unstable looking staircases led up to a mezzanine that ran above the bar. Smaller, more private tables ran along it, and two doors led back into the sleeping areas. The one on the right led to a series of dorms, each with a furnace in the center and twenty or so cots. The left one led to the private rooms, and that's where Syrina stumbled. She found her door, made sure the locks really did work, and settled in.

The bed was small, but the linens were clean. Syrina was more comfortable sleeping on the floor, anyway. One of the walls was the chimney for the fireplace in the kitchen, so it was uncomfortably warm even with the window open, which in turn was small and dirty and looked out onto the wooden face of building opposite, so close she could almost touch it. She could climb out that way if she had to. Triglav found the window a few minutes after she settled in, and perched on the sill to watch her.

———

Syrina spent two nights and three days lurking around Lees's warehouse, watching all the comings and goings, and followed some of the more interesting goings when it looked like they might be up to something interesting. It wasn't strictly necessary, but she wasn't one to jump into a situation without checking out all the players first if she had a choice about it.

She spent another two days in her room, doctoring the archived documents she'd gotten from Ormo's library, changing what she could and faking the rest, along with the seal, until even the merchant whose name she was forging wouldn't be able to tell the difference from one written by their own hand. As a rule, a Kalis needed to be more thorough than her target, and Lees would be as thorough as they came.

In the end, she was satisfied that she had all the information she was going to get without having a look inside Lees's place. She took one more night to go back to the palace and confirm a few points with Ormo, then allowed herself a few hours of sleep at The Cranky Maiden.

As she drifted off, she felt Triglav find his spot on the windowsill.

———

Exporter Row was quiet in the early afternoon drizzle compared to the rest of the District. A few warehousing goons moved here and there, and once she needed to make way for a cart laden with bricks and long wooden dowels pulled by two shaggy black camels. But an hour after noon, most of the people were already in the work yards and warehouses, doing whatever it was they were paid to do. The air stank with tarfuel smoke from the N'naradin steamships anchored in the harbor, and her eyes burned.

Xereks Lees's place was easy to find. Exporter Row was eighteen blocks long and two blocks wide, running along the northeast side of the commercial docks. His was the nicest building, if not the largest. Its wood was painted white. The high windows were cleaner than those of the Cranky Maiden's, and LEES was painted in wide red letters across the side of the warehouse and above the door of the smaller adjacent office.

Syrina entered the office without knocking, ignoring the sign that said, PRIVATE. NO ENTRY.

———

The man behind the desk had a gaunt face and pudgy body. He lingered in that indeterminate age between thirty and fifty. What was left of his thin black hair was cropped short. He looked over his shoulder from where he fiddled with a row of dark wooden filing cabinets standing along the back wall, on either side of the door that led to Lees's office. He wore loose, tailored, dark green trousers and a black satin vest, and he sported three large gems—red, black, and yellow—in rings on his right hand.

"This is a private business," he said to the boy hovering in the doorway. "Didn't you see the sign on the door? Are you lost?"

The lad appeared young, even among the N'-naradin deckhands stranded in the Foreigner's District, who averaged under seventeen. But his boyish cheeks, still free of stubble, were painted with burns, and his large green eyes were old and cold as glass.

"You mean you're not expecting me?" The youth scowled and his scarred brow furrowed.

His N'naradin accent was thick, mushing his words together and rendering him almost unintelligible.

The man behind the counter only smirked and turned back to his filing. "Hardly."

The boy sighed as if he weren't surprised, stepped into the office, and sat in one of the two straight-backed wooden chairs opposite the plain reception desk.

"My name is Silas Narn. Shenaa Marik sent me to offer a proposal to Mr. Lees. You were supposed to have gotten a messenger hawk two or three days ago letting you know I was coming. I guess it never showed up. I assume you must be Lees's secretary, Orvaan. You fit his description, anyway."

The pear-shaped man behind the desk finally turned at Shenaa Marik's name, but his expression was no more inviting.

"Yes, I'm Orvaan." He studied Silas a moment and snorted for good measure. "Marik. The naphtha merchant? I assume that's who you're referring to. You claim she's now using foreign rabble to deliver her business proposals?"

"As was supposed to have been explained already

by way of the hawk, Miss Marik and most of her regular people are indisposed at one of her refineries.
She hired me months ago as a valve operator so I
could earn passage back to Fom. I have since done so,
but I'd already decided to stay on with Miss Marik,
who has encouraged me to work toward Skalkaad citizenship. She has rewarded my loyalty with less dangerous jobs away from the refineries, and has
promised to sponsor me when my citizenship inter-
view comes up in five or six years." Silas eyed the
scowl tugging at the corners of Orvaan's mouth. "At
least, they're supposed to be less dangerous jobs." He
cleared his throat. "Again, at least some of that was
probably explained in the hawk message you say
never came."

Orvaan's expression grew even darker. "So then,
why are you here?"

Silas reached into his tattered jacket and produced a folded letter, sealed with a blob of white wax
and stamped with Shenaa Marik's seal—the eight an-
gular-pointed petals of a stylized navaras flower.

"As I said, I have a letter to deliver. A
proposition."

Orvaan reached out to take it, but Silas pulled it
away and tucked it back into the hidden pocket of his
jacket.

"For Mr. Lees only. Ms. Marik was very clear. I'm
to receive his answer in person, as any further actions
I take depends on his response."

"Well, I'm not just going to let you in to see Mr.
Lees based on your word and some mysterious letter
I'm not allowed to see. He's a busy man." But there
was a hint of hesitation in Orvaan's voice.

Silas rolled his eyes. "Once again, more information was supposed to have already come by a hawk. Miss Marik, Mr. Lees, and a few others suffer from some sort of mutual problem, and Miss Marik thinks she's found a solution. She instructed me to get a response from Mr. Lees first. If Mr. Lees agrees, I'm to approach the others. If he declines, I'm to return to her. If you want more information, you'll need to let me in to see Mr. Lees, and he can read the letter himself, then tell you about it if he wants to. Which is no more my business than this letter is yours. With all due respect."

Orvaan ground his teeth, mind churning. The last thing he wanted was to grant this little foreign prat some sort of perceived victory by letting him in to see Lees. But his own options were limited if the boy was telling the truth, and only Lees would know for certain. His only other choice was to take the letter by force and see for himself what it said. But if it was indeed a proposal beneficial to his boss, Lees would have him spit and roasted for blowing the opportunity, not to mention doing irreparable harm to whatever business relationship existed between Lees and Shenaa Marik. No, the only option left to him was to go into the office and ask the man himself what he should do with this urchin.

"Wait here," Orvaan sneered after a long silence.

He turned and went through the door behind the desk, and locked it behind him.

———

Orvaan came out sometime later to find Silas leaning back in the chair, feet propped on his desk, looking around and chewing his tongue in thought. The boy's

27

gaze found Orvaan as the door opened, his smile amused. The expression made the top of Orvaan's balding head grow red with anger, but his boss had spoken.

"Mr. Lees will see you now," he said, through clenched teeth.

Silas's smile didn't change, and the boy only offered a nod of thanks as he brushed past Orvaan into Xereks Lees's office. Orvaan followed.

The room was paneled in dark wood, the floor covered with a thick wool rug the color of bronze. On three walls, nine massive portraits hung of men, alternately dour and jolly-looking, all with hawkish noses, thin lips, and slanted eyes. Nine generations of Lees. The newest one hung behind the desk, in the bold, cartoonish style that had been popular among the low merchant elite the past few years, and mirrored the man seated in front of it.

The fourth wall was covered from carpet to ceiling by a black and gold mural of interlocking tubes, concealing a door that must lead on to the warehouse floor.

The man seated behind the ornate marble desk was middle-aged, with flecks of gray salting his black hair and close-trimmed beard. His hair was pulled back into a slick ponytail, showing off a receding hairline. He wore a large tin pendant around his neck, fashioned in a Skalkaad Spiral. Despite the brooding, colorful portrait of himself hanging behind him, his smile was pleasant. His pale blue eyes gleamed, and if he felt any malice toward Silas Narn or concern over what the boy's message might contain, it didn't appear on his face.

"Orvaan tells me you're here representing Shenaa Marik." Lees's voice was smooth and baritone.

Silas nodded.

"So how is that old bird, anyway?"

Silas forced a smile. "As good as she's ever been since I've met her. Though I doubt she'd appreciate being called an old bird."

Lees grunted a throaty laugh. "Marik has always had a knack for bringing out loyalty in her employees. I'm sure she's pleased with her continued success in that regard. Now, you have a message?"

"Yes, sir." Silas reached into his jacket and produced the letter, which he tossed onto the desk.

Lees cracked the seal and was silent as his eyes scanned the page, his expression unreadable. "Do you know what this says?"

Silas nodded. "Not exactly, but I know the general details. She wants you to break a contract with someone, so she can legally do the same. Then you both can resume your business with someone with more stable prices. If you agree, I'm to go to the other merchants on my list and convince them to do the same."

He ignored Orvaan grating his teeth behind him.

Lees nodded. He traced his gaze over the letter again before turning his attention back to Silas.

"And if I decline?"

Silas shrugged. "Nothing, as far as I know. I go back to Miss Marik and tell her you weren't game."

"So my participation will determine whether she proceeds with the contract dissolution or not?"

Silas shrugged again. "Miss Marik doesn't want to break her contract unless everyone else does, too."

"Yes," Lees nodded, "that would be the most legally expedient thing to do."

Silas shrugged a third time. "She seemed to think that if you were on board, the rest would be easy enough to convince. She told me to start at the top."

Lees's smile was gaunt. "Flattering, but not inaccurate." He sat in silence for a minute, thin lips pressed together. "Hmm," he grumbled. "I realize there's a legal precedent in what Marik seeks to do, but I must still decline. I've worked with Skaald for many years, and we've formed a trusting relationship with each other. A rare thing when one has done business in Skalkaad as long as I have. I wouldn't throw such a commodity away for a temporary savings of tin, no matter how much tin it might be. After all, Skaald's prices are the result of security issues that Marik and I have avoided only by chance."

"So that's what you want me to tell Miss Marik?"

"With my sincerest apologies."

Silas stood and bowed. "Then my business with you is done. Thank you for your time, Mr. Lees."

Lees remained seated as Silas turned to go. "Orvaan, please show Mr. Narn to the door."

———

The sun was setting sharp and bright into the east end of Exporter Row. Syrina bobbed out of Lees's office and turned west toward the District, glad to keep the light out of her eyes.

The Row was busy this time of evening. Camel carts rumbled by in both directions, their drivers cursing and shouting at the snarling, spitting animals, themselves as ill-tempered as their beasts, which were still shaggy from the brutal winter. A few steam trucks operated by the wealthier traders bumped along the roads, too, engines bleating, not any faster than the camels in the crowd. High tide wouldn't peak for another three or four hours, but already a steady trickle of sailors and cargo was filtering toward the docks. There was a chill to the breeze, but it was still warm for so early in the spring. The air stank of smoke and oil and fish and camel shit.

Syrina was glad she'd been able to weasel into Lees's office. She couldn't glean anything concrete from the encounter, but the only reason she'd gone was to get a look around. The low merchant's background had all but assured her that he would decline Silas's proposal. Whatever else anyone could say about Xereks Lees, once he signed a contract, he stuck with it. Good thing, too, because if he'd accepted Marik's non-existent offer, it could've made things awkward down the road.

She turned south toward the docks, taking a casual look along the Row, memorizing faces. She didn't think she'd roused any suspicions, but she still wanted to be certain Silas wasn't being followed.

Whoever he was, Orvaan hadn't been an ordinary secretary. One of his rings had a hidden hinge where he could conceal poison or something more unpredictable. And from the way he stood, Syrina was guessing he had a knife hidden under his left pant leg. Probably other weapons, too. He was confident that he could tell when someone wasn't being honest with him. He was probably good at it, too, when it wasn't a Kalis doing the lying. That meant his boss had confidence in him. Lees's profile didn't carve him out to be the sort of guy who hired people as egotistical as Orvaan unless they had something to back it up with. Orvaan was a hit-man and an interrogator, maybe a straight-up torturer.

One other thing was also certain—the files in the lobby that Orvaan kept pretending to be busy with weren't going to tell her much, even if she did ever manage to see them. No successful business in Skalkaad kept their records in the most easily accessed room in the building, in plain view of anyone who wandered in. Whatever was in those cabinets was probably real in the sense that if Syrina looked into them, they would cover legitimate transactions. But she'd bet her tattoos they weren't going to tell her what Lees was up to. The whole setup begged to show everyone who walked in how clean everything was, and only criminals were that proud of looking like they weren't committing crime.

Back at the Cranky Maiden, Syrina went up to Silas's room for a while, then back down, still wearing the boy's face. Triglav didn't make an appearance, but she could sense him somewhere above the inn, waiting for her to come out again. Near the front door sat two inconspicuous dock men she'd seen earlier on the Row. First, a few minutes after leaving Lees's place. Then again as she passed the piers a few blocks from the Cranky Maiden. Both were stocky, with round noses, wide-set eyes, and black hair, though one was balding and the other sported a ponytail similar to Lees's. The latter was a head shorter. Brothers. Now they were clinging to clay mugs of glog, lifting them to their lips without drinking. Too-restless eyes settled on Silas for too long before turning away to look anywhere else.

Syrina sauntered to the bar and ordered her

own mug of glog, buying a little time while she decided what to do. She was sure her performance as Silas Narn had been flawless. The fact that Lees was so paranoid that he had the boy followed anyway didn't bode well. If he was having Narn watched, he was going to check out his story, too. In a day, maybe two, Lees would hear back from Marik and find out that she'd never heard of the kid. Then Narn would have both low merchants on his case. Lees would keep these goons on him until then, and then hand down the order to nab him so Lees and Marik could take turns with him on the not so proverbial rack until they found out who he really worked for, then dump whatever was left of him into the harbor.

Of course, it would never go that far. Syrina would dispose of Silas Narn long before that happened, but that in itself was going to cause problems. Lees would still find out that Narn didn't work for Marik, and when Narn disappeared under the noses of his two hired goons, it wasn't going to help Lees's paranoia problem one bit.

Well, first things first.

———

Kakrik jabbed his brother with an elbow, making him dribble a few drops of brown glog onto his dusty tan work vest.

"There he is."

Lasaav, who'd been staring into the crowd boiling within the Cranky Maiden with a vacant look, made an annoyed grunting sound and turned to follow his younger brother's gaze while he dabbed at the spill with his free hand. Silas Narn stood at one end of the bar, nursing his cup.

"Ah, yes. That's him, all right. Good. I was beginning to think he wasn't going to come back downstairs until tomorrow."

"All right, all right," Kakrik said, his voice low despite the din of the common room. "Don't let him catch you staring at him."

"He's not paying any attention to us," Lasaav grumbled. He turned back to face his brother. "So, now what? Does Lees want us to just follow him?"

"That's what Orvaan said. Whenever he goes, we follow until he gets where he's going. Then we report back. Easy. He's supposed to be heading north somewhere, tonight or tomorrow."

"If Lees knows where he's going, then why do we have to follow him?"

Kakrik shrugged. "Suspicious, I guess. You know how Mr. Lees can be. Not my job to ask Orvaan why the boss wants us to do anything, and it's not yours either. Just needs to be sure the kid is who he said he was. Simple as that. Far as we're concerned, anyway."

Lasaav frowned. "So who did he say he was?"

Kakrik gave his brother an annoyed look. "You know as much as I do. Did you just not pay attention at all when Orvaan gave us the job this afternoon?"

"I did," Lasaav protested, but didn't add anything further, and his brother rolled his eyes.

They sat in silence for a while. Then Kakrik elbowed Lasaav again, who was ready for it this time and moved his mug to avoid another spill.

"He's going back upstairs," Kakrik said.

"I see that. Do we follow?"

"No need. Just wait here."

There were another few silence-filled minutes between the two.

"What if he's going to bed?" Lasaav asked. "Are we supposed to stand here by the door all ni—"

"No, and shut up. He's coming down. Looks like he's got his stuff. Checkin' out late. Let's move away from the door."

They jostled to a subtler vantage point toward the middle of the room, shielded from view by the growing crowd of vagrants, foreigners, and affluent citizens looking for the kinds of fun not easily found on the streets of Eheene-proper.

Silas Narn brushed through the mob, unaware of the eyes on him, and out the front door into the District. Thirty seconds later, Kakrik and Lasaav followed.

"I wonder what he's doing leaving now?" Lasaav said.

They wound through the packed dusty streets, struggling to keep track of the back of Narn's head a half-block in front of them.

"It's dark out now," Lasaav said. "He can't take the roads north in the dark. He should at least wait until Eyerise."

Kakrik didn't bother answering. And as Lasaav spoke, his voice trailed off. Narn wasn't heading north, but south toward the public docks.

The press of bodies grew thicker as they approached the harbor, and the tide began to reach its peak. The flow of people was still surging toward the moored ships, but like two leaves caught behind another in a river's current, it was impossible for the brothers to get any closer to Narn than they already were. Narn's short stature made any glimpse of him through the mass of humanity, lumbering steam trucks, and camels less and less frequent. By the time they reached the docks, the boy had vanished somewhere between the islands of light cast by the rows of naphtha lamps that lined the piers.

Kakrik looked around with building panic, while Lasaav climbed up a naphtha lantern pole to see above the press, ignoring the looks of irritation cast his way by the people swarming around him. It was no use. Silas Narn was gone.

"Well, at least we know he boarded a ship." Lasaav hopped down from the lamp.

"Yeah." Kakrik scowled. "Which one?"

Lasaav shrugged. "Well, it's not like we don't have anything at all tell Mr. Lees. He thought Narn was heading north, but he got on a ship instead. That's something. It proves the kid is a liar."

Kakrik took one more futile look around, desperate to spot the short form of Silas Narn on the deck of one of the nearer ships, but there was no indication as to which one he'd boarded.

"Yeah." He sighed. "It's something, I guess. Let's get back to Mr. Lees. Orvaan'll probably have some shit job for us to do, now that we bungled this one."

———

Thanks to her timing with the high tide, it was easy for Syrina to lose the two goons once she got to the ships. Then she slipped into the murky, frigid water of the harbor, unnoticed by the seething hoard around her. She held her breath under the hull of a N'-naradin loading barge and peeled off the clothes and face of Silas Narn, then hauled it all to her favorite drainage chamber under the docks. It was muddy, damp, and cold, and stank of rotting fish. She'd used it before, and she'd stayed in worse places than that. There, she burned the whole outfit after dousing it with the naphtha she kept there for that purpose. The chamber filled with steam and gray smoke, and the scent of burning wax. And so, she thought, thus ends the life of Silas Narn.

Syrina reflected that Lees was hearing about Narn's disappearance right about now, which meant she wasn't even going to get the luxury of a couple of days before the exporter found out that Narn didn't work for Marik. Then the question became, what would Lees think? Corporate espionage, most likely. Someone trying to sabotage his relationship with Skaald. That sort of thing was common enough in Skalkaad. Or maybe, given Narn's origins and his flight to the departing ships, a spy for the Church of N'narad. Either way, it meant the same thing for Syrina—Lees was going to beef up his watch at the warehouse before she could get back there and do anything unsavory.

The extra security might be a hassle. Still, she couldn't bring herself to be too concerned about it. She had yet to come across a mercenary detail she wasn't able to handle, and it was worth it to go in already knowing the layout of his office. As long as she didn't screw anything up, they wouldn't even notice she'd been there.

———

Syrina thought the Eheene docks at low tide were some of the most disgusting and impressive things that existed anywhere on Eris. When the tide was out, the biggest ships needed to move four spans out into the bay, or else sink into black mud six or seven hands deep. They carried smaller barges they could deploy to dock, where they perched on decaying wooden posts so they wouldn't get stuck when the tide came back in. Sometimes they got stuck anyway. There were always at least a dozen huge steamships waiting in the deeper water, belching black smoke that wafted on the eternal wind blowing across the bay, occasionally drowning Eheene in its stench. Only a few of the wealthiest shipping companies in N'narad used clean-burning naphtha engines, and half of those were tankers that trafficked naphtha anyway, so could bear the cost.

Workers got to the ships across wooden walkways, which rested on the muck when the water was out and floated when it was in. They were composed of slimy gray planks, dangerous even when people weren't carrying heavy merchandise or naphtha kegs between ships. Everything was on a strict timetable. If one ship fell behind, they all did. If profits suffered, so did the workers.

Syrina hunkered on the eves of a dilapidated warehouse, overlooking the docks. Triglav settled down next to her, his gaze following hers across the piers and mudflats. She watched the longshoremen and stevedores, toiling and oblivious. Her thoughts kept turning back to Ormo.

"Why did he give you to me?" she asked Triglav, who turned his head to study her, eyes narrowed.

The question didn't seem right, anyhow. The owl didn't feel like a possession as much as a companion. She supposed she could've asked, *Why did he give us to each other,* but the thought was too sentimental. Anyway, it didn't matter. Kalis had neither possessions nor companions unless you counted the Ma'is they served. And the Ma'is did everything for a reason.

Her sudden doubt brought her thoughts around to her childhood and Ormo's reasons back then.

———

She had had many instructors on her path to becoming a Kalis, each one crueler than the last. All of them but Ormo. Zigra stood out the most, her memory of the unassuming old man sharp even now. She smiled to herself. It had been a long time since she'd given much thought to Zigra and his tests.

She had been seven or eight. Zigra was a language instructor, gray-bearded, and wiry. His test took place in a massive room filled with junk. Crates, broken naphtha machinery, heaps of rotting ropes. The objective was to stay hidden while answering the questions he shouted to her, about history and politics. She realized later that the questions and even the answers were secondary. It was instead a test of her responses under pressure and in pain. He would ask them in Skald and required her to respond in whatever language the question pertained to. A question about the Church required an answer in flawless N'naradin. A question about the Black Wall required her to use the proper nomad dialect, depending on the details of the question. While she answered, she was to remain hidden. It was a lesson in history, language, and the use of her tattoos.

Every time he found her, every time she answered

wrong, or Zigra heard a hint of her accent, he would break one of her fingers. The first few times, he summoned her to the center of the room to do this, but then she caught on and remained hidden. Then he would need to find her himself, still asking questions, her still answering.

It was the worst of the days she always remembered when she thought of Zigra. He'd already broken all her fingers on her right hand, and all his questions were about obscure tribes in the Yellow Desert because he knew she always mixed them up and got the accents wrong. Even distracted by her pain, she managed to evade him for seven more mistakes before her involuntary whimpering gave her away.

So defiant she'd been when he'd grabbed her by the neck. Seven mistakes and only five more fingers? What more could he do to her? She refused to cry as he broke the fingers on her left hand, starting with the thumb, his expression bored. But when he snapped her arm over his knee at the elbow, she screamed, and her cries grew shriller when he did the same to the other one.

Syrina smiled wryly down onto the docks when she thought about it now. Twelve mistakes and only ten fingers. What else was he supposed to do?

As she lay crying on the floor at Zigra's feet, broken arms laying like dead branches on the floor at her sides, the old man's face still bland and unassuming, Ormo appeared, lifting her up. He carried her through the palace to his own bed, set her bones himself, and fed her chocolate with his own hands. He had always saved her from the cruelty of the instructors, but it was then, as she lay in his bed chewing on chocolate through her tears, that she realized she would do anything for him. She loved him more than a father, with every fiber of her being, just as he loved her. He fed her all her meals himself for three days, scooping food into her mouth with a spoon like she was a baby until her arms and fingers had healed well enough to endure more training. But it was on that first day that he owned her, and every act of kindness after that only reinforced her loyalty.

And then came Triglav. No, Ormo didn't do anything without a reason.

"So what's the reason for you?" she asked the owl, giving him a scratch on the top of his head.

He blinked at her and gave a little sigh.

———

As the tide began to trickle in again a few hours after sunset, the night following Narn's disappearance, she headed toward Lees's warehouse, across the rooftops, naked and unseen. Triglav soared above her.

3

CRIME

SYRINA SENT TRIGLAV AHEAD. AN HOUR LATER, she followed him, thankful the spring cloud cover was thick enough to mask most of the light from the Eye. She stuck to the rooftops, relishing the feeling of the wind and the rain. She circled Lees's building until she found a storm drain she could shimmy up, but halfway to the top, wild barking erupted across the tar-covered roof.

Dogs were usually reserved for the city watch. Only the High Merchants and a few of the aristocracy could afford the licenses for hounds and the mercenaries that used them. Lees really was at the top of the food chain. It also meant her tattoos wouldn't be any help.

She got to the roof's edge at the same time the dog did. It was a gray and black purebred tundra hound, judging by the size of it. Its shoulder stood almost as high as her. She'd only clambered halfway to her feet before it clamped its jaws onto her forearm and thrashed its head with a guttural snarl, tearing into muscle and snapping bone. It would've knocked her backward off the roof if it weren't for its death grip.

Blood spattered her neck, and pain screamed up her arm. This already wasn't going very well. Someone shouted, and she heard the buzz of a crossbow bolt whiz by her ear. Someone had already seen her. What a disaster. People didn't see Kalis. Kalis didn't even exist. Stories would spread.

There was only one thing she could do now. She rammed the flat of her left palm into the dog's nose. It yelped and let go, but dropped back on its haunches for another lunge. Meanwhile, the shouts coming from the other side of the roof turned to screams of agony, and a commotion went up somewhere in front of her.

Before the dog could finish taking her arm off, Syrina twisted to her feet and swung her right foot out, kicking the thing in the side of the head as it charged, which sent it flying off the roof. It yelped, and after a pause, started to bark. She was glad she hadn't hurt it. She liked dogs.

Syrina turned her attention toward the screams that came from the opposite side of the building. The man who'd shot at her was staggering around in agony, the crossbow forgotten near his feet. Triglav's had latched his talons onto his face, the owl's short beak buried deep in the socket where his left eye had been. Blood gushed down his face and off his chin, pattering on the roof, like rain. Triglav's wings were silent even as he flapped them wildly, trying to hang on as the man flailed against his back.

There were red splatters all over Triglav's white feathers, but how much blood was his and how much had come from the watchman, Syrina couldn't tell. She sprinted over and struck the man on a nerve center at the base of his neck. He dropped and the screaming cut out, but the dog was still barking in the street. By now, anyone on the block knew something was going down at Lees's place. So much for subtlety.

She stretched out her arm and Triglav drifted over to land on it. She checked for cuts and found none, then felt along his back where the man had beat against him. Ormo hadn't provided a book on owl anatomy, so she couldn't be sure, but it didn't seem like he'd broken anything.

"Good boy." Syrina felt like she should say something.

Triglav gave her a curious look and flapped off to circle the building. As an afterthought, she bent down and stabbed the dead man in the chest with his own knife. Might as well do what she could to make it look like a burglary, never mind the claw marks and the missing eye.

All the warehouses in the District had roof hatches. It didn't snow often this close to the coast, but the roofs still needed to be cleared off a dozen or so times every winter. This one was locked, but there was a key in the guard's pocket he wouldn't need anymore.

Lees had upped his security since the visit from Silas Narn. It was a good thing he'd underestimated who was going to break into his building. Still, the dog had put her off. Her right arm hung useless, drenched in blood below the elbow. She tore a wide strip of cloth from the dead man's shirt to bind it and grimaced at the white and red band. She'd need to set the bone later. By morning, the tattoos would do their job and sew everything back together again, even if it would be sore for the next week. Tonight though, she had a big bloody bullseye tied to her flopping, useless arm. So much for subtlety, part two.

She couldn't spend any more time worrying about it though, and she dropped into the hatch and fell forty hands to the packed dirt floor of the warehouse. Normally, Syrina could handle a drop like that without a thought, but she hit the ground crooked, overcompensating for her injury. She landed with her weight on her left arm. It compressed, followed by her head into the ground.

She jumped to her feet, fighting off the haze that came when she jumped off a roof and landed on her face, pushed a tooth back into place with her tongue, and rolled over to a stack of crates, concealing her bandaged arm as best she could with the rest of her body until she could regain her composure. She wiped the blood and grit from her eyes, but her nose and lip had already stopped bleeding.

The interior was a maze of crates and stacked pallets, reminding her of Zigra's test. The panicked, unintelligible whispers of people who think they're under attack murmured in the dark, audible under the barking still coming from outside. Syrina couldn't tell where the voices were coming from, but she could gauge which direction Lees's office was. She began to move toward it, trying to keep her useless, obvious arm between her body and something else.

She crept toward the office, then paused, eyes closed. Two voices came from ahead, and there were two others she couldn't pinpoint, somewhere off to her right. Two at the door to the office and a patrol. They would've been easy to avoid if things had gone better on the roof. Now she needed to hurry. She ducked behind a huge wood and iron box that smelled of oil and metal and risked poking her head around the corner.

The entrance to the office was more obvious here than it was from the other side, where it had been concealed by the mural. There were no more dogs, but two men stood by the door, in a pool of lantern light. The brothers that had followed her the night before. She felt bad for them. Their presence here was probably punishment for losing Narn. They cradled loaded crossbows across their chests, wore long ceramic knives at their waists, and peered into the shadows of the warehouse, back to back, eyes wide, bickering in whispers that Syrina couldn't quite make out. The other two were still back in the darkness somewhere, searching for the intruder.

Syrina ducked down again and sighed. She'd need to kill the brothers. She couldn't slip by with her arm like it was. If Lees was backed by another High Merchant and it got out that a Kalis was responsible for the break-in, Eheene, and then the rest of Skalkaad, would implode into chaos, starting with the Syndicate. And if she didn't kill them quick, she'd need to kill the two on patrol, too.

She closed her eyes, letting all thoughts drain. The last one was that this was really going to hurt her arm. The world shimmered in front of her, and she felt her heartbeat slow, then stop. She strode out from behind the crate and stepped through the Papsukkal Door. The two men stood motionless at first, before one, then the other's eyes widened, focusing on Syrina's bandaged arm, which now swung wide from the rest of her body, unable to keep up with it.

They were bringing their crossbows up to target her, the speed of cold honey oozing from a jar. One began to yell something, but it was drowned out by the roar that thundered in her ears. She was halfway to them when the bolts released almost as one. They floated toward her like feathers in a soft breeze. She stepped around one, but the other's obsidian edge sliced through her lagging, mangled arm at the shoulder. She saw a mist of blood drift upward out of the corner of her eye. Before the first drops had hit the ground, she was on the men. With her good hand, she found the hilt of the shorter man's long knife and arced it up and through the other's eye, which was still focused on where her arm had been. She continued the momentum all the way around, releasing the knife still lodged in the taller man's head, smashing the throat of the other with her dangling forearm like a flail, crushing his windpipe and shattering his spine.

Far away, she heard a bone pop, and a distant voice in the back of her head said it was hers. Continuing the same motion, she dropped her body down, leaped, and arced her right foot up to kick in the locked door. She dove into the dark doorway to find herself in the Lees's family portrait office. She was running out of time and energy. Over the roar in her ears, she could hear the thudding boots of the patrol, ponderous but getting closer. Her body could only keep up ten or twenty more seconds of being on the other side of the Papsukkal Door before it was going to drop her out whether she was ready or not.

Ten or fifteen seconds on the other side gave her at least a minute from her perspective. Maybe two. She'd have to be clear of Lees's place before then, or she was doomed. She had no idea where to begin looking for clues either, but she could make an edu-

47

cated guess. If she was wrong, she'd have to come up with another plan after she'd slept and eaten.

Syrina began to ransack the office, figuring it was a good thing to do anyway. The more it looked like a robbery, the better off she'd be when corporate security showed up. From the other side of the Door, everything she flung across the room was doing a lot more damage than it would have in a normal burglary, but she didn't have the luxury of moving slower. There'd be all sorts of wild accusations, but it was the sort of thing that happened in Eheene sometimes. Without any proof, the investigation would go nowhere.

There was a long, thick iron box hidden between the upper drawer and the top of the marble desk, concealed behind the flowing stonework of leaves and elk. It slid out, was heavy, and rattled and clanked, making her think at least one of the things in it was tin. So much the better. Even if nothing else useful was in it, it would help point the finger at a burglar.

It would have to do. She felt the Papsukkal Doorway charging in at her and the pain in her arm intensified, while the rushing in her ears grew to a moaning thunder she couldn't ignore. An alarm telling her she was out of time. Her chest ached from where her heart longed to beat again.

Syrina tucked the box under her good arm, then burst into the lobby and catapulted over Orvaan's desk. She tossed aside the bar that locked the front door and fled into Exporter Row. A clamor of alarm bells pealed from somewhere towards the District, and the dog still barked on the other side of the building.

She used the last of her momentum to run up the

wall of a warehouse a half-block down and crawl under the overhanging eaves of the higher building backed against it, into shadows and mounds of ancient pigeon shit. A pipe jutting up from the lower roof squelched greasy gray smoke. She braced the wrist of her ruined arm between her knees and pulled back with her body, biting her lip against the pain, until the bones aligned. Then she made sure her damaged arm and the box were between herself and the wall, and passed out, wondering if Triglav would figure out where she was.

4

SUSPICIONS

When Syrina woke, it was dark. Triglav perched on the roof above her. That she woke up at all was good news. Going through the Papsukkal Door without an exit plan was a good way to get killed.

She looked up at Triglav, who'd noticed her wake and stared down at her with his giant slow-blinking eyes.

"Good boy," she said.

She took her time hopping rooftops back to her drainage chamber where she could examine the box. It was a normal key lock, well-made. She jammed a chicken bone into it, one of a handful she'd picked out of the garbage on the way back, and pulled it out again. She did it with a few more and studied the scratches on them. Then she took out a small knife from a tool kit she'd stashed with the naphtha supply she kept there and went to work carving up a passable key. It was time-consuming, but she didn't want to smash it open without knowing what was inside.

Thirty minutes later, the box was open. There was a leather sack crammed with two hundred Three-

Sides, including more than a few stamped with the Sun-and-Moon of N'narad. There was also a thick ledger, which she began to thumb through.

The numbers were in order, or so it seemed at first. Expenses of production and materials were right in line with what she'd expected, considering Skaald's troubles with the Corsairs. But the profits from sales were low despite the high production costs from what looked like a large number of custom orders. The more she read, the more she realized that the amount of product shipped to Fom vastly outweighed the profits coming in. Someone down there was getting a hell of a deal, which solved one mystery and created another. Either Lees was fudging his numbers to avoid paying taxes, or he was shipping a sizable chunk of his merchandise to Fom for free. Especially the special orders—advanced stuff, from what Syrina could tell by looking at the ledger—seemed to be going out with no one paying for them.

The N'naradin importer listed in Fom was a woman named Stysha N'nareth. There was a good chance she wouldn't know anything about the missing parts or money even if Syrina ever made it to Fom to ask her, but it was worth remembering the name just in case.

There was another name in the ledger that stood out, too. An accountant in Eheene—Ehrina Ka'id. Syrina knew of her. Ka'id was a big player in Eheene. She worked for many local politicians, and Syrina was willing to wager the woman had at least an inkling that something shady was going on with Lees.

Syrina spent the rest of the night going over the numbers, but that was all there was. Enough to confirm Ormo's suspicions that Lees was up to something, but not enough to know what it was. The simplest explanation was tax evasion, but something about that theory didn't quite sit right. It seemed too elaborate. There were easier ways of not paying taxes for a man as connected as Xereks Lees.

What troubled her even more was that Ormo would've already known most of the details in the ledger before he sent her in. She tried to ignore the spark of anger that lit in her belly. She shouldn't care. She was his Kalis. He could tell her to do anything he wanted, and he didn't need to explain himself to anyone, least of all her.

A little after midnight, Triglav came into the drainage chamber. He'd caught a rat somewhere, and he perched on a stump of crumbling clay pipe, holding its limp form in his beak a moment before tipping his head back and gulping it down whole. When he finished, he turned his attention back to Syrina and gazed at her with his big questioning eyes. She watched him eat and thought about all the little things that weren't adding up. She kept going back to Lees's supposed Syndicate backing. If Ormo was going to sick her or another Kalis on Lees—or any of the names she'd found in the ledger—he needed some serious evidence that misdeeds were being done. The ledger told the story without revealing the plot or most of the characters.

Anyway, if Ormo asked Syrina to make a ledger look like money or materials were disappearing in Fom, she'd have one for him in fifteen minutes. She could even make one up in Lees's own handwriting in a couple hours, as long as she had a sample of the real thing to work off of. If this was the only evidence Ormo took to the other High Merchants, he'd be shamed out of the Syndicate and then assassinated. The ledger by itself couldn't be used as evidence. Just as well, since it was too risky to keep.

The next morning, she hammered the lock on the box with a rock until it broke, put the ledger back in it, and ditched it under one of the piers where someone would find it after the tide went out again. She left the money in the muck in the drainage chamber to give to Ormo next time she saw him.

———

She waited until her arm was working again a few days later. The flesh between the tattoos was pink and raw, but the lines had re-entwined over the scars, and the bones were straight and solid-feeling. Her shoulder was still sore. The bolt had cut deeper than she'd thought, and she must've fractured something else when she swung her arm around on the other side of the Papsukkal Door. At least the limb wasn't a target anymore. In the meantime, she sat in the drainage chamber and watched Triglav sleep. She was glad he was there.

She was down to two possibilities outside of going to Fom, which, thanks to the Church of N'narad, would add complications she didn't cherish dealing with. The accountant Ehrina Ka'id, and Lees himself. Lees obviously knew what he was doing, and Ka'id did insofar as much as it was her job to keep track of it, numbers-wise. She probably didn't know anything she didn't have to. After all, the damning ledger was at Lees's office, in Lees's handwriting. Still, Ka'id would be too smart to not realize something underhanded was going on. She'd also be smart enough to pretend she didn't see it.

There wasn't anyone else. Even if Orvaan knew all the dirty details about his boss, he wouldn't rat, and he probably knew very little anyway. He was a hired goon, and good goons stayed ignorant of their employer's business.

In the end, poking more around Lees and going to Fom were both beehives she didn't want to jab sticks into, at least not until she'd run out of all other options. So it was back to the accountant.

Syrina decided she'd pay Ka'id a visit.

5

ACCOUNTANTS

THAT NIGHT, SYRINA MOVED BACK INTO THE CITY
proper and checked into a hotel called the Mercantile
Oasis as an exporter named Rina Saalesh. She'd used
Rina before, building the woman's history and reputation over the past five years as someone she could use
to interact with the upper echelon of Skald society
without drawing attention to herself. As a result, Rina
Saalesh was a name almost everyone in the higher so-
cial circles had heard of, but almost no one had met. It
was rumored, however, that Rina was quite eccentric
and fabulously wealthy, and it was well known that
she preferred to do business in person.

The Mercantile Oasis was the most opulent hotel
in Eheene, consisting of five floors of rough-hewn vol-
canic glass. The ceilings were each two stories high.
From the street, it was a black obelisk that towered
above the white marble townhouses around it. Door-
ways and windows were framed in pillars of white
marble, carved with angular, abstract patterns.
Within, above windows and doors jutted white
marble hands, lither and more stylized than the ones
in the Syndicate Palace, palms upturned, holding

their steady gas flames. Naphtha lamp chandeliers made the black walls of the lobby and hallways glitter like stars.

Rina got a room on the third floor with a perfect view of the Walk of Bridges. Her balcony overlooked granite dikes sculpted like plants and fish, slowing the violent spring runoff into a series of soothing waterfalls, cleaned every week by indentured laborers from the District. Pink cherry blossoms freckled the eddies beneath the eves of the marble buildings, while couples sauntered over the delicate arches, glittering with jewelry and bright spring fashions, pausing to watch the water and steal kisses when they thought no one was watching.

The room faced south, and it received all the glory of the sun and the Eye. The floor was planked with polished, golden pine, and the rough stone walls were blanketed with tapestries woven in bright, intricate patterns bearing some version of the Spiral. The huge bed was draped in velvet and supported by four posts of dark wood that almost reached to the ceiling, which was covered in an abstract mural of pale interlocking shapes. Both the washbasin and the sunken tub were filled by a hidden tank which was refilled daily and heated with a naphtha flame that could be adjusted by a brass chain hanging from the ceiling.

The first night, Triglav tapped on the window until Rina padded over and opened it. He hopped onto her shoulder, gave her a quick nuzzle of greeting, then flapped up to stare at her from the top of a bed post. The tops of his black, ear-like feathers brushed the ceiling.

Rina spent the next week mingling with the upper class. She never came across Ka'id and found out that she was as rare a sight as Rina, even at the trendiest parties. She also learned that the accountant was from N'narad, but Syrina had already guessed that from the woman's name. From Pom, to be exact. Not to be confused with Fom, the biggest city on Eris, but Pom, the small but well-off port town across the sea of N'narad from Fom, on the Island. Rumor had it that most of Ka'id's clients had dealings with the Church on some level. By itself, that was far from suspicious. Ka'id was from there, spoke the language like the native she was, and was versed in the complex laws that governed trade between the Empire of N'narad and the merchants of Skalkaad.

The accountant was single, though she had two daughters, both grown and off to their own lives, and it was common knowledge that she preferred women over men, in business and personally. She managed accounts not just in Eheene, but all over Skalkaad, including, it was whispered, those under direct ownership of one or more of the Fifteen. Everyone said she was distressed by the break-in at Lees's and the subsequent murder of three guards, but then, so was everyone else.

Of course, none of that came from Ka'id herself, and most of it came from people who seemed more interested in looking like they knew Ka'id than telling Rina what the woman was like. It was time to track down the accountant herself.

———

Rina emerged from the Mercantile Oasis a half-hour before noon. She wore a black and cobalt high-collared dress highlighted in red. It hung from her compact figure and folded at the shoulders in a way that gave her the casual impression of being larger than she was. Three black stone hairpins carved like snakes held the black hair piled on her head, leaving a few curls to trace down from her temples and over her ample breasts.

She summoned a palanquin since the noisy steam cars weren't allowed in the city center, save those used by the High Merchants themselves. It was an hour-long trip, and she reclined on the silk pillows, enjoying the ride. She opened the gossamer curtains as far as they could go so she could bask in the slanted sunlight. It was cold outside, more like late winter today than spring, but hidden naphtha burners kept the interior cozy. Eight tall men carried the palanquin, clothed in white linen but still drenched in sweat under the weight of the conveyance. The entire thing was gilded in polished tin and bronze that had been worked into fine abstract swirls that ran about the lower half. The compartment was all high crystal windows and warm polished wood.

She watched the sunlight dapple the flagstones. Passers-by greeted her with looks of curiosity coupled with either disdain or envy, but they were too busy earning their own tin to give her more attention than that. Outside of the Foreigner's District, there was no poverty in Eheene, only varying degrees of wealth. Even servants were well-provided for since by law, they had to be citizens to live in the city proper.

Her route meandered down the widest boulevards to the financial district. Her behemoth of a palanquin wouldn't fit through any of the narrow, more direct routes, and she crossed a dozen of the twenty-five canals that slashed through Eheene before she reached her destination. Each one signaled the path over it with a faint metallic oozing scent, so she was aware of their progress even when her thoughts wandered from the view. The breeze blew from the west today, so the stench from the steamships waiting in the harbor was blessedly absent.

Ka'id's office was in the Third Merchant's Trust and Depository Bank, which was one of five companies in the area that catered to businesses dealing with N'naradin finance and law. The front of the building was three stories of sheer windowless white marble that gleamed in the sun until it was hard to look at.

Two of Rina's bearers helped her down from the box, and she tipped their open palms with a kiss each. They thanked her generosity with scowls, but she was already making her way up the short wide stairs, hobbled but still graceful in the clinging dress. She shuffled to Ka'id's office after the receptionist absentmindedly pointed the way. She ignored his pleading calls to her back that she needed an appointment, too late realizing his mistake, and burst in on Ka'id while she was writing letters. Rina introduced herself in the doorway as security appeared to escort her out, and her reputation paid off. Ka'id waived the guards away and gestured for Rina to sit down across from where she sat at a polished wood desk, dark and mesmerizingly grained. The walls were lined with books from floor to ceiling, and the afternoon light glowed through the tall arched window behind Ka'id's winged leather chair.

Ka'id was a pleasant woman, younger than Syrina expected for someone of her status and with two grown children. Her hair was brown and pulled back in a taut braid that started at the nape of her neck and ended at the small of her back. She was plump and smelled of vanilla. Her nose was small. Her eyes were soft and brown, wise and kind. Eyes people liked to trust.

"So you're the infamous Rina Saalesh," Ka'id said, voice pleasant. Her smile was almost shy.

"And you're the famous accountant, Ehrina Ka'id." Rina smiled back and gave a nod of greeting from where she still lingered in the doorway.

Ka'id laughed. "If accountants can be famous."

It was Rina's turn to chuckle. "If they can be famous anywhere, it is in Eheene."

"I must confess," Ka'id said after another light, pleasant laugh. "Though I've heard your name, I'm ignorant to the type of business you're in and what reason you might have to honor me with your intrusion."

Rina gave an apologetic little bow. "Up until recently, my dealings have been with Valez'Mui. Sculpture and raw stone."

"Ah, that would explain why we've never met."

"Yes. That, and because we're both bored to tears by the society gatherings that neither one of us attend."

Ka'id smiled, leaned back in her chair, and gestured for Rina to continue.

"It's why I've come to you now." Rina finally took the invitation to sit and settled on one of the two simple plush brown chairs placed opposite the desk. "I do apologize for showing up without an appointment like this. I realize how irritating it must be, so I'll get to the point. I've come into some foreign machine parts I've not had many dealings with before, and I wanted to know more about the legalities of unloading such things in Fom, as well as find someone to handle my accounts. I'd like to get rid of them as quickly as possible. And yes, I know that'll affect the price. But quickly, and you are a difficult woman to get an appointment with. Hence, my reason for barging into your office and interrupting your affairs."

Ka'id nodded through the soliloquy and studied the other woman in silence for a moment. "Your reputation for spontaneity precedes you. It's true that better prices can be found in N'narad, but even in a hurry, such things can take time. Could you be more specific on what sort of merchandise you have?"

"So you'll take me on as your client?"

Ka'id shrugged. "You're still here. I'm still listening. Let's leave it at that for now."

"I obtained them from a Ristroan airship wreck off the north coast of the Upper Peninsula." Rina settled in, crossing her legs and draping her arm across the back of the empty chair next to her, pleased to tell a story. "I got lucky. Twice. First, that we survived the storm at all. And then there it was, dashed against the cliffs that would've been our fate had the squall lasted another thirty minutes. Quite the nightmare to scavenge it, but we waited for low tide and picked our way on foot. In the end, I only lost two men, and them only because of their own foolishness."

As she spoke, Rina let her gaze fall across Ka'id's desk. Several letters were lying in a stack face down, and Ka'id flipped each one over long enough to fold and seal with blue wax, bending them toward her so the other woman wouldn't be able to get more than the briefest glance of their contents. Rina watched without much interest.

"What did you recover?" Ka'id dribbled wax onto the last letter and pressed her seal into it.

"Some parts from their engines—tarfuel driven. Or something close to it, according to my engineer. A couple weapons—those fire-thrower things you've no doubt heard they sometimes use. A few items from their cargo, which nobody could identify that may or may not be valuable."

Ka'id raised her eyebrows. "Well, the parts are all right, and they'll fetch a good price. I may even already have a buyer, in fact. I can look into it. The weapons though..."

"Oh, no, no." Rina laughed and shook her head. "I won't be selling those in N'narad. I plan to keep them myself. For my own people."

"Well, there's no law against that." Ka'id smiled.

"Does that mean you'll assist me?"

"We can work together. Of course, I'll need all the details before we can hash out a contract, but I don't see why not. I'm afraid I'll have to take forty percent."

"Forty?" Rina froze where she'd half-stood to shake on the agreement.

"Yes. Twenty for the accounting services, and another twenty if I'm the one that finds you a buyer."

"Ah, I see. Well, I hear you're worth it, but I'll need to think about it."

"Of course. I'm sure you'll find that you'll still make a tidy profit. More than you would unloading them anywhere in Skalkaad after the add-tax on acquired or found merchandise. Let me know when you decide. You know where to find me. Although, if you wouldn't mind, make an appointment next time. I do tend to be out of the office a lot. Don't worry. I'll make sure Tiab knows to squeeze you in at your earliest convenience."

"Thank you." Rina stood. "Once again, my deepest apologies for the intrusion."

"Think nothing of it. If it leads to profit, I can't complain."

Rina lingered in the doorway a moment longer, looking around the room until Ka'id stood under the guise of courtesy and escorted her out.

———

On Syrina's ride back to the Oasis, she leaned back and closed her eyes to let the images of the letters she'd been able to glimpse well-up from where she'd stored them. She hadn't been able to see them all, but there was a handful she'd been able to mentally file away. They came to her upside-down, just as she'd seen them, so she turned them around one by one until they stood against her closed eyes. Most were irrelevant personal and business correspondences, interesting to someone looking for juicy gossip or blackmail, but useless to her. One, though, looked lucky.

N,

Please do not misunderstand. The incident regarding L is troubling. Nevertheless, do not act in panic now, only to do something you will regret. You still have the support of all interested parties. As things stand now, your funding will continue unless you halt it. My clients and I realize how important your research is, and I am confident that with our continued resources, you will be able to proceed in your work uninterrupted.

All the documents have been recovered, and there

*is nothing in them that would cast a shade of suspicion
in your direction in any case. While the loss of life is
unfortunate, robbery seems to have been the sole mo-
tive. There is a high-level investigation underway, and
you will be the first to be notified if evidence contrary
to these assumptions are found.*

In Solidarity,

K

Syrina frowned and looked out the window.
Clouds had moved in while she'd talked with Ka'id.
Buildings that had been dappled in sunlight were
now dull gray and black in the dim light.

"K" was for Ka'id, of course, and obviously it pertained to Syrina's show at Lees's place—"L" for Lees.
It could be a coincidence, but the timing was too
good, and all the details fit. She didn't know who the
recipient might be. It was a formal letter, so "N"
would be from the family name. Unfortunately, "N"
was one of the most common initials in N'narad,
where "N" was a particle, meaning dependent on
context—*the, a, that, from, of,* or *those*—and was tacked
on to nearly everything, including a thousand sur-
names. Syrina had always been lucky, but she wasn't
ready to assume it stood for the importer Stysha
N'nareth before she found some real evidence. Still,
it fit.

She didn't like the sound of *high-level investigation.* Those words had connotations within the more
influential circles in Skalkaad. It meant the corporate
police force that handled things like breaking and entering had been called off, and one or more of the
High Merchants had become engaged, which may or
may not mean another Kalis snooping around. Syrina
didn't like the possibility that there were High Mer-

chants besides Ormo involved, and that she could be working against them.

Everything was getting too gray for Syrina's liking, and she still had no idea what was going on, other than it seemed to be going on in Fom.

Syria looked. Ormo. Involved. Could t... she might be
working it somehow there.

Everything was a matter... ...pieces her sitting the...
ing and there it had... out of... ...was something... that
there seemed to be... ...right to...

6

MACHINATIONS

Syrina got to Ormo's Hall just before
sunrise the next morning. She was naked, nothing but
a passing glimmer in the fading darkness. Triglav
perched on her shoulder, shifting his weight from one
foot to the other and back again, talons clinging but
not breaking the skin. Ormo was late, so she took the
liberty of sitting in his Seat while she waited for him.

An hour later, her Ma'is emerged from the hidden
door under his dais, and she wondered for the thousandth time what was under there. He looked surprised to find her sitting on his throne, as much as she
could tell how he felt about anything as she peered
under his hood at the black and white checkerboard
of squares, circles, and triangles painted on his face.
She saw his gaze wander to Triglav as he mounted the
stairs, but it was probably because the owl was easier
to see.

"Kalis Syrina!" he said with uncharacteristic en-
thusiasm as she relinquished the throne.

He seemed sincere, but then, he always seemed
sincere.

"You have information, I guess, or you wouldn't

be here." He looked at Triglav again.

"You already knew Lees was sending stuff to Fom for free, or at least making it look that way. You set me up to find the evidence." Syrina shocked herself by saying it before she was aware of what was coming out of her mouth.

It shocked Ormo, too. His smile faded from his voice, and he narrowed his eyes.

"Of course I knew. It was necessary to have the appearance of searching for the cause of financial discrepancies so that my involvement in the matter won't look unseemly if it were ever to come to light."

She could see him growing tense, and she swallowed.

"That is, Kalis Syrina, if you have done your job?" He was still staring at Triglav.

Syrina's remaining questions all drowned in a sudden swell of guilt. She couldn't believe she'd called him out on her suspicion, or that she even cared. It was one thing to experience a personal moment of doubt. It was another to bring it up.

"No, Ma'is. There's more. I'm sorry."

The guilt subsided a little. She cursed herself for not coming up with an excuse, any excuse, but his tension slackened. He leveled his gaze at her eyes and waited for her to continue.

"So, um." Syrina cleared her throat and did her best to pretend nothing had just happened. "Lees seems to be sending his stuff to Fom for free. Either that or it just looks that way because he's hiding his profits with the help of the accountant Ehrina Ka'id. That, I guess you already knew. Embezzlement is the easiest explanation, but I think he's sending stuff down there. There's no telling where all the tin is coming from, but it seems like he's involved with some sort of research."

Ormo's eyes widened, and she knew she'd told him something new.

"Really? What?"

"No specifics." She told him about the letter.

"That seems to be another piece of the puzzle, even if the lack of names prevents it from helping us. Still, a lucky find. People like Ka'id are rarely so careless. It's a shame you weren't able to take it."

"I'm sorry. I can still get it out of the post before—"

"No, no. You did the right thing. Its disappearance would cause suspicion, much more than Lees's ledger, which you were wise enough to let them find again. If another High Merchant is involved, more evidence will be needed anyway. Go back to Ka'id. Tell her you've decided to accept her offer. I will provide you with counterfeit items that will support your story. But tell her it's on the condition that you go to Fom yourself. She'll want to know why, and I'm sure you'll have a reason."

"Of course, Ma'is." She hesitated. "May I ask you something?"

He frowned under his paint, probably thinking that his Kalis had asked enough already. "You may."

"If another High Merchant is involved, shouldn't we let it be? Couldn't my involvement be construed as treasonous?"

She exhaled a mental sigh of relief when Ormo didn't snap at her. Instead, he nodded, making the silk of his hood whisper.

"If this other High Merchant is involved with the Church, then it might be they who are treasonous.

Until we know more, we must go on that assumption. Act with caution. More caution than you displayed at Xereks Lees's warehouse." He let that hang in front of her for a second. "Remember when I gave you Triglav, Kalis Syrina?"

"Yes."

It dawned on her before he finished saying it. She couldn't help wondering what else she didn't know and how much he'd known all along.

"I asked you if you would return my gift with your loyalty. Do I still have it?"

"Now and always, Ma'is."

"Good. I'll have the materials for you tomorrow. As usual, I entrust the details to you."

Syrina went back to the Mercantile Oasis and lay down for a while before another appearance at Ka'id's office. She was beginning to see a few of the benefits her relationship with Triglav provided Ormo. The Kalis that had existed before the owl would've had serious reservations about acting against another High Merchant. It was ingrained since birth—loyalty to the Syndicate first, her own Ma'is second. Whatever the job, a Kalis never worked against the greater good of Skalkaad. The members of the Syndicate might compete for power, but the key to Skalkaad's vast influence and thousands of years of stability wasn't just the Kalis. It was the unspoken rule that the Fifteen left each other alone.

Ormo must've known that the connection he'd created between the bird and her would lead to more independent thought. In fact, it was beginning to look like he'd been counting on it. Which meant he'd had something planned even back then.

The idea fed into the suspicion she was trying to ignore. Still, the crushing guilt she'd first felt when she'd questioned Ormo lifted a little. He wouldn't have tolerated her insubordination unless he thought he could get something in return.

———

Rina insisted on going to Fom to meet the importer in person, and Ka'id had agreed to arrange transportation. Rina's reputation for doing business face to face was well-known, after all.

A week later, she was on a cargo ship. The wind moaned from the north, warmer than it had been but still carrying the distant smell of the taiga. The Hound's Cry was a huge three-stack naphtha turbine ship with a hold filled with parts and gizmos salvaged from the Corsair wreck.

They pushed south in the general direction of Fom for the first few weeks, before the ragged green slash of the Upper Peninsula appeared on the southern horizon and the ship was forced to swing due west. Syrina had never had much of a problem with seasickness, but she had the impression that Triglav wasn't feeling good and it was making her queasy, too. The owl spent most of the time perched on the rail, head tucked beneath his wing, or flying parallel to the ship, skirting a dozen hands above the rolling waves. At least there seemed to be no shortage of rats for him to eat.

She knew it was a gamble to bring him. If Triglav ended up helping her the way he had at the warehouse, it would be the type of thing that people would remember. But as long as no one saw him doing anything untoward, she could explain his presence. Rina was an eccentric woman known for her exotic tastes. A pet owl wasn't too far-fetched. She'd just need to be careful.

Ka'id refused to let her people deal with Maresg. The accountant was back in Eheene, but it was still her ship, so the captain avoided the canal through the mangroves and took the Hound's Cry the long way around. It was another ten days skirting the forested hills of the Upper Peninsula before they swung south again, and then after another day around the cape, back again to do it the other way.

A day after they passed the south side of Maresg, they turned south again, parallel to the mainland's coast. The mountains along the eastern horizon diminished to grassy hills, and a few days later she could glimpse the suburbs of Fom along the tops of high limestone cliffs. Wooden peaked roofs and a few stone spires poked out of the perpetual mist that rested on the city, the tailings of the Tidal Works that made Fom one of the great miracles of Eris.

Thirty minutes later, they began to round the northern spike of the crescent-shaped double peninsulas that formed the bay, and Syrina could make out the latticework of wooden platforms, shanties, and piers that could only be the Lip. In front of them was the famous sea wall which, unlike the mud-flats that comprised Eheene's harbor at low tide, helped keep the Bowl of Fom flooded. Along the tops of the inner curve of limestone cliffs forming the harbor rose thirteen brass-domed towers, numbered in thick black N'-naradin script, robbed of any other detail by the fog.

Even with the high breakwater of the seawall protecting the Bowl from the rage of the sea, entry into the port of Fom was no easy feat, as the rusting hulks that had failed to dock attested. They surged and groaned against the tide where they wedged against the cracks between the water-smoothed rocks, never completely washing away before a new one took their place.

Syrina watched the waves roll up and crash against the walls and ruins of the steamships, a display both lazy and violent. She inhaled the scent of the ocean off the spume of the fifty-hand-high breakers as they pummeled the massive stones and twisted remnants of the dead ships, all of it green with algae. The surf pushed the Hound's Cry through the gap in the wall in slow, steady surges.

Timing had been good. At low tide, their way would've been blocked by the low center of the dam, and they'd need to join the queue that always formed outside. The tide was almost at its peak as they passed between the two spires that marked the entrance to the bay, both high enough that the yellow-tinted glow lights at their apexes were hidden as the Hound's Cry passed beneath.

It was sunset by the time Tower Ten flashed them the signal to dock far out near the end of the long pier beneath it. They were on the outskirts of the forest of masts and smokestacks, close to the southernmost arm of Fom. The sun was setting between the white and gold spikes of the harbor towers, making the perpetual mist over the city glow silver. The tide had gone out enough again that the sea dam was poking above the waves, slimy and barnacle-covered. The air was rich with the smells of fish and salt, steam and smoke.

Syrina had barely stepped on the pier, when Triglav, with obvious relief, soared up and away toward the city. She stopped herself from calling him back to her, telling herself he would find her again, just like he always did.

———

Most of the time between docking and entering into Fom-proper was spent filling out forms and standing in the lines that switched back and forth through the low-ceilinged, damp stone hallways of the underground Customs House sprawling behind the cliffs of the harbor. The arduous process was done in silence, punctuated only by the questions of the border agents and the answers of the travelers echoing from the distant guard kiosks. At times, the lines of exhausted travelers were so quiet that the gurgling of the tidewater could be heard as it flowed between the sea and the Tidal Works through wide bronze pipes running under the floor.

It wasn't until late the next morning that they were allowed out of customs, into the city. Rina Saalesh went to the nearest worthy inn. It was one of the multitudes crowded near the harbor, this one called The Grace's Hospice. The moment she checked in, she disappeared into her room and didn't emerge again for several days.

———

Syrina woke up on the floor next to the bed, almost twenty-four hours after she fell asleep, Triglav was outside on the windowsill, gazing in at her with curious sleepy eyes.

She felt more rested than she had in a long while, despite her lack of need for much sleep. She'd found it hard to relax at sea and allowing herself an extended rest fit with Rina's image if anyone was watching. She let Triglav in through the window and dressed not as Rina, but as a peasant boy in the rough clothes of a temple messenger. She wanted to breathe in some of the sights of Fom before she got to work. But first, she filled the round limestone basin with hot water and took a bath.

———

It was drizzling, but it was summer this far south, and it wasn't cold. She didn't mind the rain—good thing since it was almost always raining in Fom—and she jogged along, taking in the sights and smells and sounds of the Crescent City while looking like she knew where she was going. Sure enough, no one messed with a temple boy while he was working.

As Syrina's first time in Fom, the thing that struck her most was the absurd amount of people everywhere, and that was coming from Eheene, which wasn't a small city by anyone's standards.

They crowded onto the wooden sidewalks and spilled into streets paved with mud or stone. They huddled in alleys and sat along the curbs and bunched in clusters between covered holes along the lanes which vomited coils of greasy gray steam. In Eheene, no one was poor. If you were poor or got poor, you lost your citizenship, and it was away to the District with you or one of the coastal peasant towns where you could eke out an existence fishing or farming until you got rich enough to move back to the city.

Here, everyone seemed poor. Everyone but the handful of wealthy merchants and Church officials who hurried by, sequestered in carriages pulled by disgruntled camels which grunted and spit at anyone in their way, or in rickshaws pulled by disgruntled men who swore at the crowds under their breath. Everything, everyone was saturated in the combined stench of brine and mud and mildew, and over all of it was the stink of humanity.

Most of the buildings in the section of Fom behind the harbor were packed together, two or three stories high, and made of wood painted with faded shades of red and white. Syrina recalled the maps she'd mulled over on the voyage and made her way into the heart of the city, where the exporter Stysha N'nareth kept her residence and her office.

She trotted for a little more than an hour until she reached the Grace's Parish. Homes here were palatial, built from the same grayish-green limestone as the cliffs the city was built on. The docks were all muddy streets and wooden houses, but parks scattered further inland, filled with trees and wide-leafed ferns. Streets in the Grace's Parish were paved with reddish flagstones, and the stout, flimsy houses near the harbor turned into gated estates that slouched behind high sandstone walls. The vents to the Tidal Works, shoddy manholes and moldy clay pipes manholes around the harbor, were sculpted here into fish or dragons, and the steam came in puffs from their noses or mouths.

N'nareth lived and worked out of one such estate.

It loomed out of the rain behind a high hedge and a thick bulwark of pocked, greenish stone. Syrina ran past it as if the temple boy was heading to the Parish's Cathedral another three long blocks further on.

Then she doubled back, looked around to make sure no one was paying attention, and dropped behind a billowing fern where she could get a clear view of the gate. She'd thought about coming here naked to check things out, but she wanted to look like something other than a Kalis if she decided to talk to someone. There were two entrances. One was a small unmarked bronze gate in the stone wall surrounding the three terraces of the house. Syrina figured that one must lead to the N'nareth residence. The other one was made of heavy wood. It stood open to the wide stone path that led to the front door, marked by a sign written in elegant N'naradin—Stysha N'nareth, Importer. Syrina hunkered down on her heels as comfortably as someone squatting in a fern was able to, and spent the rest of the day watching the comers and goers.

If there was one thing she'd learned through the lens of Rina Saalesh, it was that it was good to see what sort of people someone did business with before going into business with them herself. Even if her business was to pump them for information and then maybe kill them. Especially if her business was to pump them for information and then maybe kill them. So she didn't regret spending the rest of that day or the next three squatting in a bush, even if only nine people came in and out of N'nareth's office the whole time. Sometimes, nine was enough.

The first one was the biggest surprise. Judging by his weathered skin, colorful clothes, and the emeralds studded across the top of his bald head, he was from Ristro, and not just a Church convert either. It wasn't unheard of for the N'naradin to do business with the Corsairs, but Syrina had thought it was in the tolerated black market, not with a prominent importer. People who paid their Salvation Taxes usually didn't want to risk such shady associates.

His presence made Syrina begin to worry about her supposed in with N'nareth. If the importer's customer already had a line on actual Ristroan merchandise, what chance did Ormo's counterfeits have at holding up to either N'nareth's scrutiny or her interest?

The majority of the other visitors were Church officials. They wore the red and white of the Grace's officiates, and some were women, and some were men, but beyond that, it was impossible to glean anything. Some were in and out in five minutes, others were there for the better part of an hour. Their presence could've been nothing or the answer to all Syrina's questions. She didn't know enough to get anything out of it either way. She noted the faces in case they came up again and waited more.

The last one came a half-hour before dark on the fourth night. The servant was just coming out to lock up the gate. He was tall, maybe twelve hands, and balding, though he sported bushy gray eyebrows and an even bushier black mustache. What was left of the hair on his head was black with streaks of gray, pulled back into a short, taut ponytail. He carried a leather satchel small enough to carry with one hand and big enough to hold just about anything. When he came out, he was empty-handed and looked angry.

Syrina hesitated a second to consider what she

might lose by not squatting in the fern any longer, then hurried after him, forcing a few tears down the artificial flesh that covered her face.

———

"Sir?" the boy mumbled. It took Helrith Caff a second to realize that the kid was talking to him.

Caff slowed his pace to let the boy catch up while he fought down his own rising impatience. The child's life had been a lot harder than his. He sighed, thinking of Heaven. If it got back to the temple that he'd blown off one of their messengers, the Grace only knew how high they'd jack up his Salvation Taxes just so he could get into the same middling level of Heaven he was already paying through the nose for.

"Yes, boy, what is it?"

"I... I think I'm in trouble, sir. Can you help me?" The kid—not quite a child, Helrith saw now, just stunted—sniffled and waited for him to nod before continuing. "I was sent with a message from the Customs House for a Miss N'nareth. It's just that I don't read and I got lost. I... I took a nap, and now I lost the letter, too."

Helrith raised his eyebrows, but he wanted to go home. This shouldn't be any of his business. Anyway, it was embarrassing to be seen with the boy.

"I'm sorry to hear of your troubles, but I suppose now you've learned that you shouldn't sleep when you're supposed to be doing your job."

"Please, sir. You don't understand. He'll beat me. He might kill me if he finds out I lost it."

Helrith paused. "Who will kill you?"

"Master N'nef. Keeper of the Boys down at the Custom House."

"He beats you?"

"If we make mistakes. Will you help?"

Helrith frowned. "I don't see that there's much I can do."

Fresh tears were began to swell in the boy's green eyes. "I just want to find Miss N'nareth. Maybe she'll, you know... lie for me. Tell N'nef she got the message. Maybe she's just, you know, nice. Do you know where she is?"

Helrith had stopped walking and turned to face him. "What's your name, boy?"

"Everyone calls me Cavi, sir."

"Well, Cavi, I know Miss N'nareth, but I don't know if she'll lie for you like that or not." Helrith narrowed his eyes. "Do you know what the message was? Maybe we could deliver it together. You know, just tell her."

Cavi thought for a moment, frowning and wiping his eyes. "Like I said, I don't read, and they never tell me anything. I'm just a temple boy. N'nef was really mad about something before he gave me the letter, though. He was yelling about Salvation Taxes and other stuff to another man I never saw before."

"Other stuff? Like what?"

"Fees or something. I don't know. Maybe the yelling didn't have anything to do with it, but he gave me the message right after, and he said to hurry. That was this morning, and now I've been out here all day..." Cavi's his voice quavered. He bit his lip.

"There's no need for slavering." Helrith tried not to roll his eyes when the boy could see him do it. "Clean yourself up, and we'll go back to Miss

N'nareth's place together. It's not far from here. We'll think of something to tell her. Now tell me everything you remember."

They started walking back to N'nareth's building, Helrith keeping pace with Cavi's uncertain steps. The boy sniveled and never looked up from where his worn shoes splashed on the wet flagstones. Caff couldn't help thinking of the kid as a child, even though he was at least twelve or thirteen. It wasn't just his diminutive size. There was something miserable about him that filled Helrith with pity, like a toddler looking for his mother in a crowded market.

"What am I going to tell her?" Cavi whined. "From what I hear—" He gave a furtive glance at Helrith before turning his eyes back to the ground.

"Hear what?" Helrith tried not to look interested.

"Just that, Miss N'nareth, that... maybe she's nice enough, but if you mess up she can... you know. She knows people."

"That's ridiculous. I've been N'nareth's accountant for years, and I can assure you she's no one to be afraid of. I—"

"Oh, no, no. Of course not. I never—I mean, I bet that bastard N'nef talks like that because he's the crooked one. Maybe she's got something on him."

"Ah, you heard this from this N'nef, did you?" Helrith slowed his pace and stopped a half-block from where N'nareth's gate stood closed. He turned to Cavi and leaned down. "Can you can remember what N'nef was yelling about before he gave you the message? I mean, specifically?"

"I try not to pay too much attention to what N'nef is yelling about unless he's yelling at me. Something about Corsairs and accountants who hid money. And some name. Lees, I think."

"Lees? What about this Lees?" Helrith didn't hide the sudden tinge of urgency from his voice.

"Um, I don't know. His stuff is disappearing or something, or maybe it's money that's disappearing. I don't know. I couldn't understand a lot of it, and like I said, I was trying not to pay attention." Cavi stepped back a pace. "Look, sir, I didn't mean anything. I'm sure..."

It became obvious Helrith wasn't listening. He was looking into the street with two fingers pressed against his lips, thoughts far away.

His focused switched all at once to Cavi, as if remembering the boy was there. "I just remembered. I forgot something I have to do at home, and now I'm late for it. I'm sorry. See that building there? That's N'nareth's building. I'm sure you'll be fine. Just...I'd rather you not mention our little conversation to her, all right? For your own good, mind you. She won't want to help you if she thinks you've been telling me rumors about her."

He was already walking away from Cavi, who looked like he was going to start crying again.

"Good luck," Helrith called over his shoulder.

"Wait," Cavi called, but his voice was feeble through the rising tears, and Helrith was already too far away to hear.

———

Syrina lingered in front of the gate until Helrith vanished from view. Then she doubled around the block and began the long walk back to the Grace's Hospice.

She vaguely regretted that she hadn't approached the Ristroan when she'd seen him the first day, but she didn't have a good story ready to convince a pirate to help her. Anyway, while she was pretty good at pitching her voice to get what she wanted out of people, she couldn't plan on it working with people from cultures she wasn't familiar with. She'd gotten lucky with Helrith anyway, and she told herself she should be happy with what she got. She'd been ready with a *this is Church business* speech, but he'd seemed willing enough to help, even if it was just to see what sort of gossip he could get out of a frightened temple boy.

So Helrith was N'nareth's accountant or at least one of them, but he had no idea what the hell was going on either, except that he'd heard of Lees and had his suspicions. That meant someone else was handling the actual numbers. Syrina's tin was on Ka'id. The Skald accountant was already handling Lees, and she was versed in N'naradin law. She was safer, too. Whoever was at the top of all this would want as few eyes as they could manage looking their way. Ka'id handling both ends kept things nice and tidy. As long as N'nareth kept a legitimate local accountant like Helrith around, the Church wouldn't have any reason to look for the real numbers. It also meant the importer must know something, after all.

When Syrina got back to The Grace's Hospice, Triglav was sitting on the top of the bedpost she'd left him on, staring at the door with a curious look in his huge eyes, tinged with what she imagined was annoyance, as if he'd been wondering where she was. She decided she'd let him follow along when she went out in the morning.

7

LIES

THE NEXT DAY, THE RAIN GREW HEAVY. TRIGLAV didn't seem to mind. He flew hidden in the low clouds, but Syrina wasn't worried about losing him.

———

Rina took a steam car. It wasn't as smooth or as elegant as a palanquin, but Fom wasn't such an elegant city as Eheene. Between the mud and the potholes and the crowds, she reflected that a Temple Boy could have run there in half the time. But she was what she was, at least for now.

She'd sent a hawk from the hotel with word that she was on her way—short notice, but that wasn't her problem—and when she arrived early that afternoon, the gate was open, and Stysha N'nareth was sitting in her office, waiting for her. The walls and desk were made of plain polished wood, as was the floor. A few framed documents hung on the walls, but other than that the room was unadorned.

Rina was taken aback by the fact that the importer didn't employ a secretary. There wasn't even a foyer or waiting room, and N'nareth greeted Rina in person. She was stout and withered, with wisps of whitish-gray hair reaching out at various angles from her head, disregarding the array of glass hairpins that attempted to hold it all together. Her clothes were fine silks and linens, all red and amber. She looked like a beggar in stolen garments, complete with a large, crooked nose.

Rina bowed.

"Rina Saalesh, I presume," N'nareth said, her tone pleasant.

Her voice was low and as craggy as her face, but strong.

"Call me Rina. There's no need for formality among friends." Her N'naradin was slow, but her accent was good.

The old woman chuckled. "So we're friends already, are we?" She gestured for Rina to sit on one of the two identical wooden chairs on the other side of her desk, padded in thin, reddish leather.

Rina smiled, bowed again, less deeply than before, and sat, crossing her legs and laying an arm across the back of the empty chair.

"I've made my fortune with the belief that anyone who does business together is a friend, and you've confirmed it by receiving me on such short notice. Anyway, Xereks Lees always spoke well of you."

N'nareth continued to smile, but new lines sprouted around her eyes. "Ah, so Lees mentioned me?"

Rina shrugged and looked at her manicured fingernails. "Only in passing. Until now, our interests have lain in different directions. Now...well, with everything..."

N'nareth's smile faded a fraction, and a vertical crease formed on her brow between her eyes. "Ah, yes. Quite unfortunate, isn't it? I hear his assistant is under a veil of suspicion."

Rina's eyes widened. "You don't say? That's unfortunate. I met Orvaan a few times. He seemed quite competent. Have they prosecuted yet?"

N'nareth shrugged. "I was going to ask you. News from Eheene is old by the time it gets to Fom. No matter. Shall we get down to business?"

"Of course." Rina smiled. "As I'm sure Ka'id told you, I have some parts salvaged from a Ristro wreck that I want to unload here in Fom. Frankly, the Syndicate taxes the shit out of that sort of thing. They feel it's their right on such finds. By their logic, it was never mine to begin with."

N'nareth nodded. "Yes, I'm familiar with Skalkaad tax law, but is it not a crime in Skalkaad to circumvent the High Merchant's Syndicate?"

"As you may note, we are not in Skalkaad."

N'nareth smiled. "Very well. Please continue."

"Ehrina Ka'id gave me your name as someone I might be able to work with. I would, of course, give you thirty percent of the net after her cut if you can find me a buyer. She said Lees's former client sometimes has use for things more exotic than he could easily provide, and since I wish to sell as fast as possible, it seemed a good match."

N'nareth's widened her eyes. "Thirty percent?"

"It's small compared to the ninety-five percent tax imposed by the Syndicate, even after I pay Ka'id her considerable fee. I think you'd find me a generous business partner if we were to move forward together."

N'nareth studied the woman across from her a moment and nodded. "Forgive me if I'm suspicious about working with someone whose reputation rises from rumor."

Rina chuckled. "Nothing to apologize for. It's one reason I insisted on meeting you. You may have also heard that I prefer to do business seldom and in person."

N'nareth raised her eyebrows. "Seldom? You have a prolific reputation."

"Business done well has no need to be done often. There's more to life than work."

"I see. That's not without wisdom."

"You have a reputation, too." Rina smiled and leaned forward, green eyes glittering. "One for caution and prudence. Two things I prefer in a business partner. Especially under circumstances such as these. How could I take offense, when you display such qualities with me?"

"Well, I'm glad my reputation precedes me as well." N'nareth paused and looked thoughtful. "I would need to examine your merchandise before I could say whether I can help you. And of course, the final decision won't be up to me. I must warn you that the buyer Ka'id mentioned has already found a normal supplier for the more exotic items, and had entered into a contract with him even before Lees's troubles. The price he quotes may not be worth your time if he makes an offer at all." Her smile was apologetic.

"That brings me to another reason I've made the journey here."

"Go on."

"I would be much more comfortable meeting this

buyer before any sales were final. After all, our nations aren't always on friendly terms, and as I said, I prefer to do business in person."

N'nareth frowned. "As much as I may respect that, I very much doubt that he would be willing to meet with you. He's a private person and considers his work to be important."

"Don't we all?"

"Mm. Nevertheless, I can say with near certainty that he will outright decline any meeting with you. You must understand, the Tidal Works—if you'll forgive me for saying so—is what keeps Fom independent from the Merchant's Syndicate and their monopoly on naphtha. I'm afraid he'll be wary of anyone from Eheene sniffing around his research. No offense to you."

"Of course." Rina's smile was gaunt.

"I can give you my own personal assurances that he uses such equipment only in his research. None of it will be used for Fom's modest military or anything of that sort. I try not to trade in such matters. Arms dealing can degenerate into an ugly, unpredictable business."

"Perhaps, you could inform him that I have an apolitical reputation and harbor neither any love nor respect for the High Merchants of Skalkaad. If I did, I wouldn't be here in an attempt to circumvent them."

N'nareth made an apologetic wave of her arms. "I understand your situation. I just fear it would be unlikely to help if I were to explain it to him. Especially since he's already procured another source for similar items. Again, I would still be happy to approach him to buy with me as the intermediary, in the same capacity I worked for Mr. Lees."

"Ah, well, that's all well and good." Rina began to stand. "However, if I don't know him and cannot hope to know him, then—"

"I didn't say it was impossible," N'nareth said, a little too fast, as her commission stood to take her leave. "Just very unlikely. Perhaps you could at least leave me with your hotel. I'll approach him with a list of your merchandise and your terms. There is a chance, however slim, that he may accept your offer, under the condition that you two would only meet if he agreed to buy beforehand. With the understanding that either of you could back out of the agreement without penalty if either party were for some reason displeased with the meeting after it had taken place."

Rina looked reluctant. "I suppose if such an arrangement is clear between all, I could make an exception. Without mutual understanding and compromise, we're only animals after all."

N'nareth smiled, sincerely this time. "Excellent. Since there's a good chance he won't need your wares anyway, I'm sure I can find another buyer within a few weeks. A month at the most."

"I hope that won't be necessary." Rina frowned. "I may not have that much time before work calls me back to Eheene."

"We shall see. I'll contact you after I speak with him. Early next week." N'nareth stood with Rina to shake her hand.

Rina flashed her a smile as she bowed, then left.

———

Lees's buyer, whoever he was, would have records of what he was getting from Eheene. With a little luck, they might even say who was paying for it. N'nareth probably had some version as well, but Syrina was willing to bet they'd just be lists of serial numbers, useless by themselves, and she'd rather meet the buyer, in any case.

If Lees was just pocketing the extra tin without recording it to avoid the taxes, that would be the end of it. But if this buyer was getting free equipment, it still begged the question, why?

Before anything, though, she needed to make sure the buyer had a reason to deal with her at all. If he thought his work was as important as N'nareth implied, Syrina was sure he'd be desperate enough to deal with *anyone* if he had to, and she had a good idea where to start.

8

PIRATES

THERE WERE QUITE A FEW RISTROANS IN FOM—
descendants of Corsairs and those who'd converted to
the Church. Syrina had assumed a guy like the one
she'd seen go into N'nareth's place would be easy to
track down, but there were about a hundred thousand
Ristroans living in the city out of its five million citizens, and at least half of them maintained their native
customs and dress, whatever allegiance they swore to
the N'naradin Heavens.

Syrina couldn't take a lot of time finding the man
she needed. If the mystery buyer got back to N'nareth
and told her he had all the Ristroan parts he needed,
thank you very much, she doubted she would get another chance to change his mind.

She gave a passing thought to spending another
day or two in the ferns outside the office to see if the
pirate turned up a second time, but she didn't know
enough about how N'nareth conducted her business.
It might be months before the Ristroan needed to
meet with her again.

She spent an afternoon deliberating by way of
getting drunk on rice spirits, dressed in the skin of a

diminutive dock worker, in the seediest bar she could find—a place just a few blocks from Tower Five called The Whore's Crack. She found herself hoping for a brawl to break out around her so she could get involved and clear her head a bit, but the few other customers huddled at the bar seemed too depressed to put forth that much effort. As she sat there, rocking back and forth in front of her sixth cup, she decided she might as well try the only other person she'd met in Fom. At least he and the Ristroan worked with the same importer.

Reluctantly, she concentrated a few minutes to purge the alcohol from her system, slipped into a quiet alley where she could relieve herself behind a midden heap, and went back to work.

———

Helrith Caff's office was in another affluent parish not far from the arenas and the Market Triangle. All the buildings were whitewashed limestone and plaster, two and three stories high, with steep red tile roofs that glistened in the drizzle.

A tiny, sallow dark-skinned woman with jaundiced, watery eyes ambled down one of the dim streets that spiked from the cluster of arenas in the center of the parish. She flicked her black locks from her face by flipping her head, and her neck strained from grinding her teeth—a common side effect of delezine addiction—as she scanned up and down the streets, looking at the houses. She wore a cheap, clean white shirt with cuffs that reached halfway to her elbows, and a worn tan riding coat, dark with oil to keep out the damp, and its tails dragged on the ground.

The streets were crowded—as always in Fom—but she received a wide berth when people noticed that her skin bore the same unhealthy yellow tinge as her green eyes, and the backs of her hands and spots on her forehead were flaking and cracked.

She approached a house as the night grew brighter with the Eye rising somewhere above the fog, and paused in the gloom of a nearby alley. Behind her, a vent to the Tidal Works sculpted into a trio of dancing fish began to sputter tepid, oily steam.

A few minutes later, a large white and silver owl with tufted black feathers like horns and speckled wings floated down from the low clouds to settle on the dripping eves, studying the street with wide eyes. A sign dangling above the door depicted a quill inside a triangle, the N'naradin symbol for an accounting firm.

After a while, the lights went out in the office, and the owl took wing back up into the mist. A minute later, Helrith Caff and another man came out, locked both doors and the gate, bid each other goodnight, and headed off in opposite directions. After another few minutes, the sickly woman headed off in the same direction as Caff. Every once in a while, she would pause at an intersection, but invariably chose the same way he'd gone. The faint calls of an owl hooted from somewhere above the roofs.

In fifteen minutes, Caff arrived at his home in a building that looked much like his office—one of the white blocky, red-roofed townhouses that crowded down both sides of the street. The owl glided down to perch above the door, eyes wide as it watched the woman approach a few minutes later.

Without hesitation, the Ristroan went up to the

porch and kicked in the heavy front door with strength shocking for her small size and sickly appearance. A little girl playing with wooden toy camels in the foyer screamed and began to cry as she fled deeper into the house, calling for her mother. The intruder ignored her and marched into the living room. Caff sat in a puffy green velvet chair in the corner, next to the lacy, abstract ceramic sculpture that connected to the Tidal Works and heated his home, which, even in the summer, was chilly and damp. His shoes were off, his jacket draped across the back of the chair, but he was still dressed in his gray and brown day clothes. A book lay open in his lap, and a glow lamp sprouted from the floor behind him to hiss yellow light over his shoulder.

He leaped up, the book falling to the floor, and stumbled a few steps backward, his eyes wide with fear. The little girl and her mother were both hiding, but their whimpers could be heard coming down the stairs that led up from the foyer.

"Heaven, grant us mercy!" Caff screamed, and took another step back until he pressed against the elaborate radiator, which was hissing and ticking with building heat.

The woman drew a long ceramic knife from her belt but didn't raise it. "Relax. We am here only a person to find."

Her accent was thick, strange.

Caff blinked at her. She sat down in his chair and turned it to face him, gracefully nudging the fallen book out of the way with her foot, before raising her leg to rest it on the ticking sculpture and block Caff between it and the wall. She kept the knife out.

"What do you about the business associates of

Stysha N'nareth know?" She balanced the knifepoint on the tip of her finger, concentrating on the blade, but glancing at Caff out of the corner of her eye.

Her corneas were a brilliant green, a contrast to the watery yellow around them.

"What?" He seemed taken aback.

The woman frowned and leaned forward, her leg still blocking him in as she pointed the white blade at his stomach.

"Every time we must repeat, you will one finger lose."

He tried to back up more but could only press into the heater, which was now hot enough to make him wince.

"What? I mean, I don't know. I don't know any of them. I've met a few, but I don't know them. I'm just an accountant. I don't deal with her business. I don't meet her clients. Just the numbers. No names." He began to cry.

The woman looked uncomfortable. She leaned back into the cushions of the chair and started balancing the knifepoint again, this time on the back of her hand. She still didn't drop her leg, and Caff seemed too flustered to try to climb over it.

"We am for a man like us looking. Ristroan." Her eyes intent on the knife. "Do you a man like that who business does with Miss N'nareth know?"

Caff wiped his face with his sleeve, trying to sort out the question. "What? No. I mean, I've seen a guy a few times. In her office. I mean, I've seen him, not... I don't know him. I don't even know his name. Is that what you're trying to ask? Why don't you just ask N'nareth?"

"This man, green gems in his head?"

Caff's voice shook. "Yes."

The woman nodded. "The lady N'nareth needs know of us not. Understand? We to you come because you N'nareth knows, and she the man knows. He who can something from our employer take and to Fom come, to hide and not be found thinks he. But we him will find, Mister Caff, because we you found and you will us everything you know tell, or fingers..." The woman shrugged.

Caff's eyes grew wide again. "What?" He said again, confusion and terror plain on his face. "I don't know anything else, I swear. No name, I told you. Nothing. N'nareth doesn't do names. Not on paper. Just numbers. Please. I have a family..." He began to cry again.

"That all?" She waved the knife vaguely.

"He's from the Lip, I think. Or he keeps shop there. N'nareth mentioned something once. Unless there's another guy. If there's another, I don't..." He seemed to realize he was rambling and sucked in a shuddering breath, wiped his face with his sleeve. "That's it. That's all I know. Please."

The woman looked at him a long time, making a show of it. Then she stood and gave him a traditional Corsair bow, her arms out and one leg extended.

"To your wife and child, our apologies." She left through the broken door.

———

Syrina headed toward the Lip after ditching the Ristroan woman on a rooftop, which she hoped she could find later. She didn't relish the idea of mixing that particular skin tone a second time if she needed to use the girl again, and she thought she might be able to improve on it if she ever had the time. And she wasn't looking forward to dyeing her eyes again if she didn't have to. They still burned and watered. It had been a mistake to go overboard with the disguise like that without a good reason.

The rain poured, and she hopped from rooftop to rooftop without a sound on the clay tiles, scaling the stucco walls of the higher buildings when she had to. It wasn't late when she left Caff's house, but it was morning by the time she reached the northern tip of Fom, known as the Lip. No sign or wall advertised that she was there, but the line that separated the Lip from the rest of the city was no less abrupt for the lack of one. High buildings built from stone became wooden single- and two-story shacks that crowded on top of each other from one block to the next. Every street was a narrow alley or dead end or both, and even narrower stairs descended into the old quarries. The crash of waves against cliffs was close enough to be heard and far away enough that it was impossible to know which direction the sound was coming from.

The Lip comprised only a fifteenth of the land of the Crescent City, but it contained an eighth of the population. They lived within the layers of quarry tunnels and on the trellis of bridges and platforms running down the face of the northern cliffs, dangling all the way to the high tideline.

The rest of Fom kept its cliffs clear so the sea could flow in and out of the Tidal Works, but there were no machines beneath the Lip. None of the hot running water, central heating, or glow bulbs that the rest of Fom was famous for. The old quarries here were lawless warrens filled with escaped prisoners, refugees, and the insane. At least, that's what people in Eheene said. But Syrina wasn't going to believe anything until she saw it for herself.

Whatever else the Lip was, it was also a maze. There was no way she would find the still-nameless man she was looking for by wandering around and hoping for blind luck. She needed another face, and for that, she needed either privacy and a few raw materials or to go all the way back to Rina's hotel to do-up something more professional. She didn't want to take another day to go back to the hotel, and the Ristroan girl she'd just taken off didn't fit with what she had in mind.

The materials to make false skin were common enough once you knew what they were, if you weren't too picky about your apparent health, so that wasn't a problem. Good pigment was harder, but the light was poor in the best parts of Fom and downright dark in the Lip. The clothes—well, there were clothes everywhere, so that was easy. There was nothing she could do about hair, but bald men didn't draw attention.

Privacy proved to be the hardest thing to come by. She had to go to a rooftop garden almost a whole span back into Fom where she could take the hour or so she needed to do a decent job on the disguise. Triglav circled overhead and hooted to her when someone was coming.

She ended up being a bald, pale effeminate man with a broken nose and what might be a mild case of jaundice. It wouldn't have been her first or fifth choice to look for a businessman, even if he was a pirate, but it would do. She decided she'd used too much yellow again, but at least no one would think she was working for the Church.

Syrina filled out the image with some ill-fitting, colorless clothes that looked like they'd been stitched from sacks. She didn't have any shoes, so she muddied her feet until it covered her tattoos, and hoped no one would pay too much attention to them.

Letting Triglav ride around on her shoulder was a gamble. It drew a lot of attention, and there was a chance, however small, that someone here might've heard about Rina's pet on the ship from Eheene, but she was willing to take the chance. Even if someone had heard about Rina, they probably weren't going to place the small under-nourished peasant on the Lip with her. People saw what they understood, and putting one-and-one together was too big of a reach for most. At worst she could explain it away as one of Rina's errand boys, though she didn't want to get Rina involved if she could help it. The bottom line was, the more attention she got, the more likely that the pirate would come to her just to shut her up.

The stink of human hit her first when she first stepped into the quarries. A stench of sweat and excrement and sex and death was unfiltered by fresh air or breeze and blanketed with the tang of wood smoke and fish and saltwater.

The second shock was the ant-like efficiency of the swarm of people existing in the tunnels. Some of the passages were so narrow that barely one person could fit through at a time, but it didn't seem to slow the thousands pressing past each other through the maze of corridors. They maneuvered through halls most of them had lived in all their lives, with grace not even Syrina could come close to matching. She was glad she'd decided to wear the face. The tattoos would never hide her here in the constant press of bodies.

Children were the only ones not smart enough to stay away from the little sick man with the owl. But there were children everywhere, playing in alcoves and chasing each other around the legs of the adults, playing tag or picking the pockets of the unwary. They paid the man no heed, even when grownups hissed their disapproval.

Everyone else gave the little man as wide a berth as they were able to, and after a few forks, he came to a wider passage where vendors had set up in alcoves along one wall.

"Machinery?" he asked each one. "You know, foreign stuff? Special stuff? Know what I mean? You know where to buy something like that? Not for me, of course, of course. For the boss."

And the owl on his shoulder would blink at the crowd around them in the hazy air, sleepy and curious.

The vendors balked, shaking their heads, and muttered, "Nothing like that here."

But the rumor of his presence spread like fire through the tunnels before him, and after an hour or two they shook their heads at the owl man before he even had a chance to ask any questions.

By the time the clouds had lightened into day and darkened again the next evening, he was an expected presence, and he got an occasional nod further into the maze, toward the cliffs or further down into the tunnels.

Many hours later, he emerged on a platform of wet unfinished wood a few levels above the incoming tide smashing into the rocks below. Fishing sheds and lean-tos lined the limestone wall, and ladders of wood lashed together with rotting rope led down to the lower tiers. It was still night, but the glow of Fom lit the clouds from beneath and bathed the Lip in a sickly brownish glow. Thick wooden beams jutting from the cliff face supported the platforms. There were nine or ten tiers between the top and the dark line at the bottom which marked high tide. Black openings on each level led into the tunnels, and almost vertical stairs cut into the rock led to the crush of shanties on the top.

A crude breakwater extended about a quarter-span out, a jagged tumbling of huge boulders and discarded blocks of stone piled up during low tide in a futile attempt to quell the sea. It was illegal to port in Fom anywhere but the harbor, but they told stories of smuggler captains and murderous pirates docking along the Lip even in Eheene. Even with the breakwater and at half-tide, the waves smashed and writhed against the rocks, and it was only possible to dock along the Lip when the tide was at its peak. Murderous or not, they would need to be insane to anchor there.

The little man climbed down to the lowest platform, the incoming sea crashing and boiling some forty hands below. The structure he stood in front of was about fifty hands long and made from water-warped wood that leaned against the mossy rock. A short pier jutted less than thirty hands further out from the shack's low entrance, suspended over the water by a stout beam beneath it. Two frayed ropes tied the end to the tier above. A big, tangled fishing net hung along the windowless wall of the lean-to, but it was dry and stiff as if it hadn't been used in years.

The owl blinked once and floated up into the Fom mist.

———

Syrina realized it had been getting lighter outside only after she stepped into the shanty and was engulfed by darkness. At first, she thought it was empty, but her eyes adjusted, and she saw a battered table hunched beneath a lone pane-less window at the far end of the structure. It looked like it had been hammered together from the same gray driftwood as the shack. Behind it sat the silhouette of a man.

When the figure stood, emeralds glittered across his scalp, but the rest of his features were still swallowed in shadows. Syrina wondered what the Corsair did in there so early in the morning, sitting in the dark.

———

The owl man, now owl-less, peered around in the dim light for a chair and didn't see one. Instead, he dragged an empty crate from the clutter up to the table and tipped it on its side. He plopped down onto it with a tired grunt.

"Hello," the man behind the desk said. "My name is Velnapasi. I hear you've caused quite a commotion in your search for certain things you believe you can find. Such a commotion that I've waited here all night for you despite a strong desire for a hot meal and my bed. I would suggest you explain to me what you seek and why you think I of all people can assist you. Strange things happen to strange people asking strange questions on the Lip." He smiled, the expression barely visible in the weak light.

"Please forgive me for the intrusion," the little man whined, sounding scared enough to satisfy the pirate. "I'm Gerid. My employer sent me here with only the intention of—"

"I am no fool to be conned," Velnapasi whispered, his veneer of pleasantness dropping with his voice. "Tell me who you are and why you're here, or I'll toss you to the sea and be done with it."

The little man stared at Velnapasi a long time, green eyes glittering under sallow lids.

"You're selling smuggled Ristroan goods through an importer named Stysha N'nareth," Gerid said.

"A dangerous accusation. Unfortunately, I don't know what you're talking about, and I already grow weary of listening."

"Come on," Gerid sneered, fear gone from his face. "I know what I know. You know what I know. You tell me not to screw around. Then why you going to screw around with me? You got nothing else to do, sitting around here in the dark?"

The green gems in his skull glittered in the growing light, but Velnapasi didn't speak.

Gerid continued. "Your sales, they're interfering with my boss's business. He wants them to stop for one month. In return, you get quadruple whatever profits you would make from N'nareth."

"I don't think—"

"To prove his intentions are honest, my boss will get you half your payment within the next two days, as long as you say yes. That's double up front what you'd make this whole month off N'nareth if you can't do the math, but I bet you can. No tin shows? You can call off the deal. If it does show—and it will—then at the end of the month, you get the other half. That is, of course, as long as you hold up your end of the bargain."

Velnapasi leaned forward, his elbows on the desk. "Who do you work for?"

The little man shrugged. "My boss thinks you're getting paid enough that you don't need to know. I'm sure there are a million things you could tell N'nareth that won't raise too many eyebrows. It's a dangerous business you're in. Problems come up."

The pirate nodded and chewed on his tongue.

Finally, he grinned. "Fine. If I get the tin, I'll stockpile for a month."

Gerid stood and bowed. "Leave your numbers under the right side of that rotten fishing net you've got hanging outside before tonight. Oh, and the boss says to tell you, please feel free to round up, but if you take the money and rescind, things won't go well for you."

Velnapasi coughed a laugh. "I'm sure that's true. Fine. You've got your boss a deal. But tell him if he tries to screw me, things won't go well for him either."

Gerid smiled, revealing brown teeth. "I'm sure." He bowed again. "Keep an eye out for your first payment."

Then he stepped out the door and vanished into the Lip.

9

MODERN WONDERS

GETTING VELNAPASI HIS MONEY WAS EASY, AND if his figures were a little high, they weren't as high as Syrina had expected them to be. Ormo could afford it, so she threw in a little extra to show him *the boss* was sincere.

Three days later, Rina received a messenger hawk in the nests of The Grace's Hospice. It was from N'nareth. The buyer had agreed to meet.

Two days after that, she had an appointment with a man named Gaston N'talisan.

———

N'talisan was a professor at the University of Fom. He was from Tyrsh but had been in Fom for the past five years. N'nareth told her that he could tell Rina the rest himself.

The importer's directions led her north, away from the University, toward Wise Cathedral, the seat of the Grace near the center of the city. Rina could see the colossal church perched on its hill as the rickshaw drew closer, the chapel's white and red walls rendered a featureless gray silhouette by the drizzle.

She'd called for a rickshaw this time. It wasn't as comfortable as a steam car, but it could go a more direct route. The concierge had advised her that the streets under Wise Hill were even more narrow and winding than they were in the rest of Fom, and neither cars nor carriages could navigate most of them.

Sure enough, before she reached Wise Hill the rickshaw turned into a claustrophobic maze of three- and four-story limestone buildings roofed with green copper domes. Soon after, even the rickshaw became too wide for the streets, and after suffering through a blizzard of apologies from the runner, Rina was forced to walk the last half-span. The streets were cobbled and well-kept here, but they were clogged with people, and it was slow going.

She got lost twice and arrived over an hour late. Her destination proved to be a squat unmarked door of heavy wood wedged at the end of a dead-end alley guarded by a plain granite archway, and devoid of other doors and other people. She slammed the knocker once, and a moment later, the door cracked open. Rina stepped into a round room with a high domed ceiling coated with green copper. The centerpiece was a vast C-shaped table covered with black velvet cloth and cluttered with gauges, gears, pumps, and switches. The only light came from a ring of high, narrow windows along the base of the dome. Opposite the entrance was another door, this one square, copper, and so low even Rina would need to bend over to get through it. Books of all sizes were piled in haphazard stacks about the floor. Three people were sorting and assembling parts or looking over books, but it was clear they were the assistants.

Gaston stood at the far end of the table. He was young—younger than Syrina had imagined a university professor—with a short-trimmed black beard and sharp dark eyes. He was fiddling with some sort of brass gadget while peering at it through a glass and ceramic eyepiece. He had a bearing about him that said he was in control of whatever was going on here, and he looked up and smiled at Rina as she closed the door behind her.

"Rina Saalesh, I presume. I'm glad you made it." His voice was soft, friendly.

She held out her hand so he could take it in a gentle shake. His voice was soft, friendly.

"My sincere apologies if my tardiness is keeping you from your work," she said. "I seem to have gotten lost somewhere between here and the Grace's Walk."

He laughed. "You're not the first to get lost in Fom, and all my work is here, so you've kept me from nothing."

Rina's face grew serious. "Now then, I don't wish to be abrupt, but I see you have much to do, as do I."

"Yes, yes. I'm aware that this is a one-time deal for you, and I understand you want to make sure your inventory won't come back to haunt you later. It's quite reasonable, given the circumstances. Please allow me to explain what's happening here and why we need items that would take too long to explain to the Church were we to acquire them through proper channels."

"I couldn't care less about the Church if you don't mind me saying. Nor am I much more concerned with the Merchants' Syndicate."

"Yes, well, I hope you don't take this the wrong way, but that's good to hear. There's always the concern around Fom that the High Merchants will someday find a way to make us as dependent on naphtha as the rest of the civilized world. Although truth be told, it seems unlikely that they would ever be able to. Not that many people think that they would. Be able to, I mean. I suppose more of the concern is that they would try, and who knows what kind of damage they would do if they—oh, I'm sorry. I tend to ramble." He looked uncomfortable.

Rina chuckled, easing the tension. "You won't find me so easily offended, so pay it no mind. Anyway, did you not have a similar arrangement with one of my countrymen up until not long ago?"

"Yes. His equipment was not so rare as yours, though he did manufacture a custom piece for me, now and then. And he never asked to meet me. Fortunately for you, he's not the only supplier who's met with recent difficulties."

Rina cleared her throat. "Yes, well, I know Xereks Lees as an honest businessman. I hope whatever problems he's suffering through will resolve themselves in due course."

N'talisan was quiet for a time, but then he smiled and looked up at her from his gadget, finished with whatever he was doing to it.

"It's no matter," he said. "My work continues, regardless. Please join me. Allow me to show you."

Rina followed Gaston through the tiny door in the back of the room. The chamber beyond it was narrow but high enough to stand up straight in and dropped into a spiral stairway cut into the rock floor, worn smooth with time.

"I am an archaeologist, technically." His voice sounded dead over the dull slap of their footfalls in the tight stairwell. "But for the past five, almost six years, I've been studying the Tidal Works, and a few years ago the University of Fom was kind enough to give me a grant to come here on a more official basis. You know, the Works have been around for thousands of years. People know how to maintain it, add to it as the city above grows and changes, but generations ago they forgot how it works in the first place. That's how I got involved. I was fascinated by the idea. How it could be that the people just a thousand years out of the Age of Ashes could know so much more than we do now, after so many millennia of construction and study?"

"I see," Rina said, doing her best to feign interest.

"I found something both disturbing and remarkable," N'talisan continued, unaware or unconcerned with the lack of attention from his audience.

They reached the bottom of the stairs and entered a narrow passage lined on either side by rows of ceramic, brass, and copper piping, sprinkled with valves, levers and pressure meters that stretched on in either direction until the way became shrouded in steam and lost in the dim yellow light of the globes. N'talisan turned to the right.

"How is it possible that people can keep it working but not know how it works?" Rina asked.

"Exactly."

They came to an intersection and turned right again, down an identical passage.

"The Tidal Works is made of layers and layers of machinery, cables, and batteries that all draw their power from the tidal waters as they flow through the porous stone that Fom is built on. With, of course, a little help from the span upon span of piping that leads from here to the harbor and the southern cliffs."

"Well, yes." Rina frowned. "That's why it's called the Tidal Works. Everyone knows that."

"Yes, but this machinery isn't capable of turning the energy of the tides into energy the people of Fom can use to heat their water or power their globes. It stores it, transfers it to the surface, but only a few turbines on the lowest levels convert it to power."

"Then what's doing the rest?"

"You'll see."

They came to another T-intersection. The wall in front of them was another mass of piping and wires, and the ever-present pressure gauges. The floor down this corridor was a rusty metal mesh, patched here and there with warped graying wood. The air hummed with energy and the sound of rushing water. It was hot, and everything was slick with condensation. Through the mesh of the floor, Rina could see another passage beneath them and another beneath that, until any others were lost in the steam. Echoed shouts from distant workers, clanging, and hissing clamored all around them, but the section they were in was empty of anyone but themselves. The thick, moist air was saturated with the scent of wet stone and metal and saltwater.

Gaston led her down another stairway—this one straight instead of spiral—then down another, where the passage bent right again.

"So this is the Tidal Works?" Rina gestured to the rows of pipes and valves expanding around them.

Gaston grinned. "To make a long answer short, yes. Conduits extend under most of Fom, but the main battery is just over a span to a side, maybe seven hundred hands high. It's not one solid machine, despite what the name implies. It's been built through these caverns and tunnels just as the surrounding passages have been, and added to over the ages." He gestured to the wall of brass pipes, gears, levers, valves, and gauges in front of them. "On the other side of all this are some of the caverns with the storage tanks. The Lower Works turns the seawater to steam and filters it into the condensers. The Middle Works collects it as fresh water and pumps it into the reservoirs on this level, where it can be tapped by the city. Some of the tanks are cold. Others are kept heated by the Works's energy. Every building above has access to both.

"All the pipes to the west—here—" he pointed, "are funneling the tidal waters back and forth to the aquifers. The pipes running up and down, like these here, are pressure releases to pump out the excess steam. They can explode—and have—if they aren't maintained and periodically replaced, which is one reason I need so many spare parts. Besides research, I've become something of a caretaker of this section. The Grace has appointed me chief engineer in charge of maintaining the Central Tidal Works, and now I oversee the heart of it."

"You must be proud." Rina smirked and lifted her dress from the grimy floor.

"No, it just gets in the way of my real work. Ah, here."

They reached another passage, this one again on their right, so low it only came up to Rina's shoulders. It was dark. Only a few of the glow globes that lit the rest of the passages were strung here, as if an afterthought, and if it was hot elsewhere, it was an inferno here. It ran on for a thousand hands before stopping at a gleaming convex black wall. It wasn't smooth but covered with fine swirling indentations and ridges, like a fingerprint. Or a Kalis's tattoos.

There was a little more space in the chamber at the end of the tunnel, and Gaston and Rina could stand up straight, shoulder to shoulder.

"It took me over two years just to rebuild the Tidal Works enough to open this passage all the way through to the center. There was an access tunnel, but it ended four hundred hands back." He was bubbling with excitement. "It was another year before that just to sort out all the paperwork so that the Church would let me do it. Other maintenance passages run close to it, too, further down on the lower levels that flood during high tide, but none came all the way here.

"It's a cylinder, roughly—though of the few surfaces I've accessed so far, none seem to be flat, so it must be irregular in shape—extending all the way to the bottom of the Works, maybe a thousand hands high and two hundred or so in diameter, though again, that seems to vary depending on where it's measured. The Works around it makes it impossible to be more precise. Nor do we know how far down it actually goes. The map of its shape that we've come up with so far is based on guesses. We've seen only maybe five percent of it firsthand. Less if it extends deep underground, which in my opinion it does."

Rina looked at the black wall. There was a vibration coming from it that made her teeth hurt. It wasn't independent of the mass of machinery around it but connected by huge bundles of wires that stuck out of it in random clumps. More gauges, pipes, and valves were fitted to black rubbery tubes that seemed to ooze from it as if the thing were made from some long solidified, viscous fluid.

"What's this?" Rina asked.

"That's the question, isn't it?" N'talisan was grinning with excitement.

She looked again. Not metal or wood or stone or ceramics, or even the nonmetal of Maresg, but something else.

"It's an Artifact." She didn't bother trying to keep the awe from her voice. "A real, working one."

"Yes!" Gaston said. "This, this is the heart of the Tidal Works. And what's more, I'm sure the Ancestors didn't put it here to do something as mundane as power a city. I think that purpose was found for it centuries after the Age of Ashes."

"What is it supposed to do, then?"

"That's what I'm trying to find out. I've been trying to build something that will measure the energy it puts out and takes in, test what's happening within. It's slow and fragile work. Every precaution is taken, so we don't disrupt... whatever it's doing."

"And Ristroan technology is better for that?"

"Now you see. They're more advanced than we are in N'narad, what with such pointless restrictions laid down by the Church. Maybe even more so than in Skalkaad, at least with regards to things besides naphtha engines. I couldn't have gotten half as far in my understanding of this thing if it weren't for some of the equipment smuggled from Ristro, or at least copied from Corsair designs by Xereks Lees. Since I don't know what we're looking for, though, I don't know what sort of tests to do. I need to study everything, checking and rechecking results. Right now, we're looking at the Tidal Works surrounding the Artifact in the hope that whoever first started expanding its function as a power source knew what it was supposed to be doing. But so far, we can't even determine how the newer Works is attached to it." He pointed at a clump of wire and tubing. "It's just... attached somehow, and the connections never seem to wear out. In fact, none of the Tidal Works seems to wear out near it. All this," he gestured around their tiny chamber, "is thousands of years old. It has to be since nobody has been this close to the Heart—that's what I've started calling it—for that long, but none of it has needed to be replaced or repaired. Ever, as far as we can tell."

Rina frowned, looking around. "It looks new."

"Indeed, it does. No one understands it at all. No one understands how any of this is possible. With so many different variables—"

"You need a wide range of equipment."

"You'll sell to me, then?"

She smiled. "Curiosity dictates I do nothing less."

10

JABBING THE BEEHIVE

A LOT WAS GOING ON, AND SYRINA KNEW JUST enough to know she didn't know anything. She wrote Ormo a note in tiny shorthand and attached it to Triglav's leg before sending him out the window and closing it behind him. She stared at the rivulets of rain dribbling down the pane, wondering how she knew that he knew to fly all the way back to Eheene. She missed him already and wondered once more what Ormo had done to her. To them. On a whim, she opened the window again, even though it would be at least a month or two before he'd be back.

In the meantime, Syrina hung around Fom, watching the summer evolve into a wet autumn that was like summer, only a little cooler, and took in the sights while she waited for Triglav, though she avoided the public executions and the Pit. Famous as it was, she found the idea of betting on prisoners as they fought over scraps of food unappealing.

She did spend one wet, dim afternoon at an arena fight. One of the karakh ones, since they were the most popular and she'd never seen a karakh do more than walk around before. The ticket was outrageously expensive, but Rina had tin and loved to spend it.

The two karakh crept out of opposite gates, scuttling on their big clawed hands across the packed mud. They both stood well over thirty hands high at the shoulders, one a reddish brown, the other, slightly smaller, a mottled black and gray. The two creatures locked round, luminous yellow eyes and clicked and whistled at each other around tusks protruding from their elongated jaws. Their hands were pale and devoid of fur, with black four-hand-long claws at the ends of each of their twelve fingers. Their feet had three clawed toes, like birds, with one thick grasping talon jutting from the back.

Karakh were omnivores, scavengers in the wild, and almost comically unsubtle. The tusks were for digging up roots, rending carcasses, and fighting off rivals, not hunting. Even the deafest, lamest game could drag itself out of the creature's path long before the karakh came into view.

The riders—shepherds, to use the ancient word they liked to call themselves—rested behind the animals' heads, straddling their necks and holding onto heavy chains, which linked to brass rings pierced through the karakh's cheeks.

What fascinated Syrina most about the karakh was the famous connection between mount and rider. She'd heard stories about the nomads in the Yellow Desert forming a special bond with their camels, but that was a casual acquaintance compared to the link between a karakh and its shepherd.

Karakh lived about as long as humans. When the elders chose a tribesman to form the bond, sometime in their first year of life, he and a karakh cub were put together, raised together, trained together, until they thought together. They even spoke the same whistling, clicking language. But as often as not, the creature seemed to respond to thoughts and feelings alone.

If the karakh died, the rider usually followed within the week, if not from suicide, then out of a loss of the will to live. If the shepherd died, the karakh remembered it had twelve claws and two ten-hand-long tusks, and mad with grief, used these assets on anyone and anything nearby until it was put down or crawled off somewhere to die of grief and exhaustion.

When Syrina had first learned about such a bond while a girl and still in training, the idea of caring about anything but her Ma'is so deeply seemed ridiculous, especially a mere animal. Now she'd developed a new interest in the subject, and she wanted to see it firsthand.

The Fom arenas weren't to the death. Mounts and shepherds were too valuable for that, and whatever the details were within the treaty the Tribes, signed hundreds of years ago with the Church, it didn't include a clause that said they had to kill each other for someone else's entertainment. The karakh's tusks were sheathed in thick leather. The contestants scuttled around the oval pit of the arena, lunging and swiping at each other until someone was dismounted.

The reddish one, named Pas on the playbill, was favored to win. Rina put a thousand Three-Sides down on the gray one.

The arena was a square mud-floored pit, eight hundred hands to a side and fifty hands from the ground to the first row of seats, which were reserved for Church officials and their guests. Rina sat in the row behind them. The walls of the pit were boarded with thick bands of hardwood, replaced every week but still scuffed and beaten half to splinters. Nine thick lodgepole posts, likewise scuffed, rose in a grid from the floor, a hundred hands apart from each other and almost as high as the rim of the pit. The whole arena was built to give the karakh something to jump around on while they dueled, vaguely simulating their natural environment on the Upper Peninsula.

The National Arena itself was an immense circular marble and granite structure built the better part of five hundred years ago for the karakh fights, which had been gaining in popularity for a hundred years before then. It held almost fifteen thousand people and was always sold out.

The karakh skittered, crab-like on their clawed hands through the mud, circling each other, leaping from ground to post, post to wall and back again, whistling and clicking while the shepherds eyed each other.

The gray karakh, billed as Nazuun, made the first move, jumping from one post to another, then shifting its momentum to lunge toward Pas. Nazuun tossed its rider just before the attack, protecting him from the impact of the landing and any retaliatory swipe. It caught the shepherd with one hand as it landed, and placed him back behind its head while swiping at Pas's rider with the other in an open-handed slap. Pas was bigger, but it was faster, too. It tossed its own rider over the swipe of Nazuun, crouched down, and dropped back to avoid the blow, then snatched its shepherd out of the air and set him behind its head again. The maneuver caught Nazuun off balance, and it hadn't recovered from its own attack before Pas

117

swiped again. Its padded open palm smacked into Nazuun's shepherd, who flew thirty hands into the mud, narrowly missing one lodgepole and rolling into another one. He was still for a moment, then stood. He looked muddy, bruised, and annoyed, but unharmed. Most of the crowd thundered with cheers, but there were a few boos, too, from the sore ones who'd lost money. Pas whistled in triumph and lopped toward the beaten gate opening on one side of the arena.

And just like that, Rina was out a thousand Three-Sides. *Oh, well.* She stood to leave with the crowd filing toward the exits, losers muttering about the shortness of the show, winners too pleased to care. It wasn't her tin, anyway.

———

A month later, Rina got back to the Grace's Hospice from a day of shopping to find Triglav waiting for her at his place on the top of the bedpost. He stared down at her, eyes curious and bored, but she still got the impression he was happy to see her.

It was an Eye Night. Unlike almost everywhere else in the world, it wasn't a big deal in Fom, though many people still got the day off. It was always fairly dark under the permanent clouds belched out by the Tidal Works, and it seemed like half the city was intoxicated on something most of the time, no matter what day it was. She wouldn't have been surprised if half of Fom didn't even know there was an eclipse going on somewhere above the constant drizzle.

Syrina was elated to see Triglav and peeled off Rina so she could be herself around him. There was no logic in it. Just felt like the thing to do. He hopped down onto her shoulder, made a warbling sound, and leaned into her head. She scratched the back of his neck and untied the tiny piece of paper wrapped around his leg. The script was minute, small enough that it was hard for even her to read, and she imagined Ormo's fat hand holding a tiny pen steady enough to write it. The image made her smile, but it was smart. Anyone coming across it would only see a small paper covered in uneven lines.

L motivations beyond profit. Ambitions of an HM working outside Syndicate. Find proof. Disrupt. Remove both ends.

There it was. *Both ends.* One end was Lees because he'd overstepped his bounds and it was just a matter of time. The other was N'talisan, the guy who was getting all the benefits. Rubbing the archaeologist was the cleanest way to disrupt the operation, perhaps permanently. N'talisan was working indirectly, or maybe even directly, for a High Merchant who was going against the rest of the Syndicate. Or at least that's what Ormo believed. Syrina wished she knew what else her Ma'is suspected that he wasn't telling her, and she reminded herself for the hundredth time that it wasn't her job to care.

She could probably justify getting rid of N'nareth as well, and for that matter, Ehrina Ka'id if Ormo asked her to. On the other hand, she'd be surprised if N'nareth knew very many details. It would be too dangerous for her and Lees, and details wouldn't help the importer anyway unless she was in the blackmail business, and Syrina didn't think she was. Ka'id would know more, but the accountant was far too influential to act against without solid proof or direct orders, and Syrina had neither. Ormo might want to make their lives miserable in other ways, but they were just money movers doing what they were paid to do, and he wouldn't have anything against that.

Something still didn't sit right, though. She told herself once more that she shouldn't second-guess her Ma'is, but something was off, and she couldn't put her finger on it.

But Ormo was her Ma'is, and she was his Kalis, and he gave her a job, and she did it. That meant dealing with N'talisan now and Lees when she got back to Eheene. With N'talisan gone, whatever plot was being cooked up by the rogue High Merchant would crumble. With Lees gone, everyone would be too scared to start it up again, at least for a while.

Before she made everyone suspicious by killing people off, though, she needed more indisputable evidence against Lees, and she might be able to get to the bottom of the mystery around the Tidal Works while she was at it. She didn't cherish the thought of looking through piles of records of tariffs paid, merchandise shipped, fees collected, and the rest, but with a little less work she thought she could get someone to do it for her.

The idea of rubbing Gaston made her sad. She suspected that whatever he'd discovered within the Tidal Works was bigger than the Church or the Syndicate, but it wasn't her job to like what Ormo told her to do. Well, it was, but just because she stopped liking it didn't mean she wasn't going to do it. The thought of Ormo's disappointment was still more painful than any regret she might have over killing a N'naradin archaeologist.

She tried to shake the black feeling from the back

of her mind again. *I've needed to kill better people than N'talisan. Why should it bother me now?*

———

The auditor's robe was the easiest part since they took them off every night before they went home and left them in the coatroom of the Customs House. A little research told her that each House maintained its own supply, so there were always extras in different sizes. They were bulky, heavy affairs made of red and black silk. They bore complicated folds along the shoulders, and the Sun-and-Crescent of N'narad etched in gold thread down the front and back. She was short enough that they were all too big, but she grabbed the smallest one she could find, stashed it on the roof under an overhang to keep off most of the rain, and went back in naked to pick the lock on the Trade Commissioner's office.

She rifled through old letters and files until she found one that still had most of the broken wax seal on it and another one she wouldn't need to doctor too much to make it say what she needed it to. Then she whisked everything back to Rina's hotel room.

The streets were still busy that close to the docks, and anyone looking up saw the robes as a shapeless ghost in the fog, flapping from rooftop to rooftop, and maybe something else they couldn't get their head around before it was out of sight again.

She took her time making up the face, and even more fixing the seal and altering the letter. She was thankful she could come to Fom with Rina's absurd stack of luggage. Everything she needed was in it, including more than a hundred wigs, and this time she'd need to do more than fool a few frightened peasants on the Lip.

———

A stern, diminutive man, pallid and nervous, with a sharp nose and a jaw that protruded in an under-bite a karakh would be proud of emerged from The Grace's Hospice an hour after dawn. His hair was thinning into a widow's peak as sharp as his nose. It receded almost to his crown and was uncompromisingly black. He clutched a letter sealed with black wax to his chest with both hands, and his eyes were a serious, intelligent green. He was tiny compared to the throng of people around him, but he had no trouble weaving through the streets unhindered.

People began to flood out of the Customs House as the tide reached its peak. He merged with them for a half-span and checked into a hotel with the lofty name of Summer's Prayer. He ignored the tinkling marble fountain under the dome of the lobby and the children's choir humming on a balcony to his left. There were a few minutes of confusion at the desk. The man's reservation had been lost, and they scrambled to find him another room, but they did so with prolific apologies.

Then he slipped back out into the river of people.

———

No one in the Customs House was happy to see an auditor from the Spire. Fom fancied itself a free city, even, blasphemously, independent of the archbishop in Tyrsh. Every time an official showed up from the

Island, it reminded everyone that the Grace wasn't in charge. If the auditor felt the disdain of those around him, he showed no sign of caring.

"Where is the commissioner of this circus?" he snapped, at a cowering secretary, his voice and accent brimming with the contempt of an Islander forced to come to the mainland for a duty that's beneath him.

The secretary cringed and pointed down a short hallway.

"Xereks Lees," the little man spat as he stepped through the door.

The commissioner was an old man with a thick wreath of white hair wrapped around his ears, and a spotted, pale head. His nose was bulbous and ruddy, and he had a mole on the left side of his face that sprouted a few long strands of brilliant white hair. His eyes were clear, gray, and angry.

"Who are you?" he demanded, unintimidated.

"Hayden Temm, Under-Commissioner, Trade and Import Oversight Regulator under his Holiness, Archbishop Daliius the Third."

The commissioner shifted, but he didn't look any less irate or any more cowed.

"And what brings you to Fom?"

The commissioner's tone dripped with sarcasm, but again, the auditor showed no sign of caring.

"Xereks Lees," he said again. "Do you know who that is?"

The commissioner thought for a moment. "The name sounds familiar. Skald, from the sound of it. But, no, I can't place it. Who is he?"

"He is a low merchant and foreign exporter. Tidal Works. He uses an importer here, Stysha N'nareth. He may be the head of an espionage ring working for one or more of the Fifteen, the entire Syndicate, or some other entity."

In the commissioner's eyes, anger was falling away to suspicious curiosity.

"And you're saying Stysha N'nareth—who I do know well, by the way—is involved in this spy ring?"

Temm shook his head, but his green eyes were still hard. "We don't know. It's probable that she doesn't know of Lees's other activities. Nothing is certain. That's why I'm here."

"I'm not sure I understand."

The auditor tossed a sealed envelope on top of the papers already strewn across the desk. The commissioner picked it up and examined the seal before cracking it open. When he was finished reading, he laid it back on the desk and looked up at Temm.

"You want N'nareth audited."

"I want every page, every note that mentions or can be connected in any way to Lees or his business pulled and delivered to my room at the Summer's Prayer Hotel within the next three days. Two days would be preferable, but His Holiness is nothing if not flexible."

"Three days? One of the biggest importers in Fom? It would take..."

Temm glared at him, frosted green eyes never unlocking with his.

The commissioner swallowed. "Two days. Of course."

———

Syrina was happy. She was going to get a lot more than she needed on Lees, but she could dump it all on

Ormo and let him figure it out. She had other business.

There was a risk that Lees would hear about the audit and get spooked, but she was guessing N'nareth wouldn't say anything, and there was no one else to tell him. The woman would lose Lees's business if he was innocent and be incriminated if he was guilty. Better for her just to wait it out.

Syrina went back to N'talisan's workshop the next day, this time naked and across the rooftops. Triglav followed, skimming in and out of the low clouds. It was still early, and the door was open to let out the constant heat of the Tidal Works. Only one of the assistants was there now, tagging and documenting a collection of tiny metal pieces laid out on a dark cloth at one end of the table. A large book lay open on another table next to her. She wasn't one of the three that had been there when Rina had visited, and Syrina wondered how much help the Church provided N'talisan with. The low door that led down to the Tidal Works stood ajar. Across the alley, a vent whistled and sputtered little puffs of steam.

Syrina opted to wait. It might be easier and quieter to do the job underground, but she'd never find him down there, and Triglav would be useless if she needed him.

N'talisan and one of the other assistants came out three hours later and closed the door behind them. It was afternoon now, and brighter. The clouds had lifted a little, and the drizzle had succumbed to a fine mist. The woman she'd seen tagging earlier wasn't with them. Syrina wondered how she felt about being left behind.

She decided to do it then and there. Assistants

would be with him most of the time, and Syrina didn't have the time or motivation to spare them. She was lucky there was only one now. The wide alley to the lab was empty, but a block or two in any direction and they'd be lost in the throngs of Fom where it would be impossible to do the job unseen. Plus, it was one thing to keep the audit quiet from Lees all the way up in Eheene. N'talisan would find out by dinnertime. Syrina would be lucky to find him after that if he was smart enough to realize where it would point, and Gaston N'talisan was nothing if not smart.

She dropped into the street. He seemed oblivious as she slipped up behind him, fingers on her left hand rigid as she prepared to strike the nerves in his spine that would stop his heart. He'd have an early, unfortunate heart attack and a bruise on his back that would probably be explained away by his fall. If she was quick enough, she thought she might even be able to spare the assistant.

Gaston whipped his body around, so quick it was a blur even to Syrina. He grabbed her wrist and dropped, tossing her over his shoulder onto the granite cobbles like a sack of potatoes. She stayed on the ground longer than she should have, not from the pain that danced around her senses, but from the shock of having been seen. Not just seen, but seen by her rub. *It's impossible.*

Gaston didn't let his surprise at her attack show if he felt any. Before she'd even crumpled to the ground where he'd thrown her, his foot was coming toward her face. She rolled out of the way, noting that his gaze never left her eyes. Even when she spun away and back again, his eyes were there to meet hers. He knew what he was doing.

As Syrina rolled away, her foot clipped up into his knee, and she spun upward to bring her palm into his face. He dropped back in a blur, not quite quick enough, and her fingers scraped his face at an angle. Her hand came away sticky with tough, rubbery globs of flesh. One side of Gaston's face had peeled away to reveal his sharp blue eyes lost in a swirl of writhing tattoos.

He—she—rolled back out of Syrina's reach, stripping out of her now-useless costume at the same time. By the time the other Kalis stood, she was mostly lost to Syrina's sight, as if Syrina was finding something out of the corner of her eye. She wanted to sit down for a minute and wonder why the hell Gaston N'talisan was a Kalis, but the blurry figure came at her again. The attack didn't do any serious damage, but it knocked her off balance for a second, which was probably the point. The N'talisan-Kalis used the half-second to pause, sigh, and roll her eyes back into her head.

She went through the Papsukkal Door a split second before Syrina could, and it was enough to keep her out of it. The N'talisan-Kalis streaked toward her so fast that Syrina couldn't get a fix on her eyes, so she didn't see the other Kalis until she barreled into Syrina's chest and smashed her back into the limestone wall so hard Syrina heard her ribs pop. The N'talisan-Kalis smashed her fist into Syrina's face, crushing her nose sideways and snapping her cheekbone. Syrina felt hot stickiness flood down her face, and she realized she was going to die. Her blood-covered face gave the N'talisan-Kalis a nice red target to practice on while Syrina squinted through the rain of her own blood, looking for sudden movement.

Behind her, the vent to the Tidal Works began whistling in earnest, and the air began to thicken with brownish fog. Syrina dropped to her knees, hoping that if it happened to be at the same moment as the strike she knew was coming, it would make the N'tal-isan-Kalis miss and buy her own life a few more seconds.

A white comet dropped out of the sky and hit the other Kalis while she was still ten hands away. A spray of blood arced into the street. Through the Pap-sukkal Door or not, Triglav was faster. He shot back up into the low clouds before the N'talisan-Kalis could react, no doubt as surprised by Syrina's owl as Syrina had been by her. It was enough. Syrina felt her heart slow, then stop, and time stood still. She lunged from where she'd crouched against the wall, toward the bloody face that floated above a shadow in the middle of the alley and knocked the N'talisan-Kalis back against the opposite wall. Syrina pushed her fist hard into the woman's solar plexus but was careful not to kill her. She just wanted her to sit still for a minute. She had questions.

The Kalis's head struck the stone, but she didn't slow down, and she arced her hands up to smash over Syrina's ears. It would've killed a normal person, but Syrina just heard a bang so loud it made her see white and all other sound died to nothing as if the world was suddenly wrapped in thick velvet. It stunned her, but Syrina was still on the other side of the Door, and it looked like the N'talisan-Kalis was already falling out of it. Syrina managed to stumble back a step just in time to make room for Triglav, who arced out of the clouds for a second swipe at the N'talisan-Kalis's face.

Syrina saw the crossbow bolt arc through white

light and muffled noise. The feathers of it brushed past her face from somewhere behind her. *Someone's shooting at me*.

The bolt—she could've caught it, would've caught it if she'd thought about where it was going instead of why it hadn't hit her—drifted like a paper bird, past her head and into Triglav's back, where he was just arcing up from the N'talisan-Kalis to the safety of the clouds. He let out a soft hoot and fell like a stone to the cobbled street.

What's going on? A voice in Syrina's head that sounded almost like her own shot through the spike of blind horror that pierced her the moment the bolt struck Triglav. Then it said, *Never mind*.

Syrina leaped toward the other Kalis, who crouched against the wall, looking as shocked as Syrina had probably looked earlier, and dropped low, so her shoulder rammed into the N'talisan-Kalis's chest. Syrina grabbed the woman's wrist and broke her arm in three places. Then she spun around. The research assistant—the woman who'd been tagging innocuous pieces of metal earlier—still had the crossbow at her shoulder. Syrina darted forward, blind with grief and rage, faster than the bolt that had struck Triglav, intent on breaking the woman's neck before the N'talisan-Kalis could recover from her shattered arm.

The assistant stepped out of Syrina's way as if Syrina was just walking toward her, and brought the crossbow down across the back of her head. Syrina stumbled, fell, jumped up and spun around, but all she saw were clothes drifting down to the wet cobblestones and a flash of motion out of the corner of her eye. A few globs of a waxy face oozed in the gutter. The abandoned crossbow clattered onto the ground.

No, no, no, no, no. The crumpled white shape of Triglav lay in the street, burning behind her eyes even when she wasn't looking at him. *He'll be okay. He's okay.*

Syrina could feel herself tumbling out of the Papsukkal Door, but she wasn't done yet. She staggered over to the N'talisan-Kalis, who hunched over, drained from her own Door, cradling her arm and staring down the street in shock, toward where the assistant had disappeared. Syrina dragged the woman into the door of the laboratory. The N'talisan-Kalis was too weak to resist. Whoever she was, Syrina's training in Papsukkal was better.

Then she killed the cowering male assistant. She didn't like it, but she was about to be vulnerable in a Church city, and he knew what she was and where she would be. She tossed him into the room, too. Then she picked up Triglav's still-warm body and collapsed into the lab herself, with enough wherewithal to wedge the crossbar across the door, jamming it closed.

"You're fine," she whispered to the limp form, stroking his feathers, unfamiliar panic churning in her belly. "You're fine. You'll be fine. It's okay. It's okay."

She wanted to pass out. She was lying down to pass out, but a voice in her head wouldn't let her. *Tie her up.* It was almost Syrina's voice. Almost.

Whatever it was, it was right, and somehow she was still conscious as if some alien part of her mind was forcing her to stay awake. Syrina spun up the black cloth that all the carefully marked parts were gathered on, scattered them onto the stone floor with a clatter like hail, and tied the unconscious Kalis's wrists and ankles together behind her tight enough that the woman's hands and feet began to turn blue under the tattoos. She tied them to the woman's neck, too, so even the slightest squirming would strangle her. Then Syrina crawled over to the low door that led to the Tidal Works, slammed it closed, and broke off a thin metal rod that had tumbled from the table into the lock, not caring if any remaining assistants could still get through it or not.

The voice in her head went silent when she finished, and Syrina passed out in the corner of the lab, cradling Triglav's body like a baby.

11

QUESTIONING AUTHORITY

Syrina woke, holding Triglav. His body was no longer warm. The corpse of the assistant who'd just been in the wrong place that day slumped in the corner she'd dropped him in. She could make out the shape of the N'talisan-Kalis lying hogtied to the leg of the heavy table. Syrina didn't remember doing that, nor straightening her own nose, which seemed to have healed in place. The woman was awake, and she looked at Syrina with calm blue eyes.

Syrina realized her own face was wet with tears. She'd been crying while she slept, and she was ashamed. Even during the harshest tests of her training, she couldn't remember more than a handful of times she'd cried, and that was different anyway. Tears of a child in physical pain. This was... emotional, and she did her best to swallow her tears.

But then she looked down at Triglav cradled in her arms, and her stomach twisted in a knot of grief so hard she thought she might throw up. She heard a low, moaning sob well-up from her throat and she couldn't stop it, so she buried her face in the cold, bloody feathers of Triglav's chest and screamed, so at least the other Kalis wouldn't be able to get a clear look at her eyes.

She sat like that, sobbing and screaming and clutching him and not caring about anything until the burning pain in her gut subsided into an ache that ebbed through every inch of her body. Then she lay Triglav down and walked over to the N'talisan-Kalis, who was watching her through the blood caked on her face, with an expression unreadable under the swirl of tattoos.

She was taller than Syrina. Maybe older, though it was hard to tell. Their tattoos were similar, but where Syrina's were all curves that flowed around her body, the other Kalis had sharp angles on her arms and thighs and under her small breasts.

"It was just a matter of time," the N'talisan-Kalis said.

Her voice was soft and young and sweet, but Syrina had no way of knowing if it was her own.

"Which one is it?" the woman said. "Berdai? Ormo? Nyliik? I know you have no reason to tell me, but I can't help wondering which one you work for."

Syrina wanted to ask her the same thing but didn't bother. The impostor had nothing to gain by giving up her Ma'is. On the other hand, Syrina might be able to get something out of the exchange if she told the N'talisan-Kalis she worked for Ormo.

Not yet. Wait.

That voice. Like someone mimicking Syrina's and doing an imperfect job of it, right behind her head where she couldn't see them. She could feel it holding her grief in check, helping her think.

Well, one thing at a time. "What were you doing

here as N'talisan?" Her words caught in her throat, and she bit her tongue against more tears.

There was a certain camaraderie among Kalis, even if they never worked together and almost never met. The N'talisan-Kalis probably didn't have anything personal against Syrina, even if she could guess what was in store for her when they were through talking. At least, Syrina knew that's how she'd feel if the tables were turned.

"Same as N'talisan," the woman said, her voice grating with the twist of cloth around her neck. "Researching the Tidal Works. What its function is, how it's made. My Ma'is taught me everything he could about the Works. Then he sent me here to learn whatever I could understand. At first, I think it was because he wanted me to disrupt it. Permanently, if I could. Open up the biggest city in the world to the naphtha market. The more I found, though, the more he just had me study the thing."

"Lees was shipping you the parts?"

"Some of them. A lot of the ordinary ones that I couldn't get through the Church without raising questions. You wouldn't believe the list of stuff the priests gave me that I wasn't allowed to do. I swear they don't want to know what's going on down there. Lees did some special orders, too, but he was slow, and then he got screwed anyway, so I arranged something else."

"Did your Ma'is set that up? With Lees, I mean."

"He had me set it up, yeah. The boss cleared everything up in Eheene so Lees could ship out the extra parts under the noses of the Port Authority. He didn't want any flags raised on either end by strange shipment manifests. He paid Lees extra so that Lees would go to all the extra trouble of shipping his stuff for free and deal with the cover-up that went with it. No profits to report, no paper trail. Not unless someone started looking at a lot of different strings at the same time and knew what to look for. Someone like another goddamn High Merchant."

"What did you learn about the Tidal Works while you were here?"

"Not much more than I already knew. Six or seven thousand years ago, when humanity started to claw their way out of the Age of Ashes and Fom sprouted up, they started building the Works around the Artifact to pump hot water into the settlement. Something to keep them warm at the end of the endless winter. This was way before naphtha machines were a thing. Hell, the Tidal Works was the reason anyone figured out how to make a naphtha turbine in the first place. And the tarfuel engine, and all the rest of it. As far as I can tell, Fom is the birthplace of modern society. Anyway, they probably remembered what it was for back then and decided to use what it was doing to their advantage. As Fom grew, so did the Tidal Works, until the Artifact was buried and forgotten. Something that just always worked. It bound itself to the newer machines, and the connections don't wear out. Whatever it is, they built it to last forever, and what's more, they built it to keep the things around it from wearing out, too. However that works. And it's storing a tremendous amount of power."

"I guess it would have to if it can heat a city as big as Fom," Syrina said.

"No." The woman's blue eyes were serious. "A tremendous amount. As in, if that thing were to ever lose whatever force is holding it together, it could vaporize Fom and the coast most of the way to Maresg. Maybe shatter windows in Eheene."

Syrina stared at her, looking for some hint of deception and seeing none in the liquid blue eyes. It didn't mean she wasn't lying, but Syrina didn't think she was. Just a hunch. Something in those sapphire eyes said that the N'talisan-Kalis believed the heart of the Tidal Works was every bit as important as N'talisan had said it was.

"Oh," Syrina said. Then she took a breath and asked the question she'd been avoiding. She tried to keep her voice from shaking. "What about your assistant? The other Kalis?"

Syrina was knew the answer already, given how the N'talisan-Kalis had reacted, but she still had to ask.

The Kalis laughed at her. "You're smarter than that. She was after your friend there." She nodded toward Triglav's corpse and coughed as the gesture made the binding around her neck tighten. "I didn't know about either of you," she began again, when she could, her voice hoarser. "She was a new understudy. Transferred under N'talisan a month ago from Tyrsh. The professor's bright new student. She had all the proper paperwork. Everything checked out. Naturally."

Syrina ground her teeth. The Kalis was right. The other one had just rubbed Triglav and run. That meant—

Later. Tell her now.

Syrina took a few deep breaths until she could relax enough to speak again, forcing down every lesson her twenty years of training and ten of experience had taught her.

"I'm here under Ma'is Ormo," she whispered. "He has me investigating the finances of Xereks Lees."

The N'talisan-Kalis's eyes grew wide, and she might've looked amused under the blood and tattoos.

"Why on Eris would you tell me that, even if you are going to kill me?"

"Do you know something about... Ormo?" Syrina had almost said *me* but caught herself before she showed the woman just how messed up she was.

Not that she hadn't already figured it out for herself.

The Kalis laughed again. "Ormo. So that's who it was. I should've known."

"What do you mean?" Syrina bent over the Kalis at her head, away from her tied hands.

The Kalis managed a little shrug without strangling herself. "It must've been fifteen, maybe twenty years ago, now. My Ma'is started looking for some sort of connection between us and the Tidal Works."

"Us? You mean the Kalis?"

"That's right. I don't know how he connected the Kalis with something like that, but he's always digging around for stuff left over from the Ancestors, just like they all are. He must've found... I don't know, something. Anyway, I ended up out in the taiga at one point, checking some things out. Long story, but the short version is I ran into another Kalis. She had this messenger hawk. They were inseparable. It was weird. Being a Seed means I come across other Kalis now and again, or rather, they come across me. You're an Arm, I'd imagine, so you move around too much to run into your own kind very often. Well, you do, but you're usually not aware of it. Anyway, when two

Kalis meet, it usually goes better than this. Never saw anything like that, though. At first, the boss was interested in the idea, like maybe he thought the bird was connected to the Works somehow, too. It seemed like good old-fashioned Kalis luck at the time. Two of the Fifteen working on the same thing from different sides, you know? Mine looking at Artifacts being connected to the Kalis, the other one—Ormo, I guess—experimenting with the Kalis's connection to the old Artifacts. I guess your boss and my boss didn't play well together, though. A few weeks later, he pulled me out."

"Why?"

The N'talisan-Kalis snorted. "What? You mean Ormo gives you reasons for what he tells you to do? At the time, I assumed it was because he found out that something I did stepped on another High Merchant's toes and he backed off." She paused. "At least that's the way it's supposed to work." She twisted her mouth into a brief frown, visible under the caking blood. "Not long after that, he planted me in Tyrsh to start setting up N'talisan."

"How long ago did all this happen?" Syrina's throat was dry.

"Like I said, maybe fifteen, twenty years. I've been N'talisan so long I think I was almost beginning to believe it. Hadn't given any of it much thought since then, until yesterday, seeing you with that owl."

The Kalis tried to prop herself up a little to look at Syrina, who'd gone back to hunker against the wall, but the noose around her neck tightened again. She made a little strangled noise and lay still.

Syrina plopped down to sit against the wall she was leaning against and stared at nothing. She couldn't see the other Kalis's face, but she could hear her laughter rasping through the noose.

"My source on Ormo's Kalis experiments—the only one I found before my own Ma'is pulled me out —he was a doctor. A guy named Saadasi." The N'tal-isan-Kalis's voice was a scratchy whisper.

"Why are you telling me that?" Syrina asked, but it was what she would've done, too. She felt defeated.

"Ormo's a traitorous coward who's stabbing my Ma'is in the back by sending you here to kill N'tal-isan. Why wouldn't I screw up his little pet even more before she rubs me?" She nodded toward Triglav and snorted again. "I bet you won't be able to resist looking into it now, whatever Ormo tells you to do."

"Fuck you." Syrina stepped over, leaned down, and broke the other Kalis's neck with a twist of her hand.

The N'talisan impostor must've let her do it, or it wouldn't have been so easy.

Syrina went back to Triglav and cradled him while she watched the tattoos on the Kalis's corpse blacken and grow. There was a flash as they ignited the flesh under them, so bright it hurt her eyes. In a minute, the body had disintegrated to ash and a few fragments of blackened bone. The room filled with noxious, sweet smoke.

Syrina sat against the wall, coughing. She didn't know what to do. It didn't seem right to just leave Triglav there, so she bundled him up in the assistant's shirt and slipped into the alley.

It was dark. She had no idea what time it was. Late. She carried Triglav across the rooftops as far as she could until the maze of stone buildings straight-ened and grew further apart as the homes grew larger.

Stone walls sprouted along both sides of the road and between the estates that blanketed the steep southern slope of Fom, their ramparts forming a bird's-eye tapestry of uneven squares. The crowds that bustled all night deeper in the city thinned, until up here, she was alone.

She padded along the edge of the camel cart road, on a narrow footpath crammed against a high, rough limestone wall green with moss. For a hundred paces, the fog grew so thick that even the ground became lost to her sight, and her only guide was the rugged unbroken vertical plane of the wall to her left.

And then, just like that, she emerged onto a ridge above the rocky vineyards that sloped down to the cliffs south of the city. The Eye slashed a thin violet smile beneath an empty black circle surrounded by stars, and the dim, thick light of the crescent danced on the distant whitecaps. Behind her, Fom's clouds boiled, burning gold with the city smoldering beneath them.

Syrina jogged past stony straight rows of knotted vines, thick with brown, withered leaves. The vines ran all the way to the edge of the cliff. There, Syrina stopped running. As she released Triglav over the rim, a new twist of rage snarled in her chest. She didn't care about killing and spying for Ormo or about Lees and the fake Professor N'talisan or the Tidal Works exploding and destroying a fifth of Eris. All she cared about was making whoever was responsible for her grief suffer, but she had nothing to go on except the job she was on now and the word of another Kalis, who'd been the first to admit she was just trying to screw with Syrina's head.

Someone had ordered Triglav's murder. There

were Fifteen suspects, but all of them were untouchable. It could've been whichever High Merchant had sent the N'talisan-Kalis to Fom. That the impostor didn't know about it didn't mean anything. The machinations of the damned Merchant's Syndicate were inscrutable to their pet Kalis. As far as Syrina knew, though, none of the other High Merchants even knew about Triglav. Then again, she had no idea what Ormo knew about anything, much less what the other Fourteen knew about her. But even if they did know, none of them had an obvious reason to kill Triglav and keep her alive.

Except for Ormo. He gave her Triglav, forged some bond between them. And the N'talisan impostor said he'd done it before, if she was telling the truth, and if that other Kalis had been one of his, all those years ago. But why would he go to all the trouble just to take it away?

Maybe you were the first time it worked.

And then there was that voice. Too much, too much.

The thought came that it was somehow Triglav's voice, but she dismissed the idea as soon as it crossed her mind. Not just because it was crazy—it was, after all, a voice in her head—but because it simply wasn't his. She could feel his absence. It was infinite. A black emptiness in her heart, edges still clawing outward, consuming her. Triglav was gone. The awful truth she kept coming back to was that the voice was a lot closer to her own.

Syrina wasn't ready to believe the other Kalis or the voice in her head. Neither one of them had any reason to tell her the truth, and it was Ormo they were talking about. Ormo. He'd raised her, taught her most of what she knew, and made sure she learned the rest from someone else. Up until he'd given her Triglav, she'd been his slave and a willing one at that. Just like any other Kalis.

Exactly.

She was done in Fom. She paid the smuggler, her various personalities checked out of their various hotels, and she gathered the absurd amount of materials that had turned up in the importer's audit and shipped it ahead to Eheene.

Little things here and there, a rat in the street, a random windowsill, would remind her of Triglav, and a ball would clot in her throat. She'd need to close her eyes and force her mind empty until it sank back into her stomach and she could think again. She cursed Ormo for introducing her to love. All it had brought her was grief.

———

Syrina had a conversation with herself on the way home.

She'd been growing more convinced that the voice was just some part of her mind in denial of the swell of new emotions that a Kalis shouldn't have any business feeling. She was still almost as convinced of it after the conversation was over, but doubt smoldered in the black pit of grief that had settled in her chest.

She sat in her tiny cabin, all done-up as Rina and staring out the round brass-rimmed portal, trying to keep herself from looking for Triglav as he skimmed through the clouds, when the voice asked her, *Where am I?*

Syrina had nothing else to do. "On a boat? I don't know what you mean."

How did I come to be here?

Syrina was game. It was a long trip back to Eheene, and she needed a distraction.

"That depends on where you came from."

The voice seemed to think about that for a minute. *I was always here. Watching, like a dream I can't remember.*

"That's because you're a figment of my imagination."

It paused again, and she could almost feel it considering that, too.

No. Your heart is beating at twenty-six beats every minute. When I came into being, it wasn't beating at all, but your blood was getting pumped through your system by your external markings at an equivalent of 297 beats per minute. I could increase that rate to 405 without any risk to yourself, and, consequently, me. The unavoidable fatigue you experience afterward can be managed a lot better than you did on your own. I tried to help, but my control was limited at the time. I'm not sure if you noticed. Your markings, by the way, are an artificial bacterium that's also able to heal wounds and scatter photons, creating a confusing effect on most retinal—

"Shut up a second. You can control my body?"

Certain things, yes. Things that you don't need to think about.

"So you could kill me, then?"

Syrina didn't believe anything other than she was talking to herself.

I suppose so, but since I'm inseparable from you, it would be a murder-suicide.

"How do you know all this? What are you?"

If it could've given her an explanation half as good as what it had just told her about the tattoos and the Papsukkal Door—most of which she didn't even understand—Syrina might've been convinced. It would've been easier on her fragile state of mind than endless doubt.

It couldn't.

I don't know, it said, after another long pause. *I am as much you as you are, and I came from the same place. Whatever I know, I just... know. I just didn't know it until that day in the street.*

That drew Syrina's mind back to Triglav, and her heart snarled into a knot. She fell silent.

Who are you?

"What?"

She didn't care if any of the crew heard Rina Saalesh talking to herself through the cabin door, but she dropped her voice to a harsh whisper anyway.

You want to know what I am. I want the same from you. We're inseparable from each other. It's reasonable to think we might learn something about my nature by learning something of yours.

"You want my life story or what? You're in my head. Can't you just dig around for it?"

I don't know. If I can, I don't know how. If I could, would you want me to?

Syrina felt like she was arguing with herself and losing. "Fine. Let's see. You know about the tattoos, apparently. More than I do. I got them when I was five. I don't remember getting them, or anything before then, or the year after. I know I was trained before then, but I don't know what. Languages, I suppose, and whatever else. It's my understanding that none of the Kalis remember. Trauma, maybe. Not just from the tattoos, although that must be the worst of it. They burn out every hair follicle with needles, pull out every fingernail and toenail, everything but our eyelashes. Then they can mark us, and the nails grow back over them. Inside lips and ears. Everywhere. Otherwise, one eyebrow, one strand of hair, anything for the eye to follow and the tattoos don't work as well. And that's just the tattoos. Who knows what else they do to us. It's a wonder that any of the chosen kids survive."

Why you? Why were you chosen?

Syrina was beginning to wonder that herself. "I don't know." She forced her eyes away from the window and lay down on the bed. "Girls are chosen before birth. Or rather, our parents are chosen."

Girls? No boys?

Syrina allowed herself a little smile. "I asked Ormo that once when I was little. He told me men were anatomically unfit to be Kalis. Imagine, he said, if the most vulnerable part of your body was one you couldn't use the tattoos to hide. I didn't understand what he was talking about at the time, but I've seen men naked since then.

Anyway, we're trained, literally, from the day we're conceived. Observe, mimic, disguise, forge, manipulate, kill. My life for Ormo."

But you don't trust him anymore.

Ormo. Goddamn Ormo. He was the first thing Syrina remembered when she woke from the nightmare of the tattooing. He gave her a hug and some chocolate and taught her how to paralyze a person's lungs by tapping their neck. He was the only person she saw for the next two years, and he was the one that protected her from the cruelty of the instructors in the years that came after.

It seemed so obvious now. The harshness of the teachers and the kindness of the master. An act. A High Merchant wringing loyalty from his servant. All of it flooded Syrina's thoughts, but she didn't want to talk anymore.

"No."

The voice must've heard more than that because it didn't say anything else.

Too much. Triglav. Roiling grief. Boundless, impotent rage. A voice in her head. Confusion and doubt.

12

HEIST

SYRINA TOLD ORMO MOST OF IT. HIS EXPRESSION was as unreadable as ever when she told him Triglav was killed, but his voice seemed sad. Not that that meant anything. She couldn't bring herself to lie to him outright, but she didn't mention the other Kalis. Either of them. She only said that one of N'talisan's assistants had killed Triglav. If he sensed she was keeping something from him, he didn't press her about it.

It had never occurred to her before to keep something from Ormo, but she wasn't ready to talk about the conversation she'd had with the N'talisan-Kalis or the voice in her head.

The break-in at Lees's and the death of Gaston N'talisan had combined to create quite a stir. Lees now had a contingent of mercenaries posted around his home and his warehouse, and he traveled with Orvaan and a gaggle of bodyguards when he went out, which was rare these days. The upper echelons of Eheene had been talking about how disgusting it was that he thought he was so important, but they all were still sycophants to his face.

To Lees's credit, Syrina was going to kill him. She hoped that would vindicate him a little in the eyes of his peers. But before she rubbed Lees, she still needed to find out who his backer was. She now knew where his product was going and why, but not who he was working for. If she could find the source of his tin, she'd also find the High Merchant behind the N'tal-isan-Kalis and maybe a clue about the other one, too.

Ormo had people going over everything pulled up from the audit on N'nareth. There was plenty in it to incriminate Lees, but nothing so far that said who was pulling his strings. It was a good bet he wasn't keeping anything at his office anymore, which left his home and his accountant. His home was an *if*, and the accountant was a *probably somewhere*, so Syrina decided to check Ka'id's again. She was acutely aware of how much she'd avoided doing just that from the very beginning. More goddamn paperwork.

There was a note on Ka'id's door that said she was out for the week, but she wouldn't keep documents as sensitive as Lees's there anyway.

Syrina waited.

She waited until the end of the week for Ka'id to get back from wherever she'd been. Then she spent another month waiting for Lees to pay her a visit. No doubt she had other clients whose records were kept in the banks, but Syrina didn't know who they were or how many different banks Ka'id used, and it would take even longer to search every place the accountant went.

It was cold. The sun came up late and went down early without ever clearing the copper points of the roofs on the south side of the street. People who walked by stayed hunched under heavy hoods of embroidered silk. The ones who rode within palanquins hid behind heavy curtains drawn closed to keep in the warmth, while the bearers wore thick, hooded white robes. The chilly, still air muffled sound, and the only noises on the narrow street in front of Ka'id's office were the shuffling feet of passersby and the faint hiss of the naphtha lamps when they were lit every afternoon.

Syrina perched on a ledge across the street from the accountant's place every day, still as a gargoyle, as unnoticed as the marble hand above the door beneath her feet, holding its flame.

After Lees and his entourage showed, she needed to wait three more weeks because Ka'id didn't go anywhere with him the first time, and only went home at the end of the day.

Winter Solstice came and went, and the days began to grow a little longer, but ice still glazed the oily canals.

———

When the accountant finally did go somewhere with Lees, it was just a few blocks from the Syndicate Palace—a bank called Raymos Storage. There were a plethora of banks in that part of town that catered to the type of people that had a lot to hide and the money to hide it somewhere good.

It was easy to get the floor plans from the Syndicate Aggregate Halls. They had most of the plans of the city in there, as long as someone knew how to find them amid the rows of ancient rolled-up blueprints. Syrina had more than enough experience in that regard, but she couldn't count on them including all the details. The banks claimed to be safe from everyone, and they'd all made steps to be sure of it, including altering most of the records before they made it into the Library.

The huge marble and obsidian building was empty inside except for a long marble desk, behind which was a heavy copper door set in the floor, which led down to a second reception area. Behind the desk down there lay the vaults—three massive arched chambers deep below the streets of Eheene. They were level with the top of the naphtha reservoirs, which streaked the ground beneath the city, and a tricky architect could've put all sorts of nasty mechanisms down there. Vault One held Syndicate bonds and promissory notes as well as tin currency. Two held documents too sensitive to be kept anywhere else, and Three was arranged to hold larger items such as sculptures and iron ingots.

Syrina spent the next four days creeping over every inch of the area around Raymos Storage. Naphtha and oil traps needed ventilation to work, and she found nine innocuous vents leading under the streets, placed above where the vaults were hidden. The shafts around Vault Two were set into the base of the Skalkaad Trade Union building, with another in the roof of the Feraas Wells Investment Corporation across the street.

The vents told her there were traps but not what kind, besides either fire or gas. Both could cause problems for the bank. Venting toxic gas into the heart of Eheene would be frowned on by the Merchant's Syndicate, but fire was also tricky, in a room full of papers valuable enough that someone would pay a lot of tin to keep them there. Whatever the traps did, though, they wouldn't be good for whoever was down there when they went off.

The whole thing would need to look like a false alarm. Lees was already on edge, and if there was an incident in the vault that Ka'id kept his life in, he would hear about it long before Syrina had a chance to finish him. Any suspicious corpses or missing documents and Lees would vanish in a puff of self-entitled smoke. True, if he disappeared thoroughly enough, even Ormo might think he was dead. But if her Ma'is ever found Lees alive after she told him the job was done, Syrina would be as dead as Lees should have been, favorite pet or no.

She wouldn't be able to take anything out of the vault, but the stack of evidence from the audit was already damning enough to Lees. Syrina just needed the end of a string that would lead her to the High Merchant at the top of the pile.

She did more digging, this time at the city planner's office. The openings she'd found doubled as drainage. Air shafts went from angled to vertical about ten hands in to let water drain into the sewers. The vents to the vault continued two hands further down, set in the far wall of the shaft.

When she was satisfied she'd learned everything she was going to, she traveled across town to the rickshaw depot near the District Gate, nicked a spare wheel and stashed it on the roof of the building across from one of the ducts.

At the Stone Mason's Quarry—not an actual quarry, but the part of Eheene outside the Foreigner's District where they worked the raw marble and obsidian from Valez'Mui into blocks—she spent the next night gathering enough dust and marble tailings to fill a sack that weighed about as much as she did. She stashed it on the roof with the rickshaw wheel.

In the morning, she went down to the dry docks, wearing the face of a ship builder's apprentice, and with a half-day's work carved into shape a long, narrow plank that curved into a dip on one end and was concave down the middle. After the shipyards had closed, she went back to get it and brought it to one of the shafts at the base of the Skalkaad Trade Union.

It wasn't too cold. A blanket of clouds had rolled in at sunset to seal in the faint warmth of the day and block whatever Eyelight might otherwise filter through. It was hard to see, but she still needed to interrupt her work to freeze in place a dozen times as mercenary patrols made their rounds. It wasn't until the predawn light was graying the sky to the east that she'd maneuvered the long piece of wood inside the shaft the way she wanted it.

Hoping it wouldn't rain, she went back to the palace and slept a while before dressing as a rickshaw runner, strong and stooped, and jogged back to the depot. She selected one of the rickshaws enclosed by curtains instead of a convertible, and after a lengthy argument with the depot manager about the validity of her license and transfer documents, she was trotting back to the Palace district, rickshaw in tow.

———

Less than an hour before the service curfew, a tiny scowling rickshaw runner hit a curb, breaking a wheel as he trotted his empty conveyance down the lane along the Skalkaad Trade Union. It was the most heavily patrolled district of Eheene, outside the Syndicate complex itself. The watch traveled in packs of four, and a group of them was on the little man before he could even ascertain the damage.

The unit that confronted him was composed of three men and a woman. All four wore thick hoods of woven gray silk. The woman was the senior officer and carried herself with a dignified air of authority. She glared down her long nose at the man, who had turned away from their approach to frown at his rickshaw.

"You need to move off," she said.

The three men stood around her, gloomy and rough, but the woman was calm and cold, her brow furrowed beneath the gray and auburn mane that bloomed from under her hood. Little clouds of her breath gathered in the air in front of her as she spoke.

"That's helpful," the runner grunted, without turning to face her. He eyed the cracked wheel, scowl deepening as he rubbed his tan, leathery scalp.

"Look, you've got ten minutes to get this thing out of the street. After that, your boss is fined and you're going to jail."

That got his attention. He turned, wrinkled face angry and scared.

"What do you want me to do? You going to lock me away because my goddamn wheel broke at the wrong time? You might as well. Ranaad gets fined and he'll beat me to death anyway."

The woman pressed her lips together and looked at the wheel, over the runner's shoulder. It was split down the center, right through the axle.

"Look," the runner sniveled, green eyes pleading, "help me push this thing against the wall out of the way, and I'll be back here before first light with a fresh wheel so I can get it to the depot before Ranaad gets in. No beating or jail for me, no paperwork for you."

She thought a moment. "We'll be back through here at the end of our shift, an hour after Eyeset. That thing is still here, we've got your license and your face, and we're coming for you."

"Deal," he smiled. "Thanks. I promise I'll be long gone by then."

———

When it was dark, Syrina returned, naked and slathered in fish oil, which made her want to throw up but would cover her scent from any dogs. Of course, they'd notice the overpowering stench of fish—the dogs and everyone else—but she hoped they wouldn't be able to smell a human intruder under the stink.

The rickshaw was still where they'd pushed it against the wall in front of the vent. The board she'd banged out at the dry docks remained in place, protruding from the Trade Union building, three fingers out. As far as she could tell, it still reached over the sewer drain to the shaft on the other side.

She climbed up to the roof, got the spare wheel, and repaired the rickshaw well enough to get her the short distance she'd need to go. Then she hid the broken wheel on the seat behind the curtain and went back up to the roof to get the bag of marble tailings.

Hidden behind the repaired rickshaw, she began pouring the gravel and dust down the plank, slowly at first, so she could listen. There was a faint hiss and clatter as it flowed across the sewer shaft, and a distant rattle as it pelted through the vent into Vault

Two. Syrina stabilized the board with a spare chip of wood from the broken wheel and began to dump the bag down the ramp.

She was about two-thirds of the way through the sack when there was a deep thump from somewhere underneath the ground, a quick suction of air and a thick pop. A second later, a lone bell began to toll over Raymos Storage, and red smoke floated off from the roof, west over Eheene, under the soft purplish glow of the thinning clouds lit from above by the Eye.

She yanked the plank from the vent, snapped it twice over her knee so she could fit it into the rickshaw, sprinted everything the two blocks to the nearest canal, and shoved it in. It smashed through the thin ice with a crack, and she watched long enough to make sure it disappeared beneath the oily water. Then she ran back to wait for security.

———

Four mercenaries trotted up the steps to the double doors of Raymos Storage. They were all men. Their leader had a small crooked nose and a jagged yellow beard that hung in knots down to his chest. He banged on the knocker, and the door cracked open enough to let them in. Syrina slipped in behind them and skittered to the top of the thick stone door frame before it closed.

The room was huge and cold and empty. Everything inside was cut from gleaming black obsidian except the long, narrow reception desk, which was one solid block of marble. She wondered how they'd gotten it inside.

Two more hired swords—a boyish man and a

middle-aged woman who could've been his mother—
stood by the desk. Junior stood by the lever that
opened and closed the outside door, and Mom held a
leash connected to a hound that was bigger than Syrina. It growled and mumbled and looked Syrina's
way, but so far that was all. The only light came from
an oil brazier suspended by brass chains above the
desk, which glittered on the black stone walls
without illuminating the room any more than
starlight. The lamps that lined the walls every ten
hands were unlit.

"Crap, Lucaan, you just come from the docks?"
the woman asked.

"Gah, I smell it," one of the newcomers stuck out
his tongue. "Was outside, too. Some monger must've
spilled fish guts in the street."

"Let's just get the damn door open," the bearded
one said.

There was a mutter of agreement, and Beard and
Mom tugged open the copper trapdoor which led
down to the bank proper.

"You been down there yet?" he asked her.

"Yeah. Chelsen and Gav are still there. Waiting to
go into the vault until you guys got here, just in case.
Doors are all still sealed. Probably just a false alarm.
Big-ass rat or something."

"Well, let's go check it out," Lucaan said.

Syrina slapped her hand against the marble wall,
and the hound, who'd been staring at her with pricked
ears while growling deep in her throat, let loose with a
torrent of barking and howling. White lather flew
from her teeth like snowflakes.

"Holy shit," the woman said. "What is it, Gracy?"

"I heard something, too," one of the other men

said. He was looking at the door. "It must've come from outside."

Junior pulled the lever that opened the front door, and he and Beard followed Gracy as the dog dragged Mom across the marble flagstones toward the entrance. The others were a few paces behind them. Everyone except Gracy focused on the open door. If anyone noticed the dog was looking at something above it, they only gave the spot a brief glance before turning their attention back outside.

Syrina sprang over their heads, rolled twice, and came to her feet at a silent run. The dog leaped up, spinning to face back inside. Her barks grew high pitched and frantic.

"Gracy! Gracy! Stop! Down!" The woman struggling with the leash yelled.

Everyone else stared at the hound, backing away and cursing. No one followed Gracy's gaze back toward the open trap door, where a shadow flickered for a moment and was gone.

Syrina got to the base of the spiral stairs cut into the foundation. The iron portcullis to the lower lobby was open. The desk here was carved from the granite floor. Three massive, round steel doors behind it led to the vaults. Behind the slab of the downstairs desk, idling in front of the door to Vault Two, was another pair of guards, a squat dark-haired man with angry eyes, and a svelte redhead holding the leash of another dog. To Syrina's right was another door, this one heavy wood reinforced with copper bands. It was closed, probably locked. Syrina scurried to the corner nearest to it, squatted and waited.

A minute later, the four guards she'd followed inside came down the stairs. The pair with Gracy stayed above, as she'd hoped. No need for two dogs down here, not if one was acting crazy. The second dog whined and growled, though at Syrina or from an unfriendly disposition toward the newcomers she couldn't tell, and everyone ignored it, in any case.

"Let's get this over with." The bearded man headed toward the wood and copper door next to where Syrina squatted in the shadows, a ring of keys in his hand. "Gah. Stinks down here, too." He scowled at the vault doors.

"What's your problem?" the dark-haired man asked.

"You ever seen someone after they've been pulled from a vault that's gone off?"

"No. Have you?"

Beard snapped the three locks open in quick succession, and the door squealed inward on copper hinges. It revealed a cramped room lined on one side with twelve ceramic and teak levers.

"When there's a controlled explosion in the naphtha chamber under the vault," he said, "the fire sucks the vents, and the door closed and burns out all the air. Clever trick. Vacuum puts out the fire before it can spread."

"So? What's your problem?"

"Five, six years ago, a little kid, maybe five years old, got caught in Three. Playing around. Parents couldn't find him, but no one knew he was in there. Never did figure out how he slipped in. Anyway, after closing time he set the plates off. We pulled him out a few hours later. His eyes'd burst, and his ears and nose had hemorrhaged all over the damn place. It's a mess, is *so*. Still got the image of the poor kid stuck in my head like it was yesterday, and I don't have any great desire to see it again. There, plates are off."

He pulled the four center levers back and headed toward the other soldiers, who had gathered around the door to Vault Two.

Syrina waited.

"Ready?" the redhead asked.

"Yeah, do it," Beard said.

The redhead cranked a small wheel on the front of the door, off to the side and closer to the floor than the main handle. There was a pop, then a hiss of air, which died as pressure seeped back into the vault.

Beard stepped up and dialed the combination. "Okay, ready?"

When no one answered, he cranked the handle, and the huge round door swung outward. It clanged as it came to a stop after six hands, leaving an opening big enough for one person to file through at a time.

"Let's go to work," he said. "Come on, Syfa. Sniff out whatever's in there."

Syfa growled toward Syrina's corner before reluctantly squeezing into the vault. Beard took the leash and followed the dog through. His three companions pushed in after him, while the redhead and the dark-haired man stayed outside.

Syrina moved.

"There's a pile of sand or something in here," she heard beard say, but then she was in the security room, pushing the levers back toward the wall.

There was a dull boom from somewhere deep under her feet. Wind blew down the stairway for a second before the vault door sucked closed with a re-verberating, heavy thud. Outside, the bell began to toll once more.

The remaining pair had been standing in front of the vault, and either the sudden drop in air pressure or the giant metal door slamming closed right next to their heads had stunned them. Syrina glided over to where they leaned against the door, blinking, hands at their temples. She slapped first the man, then the redhead over their ears, hands cupped, as hard as she could, and jabbed them each in the nape with stiff fingers, crippling the connection between their lungs and their brain. They fell to the ground, flopped, and lay still. Then she closed the door to the security room, hopped up to the top of the door frame of Vault One, and waited more.

It wasn't long this time. She heard barking on the stairs, and a second later the woman from the lobby and Gracy appeared in the doorway. Sonny was nowhere to be seen. Syrina hoped he'd gone to get someone who could open the vault again.

"Goddamn it, it stinks down here, too. Which one of... holy shit." The woman emerged from the stairway and ran over to the two bodies, letting go of the dog's leash.

Gracy stood at the bottom of the stairs and continued to bark in Syrina's direction, but the woman only gave the corner a cursory glance before turning her attention back to the corpses. In a few minutes, the son appeared with a corporate inspector and four more security in tow—the woman and three men who had harassed Syrina's rickshaw runner earlier that evening.

"What the hell happened here?" the inspector demanded.

He was about fifty, thin, with dark bags under his

eyes. His shaved head bore the spiral tattoo that marked his office.

"I think... it looks like they forgot to lock the plates before they went in." The woman's voice shook.

"You've got to be kidding me." The inspector scowled. "Mavis is no fresh pie. He knows the drill."

"I heard it go off again, too," Sonny said.

The inspector walked over to the security room and opened the door. "Shit. Door's unlocked, but the plates are still set. That idiot."

He re-pulled the levers, and as the redhead had done, then evened the pressure in Vault Two with the valve. There were no theatrics this time. He rolled the combination in its cradle and swung the door open.

———

In the next three hours, twenty people went in and out of Vault Two, removing bodies, taking samples from the pile of sand and grit that had built up against one wall, and taking inventory of the vault's contents. No one noticed the naked woman who'd slipped in during the commotion and took up residence on a high shelf in the back corner, though everyone complained that the place stank like fish.

With not quite three hours left before opening, the whole thing was written off as a false alarm set off by a collapsed ventilation shaft in the Union building above, which had led to a tragedy caused by old-fashioned human error. Further investigations were planned, but everyone agreed the most viable course of action was to open as usual and reassure the clientele their deposits were secure. They locked the door behind them and set the plates again.

Syrina finally had some alone time. There were thousands of files stacked in narrow aisles, but they were well-organized, and she spent the next three hours avoiding the floor while rifling through Ehrina Ka'id's most confidential records. Syrina ignored most of it, taking mental pictures of everything that might lead to something solid about Lees's funding. She kept the lamp she'd snagged from the hook on the inside of the vault door turned down to a tiny flicker, both to preserve her air and in case someone came back in.

When the bank opened, no one noticed a naked woman flit up the stairs and out the front door, but she overheard several comments about the stench of rotting fish.

13

THE DOCTOR IS IN

LEES HAD BEEN EVEN MORE PARANOID THAN Syrina had given him credit for. He'd panicked at the first sign of a break-in, and according to the servants left behind, had vanished at first light. His home stood abandoned, his business in confusion. He'd skipped town with his wife before he'd even had a chance to find out it was a false alarm.

Ormo wasn't going to like that, but there was nothing Syrina could have done about it. Lees had fled an hour before she'd even slipped out of the vault.

There were a few personal things she wanted to take care of, but with Lees's disappearance she couldn't risk Ormo hearing details from anyone but her, and that meant she needed to tell him now.

———

"You scared him off," he said, by way of greeting.

Syrina needed to assume he wasn't happy, even if she couldn't see his face.

"As soon as the alarm went off he was gone," she said. "He must've packed weeks ago and been waiting for an excuse to run ever since. I'm wondering how that's going to affect whichever High Merchant was using him."

"And did you find any information pertaining to who that is?"

"I might've found something. You'll need to tell me. I didn't want to take anything from the vault and scare Lees off—a lot of good that did—but I had a good look at Ka'id's records, and there was one financier who's been sending a lot of tin Lees's way without getting much in return, at least as far as I could tell. It could be nothing, but it was the only thing that stood out."

"Who?" Ormo shifted under the shapeless silken mass of his robes.

"More like what. An organization of some sort. Something called the Northern Resource Initiative."

"Ah. I'm familiar with it."

"All of the... donations, I guess you could call them, came from various other companies, but I could eventually trace all of it back to them." Syrina waited, but nothing else seemed to be forthcoming. "Anything I should know?"

"It's an energy collective of fifty or sixty smaller companies. Mostly naphtha production, of course. They also, through their subsidiaries, control three of the five iron mines on Eris. All these companies operate independent of one another, but they're all controlled by the Northern Resource Initiative. It's the kind of conglomerate that not many have heard of but has its fingers in everything. An organization that would take an interest in something like the Tidal Works. There is no question that NRI is connected to one of the Fifteen."

"Anything else you can tell me?"

Ormo rustled. "That'll do for now. Look into it. Make sure they're not paying for something else. Until you're sure, stay out of trouble. And if you come across Lees, kill him, will you?"

———

She didn't go straight to NRI. She knew she should, and that she shouldn't do anything behind Ormo's back, but there was something else she had to check first.

It could have been a lie. The N'talisan-Kalis could've made up anything she wanted, and Syrina knew it. She was going to look for this Doctor Saadasi, anyway. There were too many unanswered questions, and every time she slept, she dreamed of Triglav. Going against Ormo filled her with unfamiliar terror, but she couldn't stop. Didn't want to stop.

Maybe we'll find something out about me, too, the voice said.

Syrina pretended not to hear it.

With a little poking around in the city lists archived in the Aggregate Library, it became clear that Saadasi was at the very least an actual person and not just some creation the N'talisan-Kalis had dreamed up to screw with Syrina. Not only was he real, but he was no ordinary physician. He didn't keep offices in any of the hospitals or clinics. Instead, he headed a private laboratory funded by something called the Witt Group. Who controlled them was unclear, but the collective seemed focused on inherited traits and maladies in the blood. Syrina would've thought all maladies were in the blood, but what did

she know? She knew the convoluted business hold-
ings in Skalkaad were giving her a headache.

———

Syrina learned little about Cab Saadasi after watching
his house thirty hours a day for the next eight days,
and she wasn't sure what she could do with what little
she had got.

Saadasi was thin, on the older side of middle
age. He must've been just a few years out of school
when the N'talisan had encountered him years ago.
He had deep-set gray eyes, a hard, pale face, and a
thick mop of pure white hair that gave the impression it had been white since he was twenty. He lived
alone in one of the marble four-story townhouses
along the Central Canal, and he ate out every night
at the same place—a little, charming back-alley joint
called Fali's Atrium, though he was adventurous
enough to order something different every time. He
ate alone while he perused whatever work he
brought with him, and he always brought something.
From what little Syrina could tell, his focus seemed
more on inherited traits and less on maladies, but
she was the first to concede that she didn't know
enough about medicine to draw any conclusions
from that.

On two of the evenings she watched him, he met
another man after eating. Both times they went back
to Saadasi's townhouse and didn't come out until the
next morning when the doctor headed back to Witt
while the other man slept in.

Syrina found it ironic that someone who's work
seemed focused around reproduction had so little in-

terest in doing it himself. But then, she thought, maybe that said something about reproduction.

Besides his lover, Doctor Saadasi never broke from the routine, never associated with anyone outside those he worked with. At least, not in the week Syrina watched him.

It was better than, or at least as good as nothing. She only had another day or two before Ormo started wondering what was going on with NRI, but she wanted to get involved with the Witt Group before she changed her mind.

———

"Who did you say you were again?" Doctor Saadasi scowled at the woman in front of him.

She was diminutive and pudgy, and too young to be a doctor, whatever her papers said.

The woman brushed a short yellow curl from where it licked at her cheek and scowled. "You heard me the first time, Doctor. My name is Faax. Doctor Sailish Faax. I've been sent here to assist you." She pointed at the small stack of papers in his hand. "They weren't specific. They told me to show up here and ask what you need help with. As you can see, the Board has already paid me, so if you want me to leave just say so."

"You were sent here by whom?"

Faax nodded at the papers again with an irritated frown that asked, *can you read?*

"The Board." She let out an irritated sigh, rolling her green eyes.

Saadasi considered. The Witt Board of Directors —and the Eye only knew who was pulling their

167

strings—had been saying they would send him some extra help for months, and he'd been asking for it, but he didn't like the way she'd just shown up like this. Still, since Kaandri had disappeared three days before, the research department had been grossly understaffed. He'd be a fool to turn anyone away. Her papers checked out, and since she was contracted by the Director's Panel, she wouldn't even be around all the time. They liked to keep their temps busy. If she didn't work out, she'd be easier to get rid of than most of the buffoons that cluttered his lab.

"All right." He gave the documents in his hands one last glance before handing them back to her. "Head down to the FHASyL and see what Stefaan needs to have done. Don't bother me again unless you're quitting or you have something useful to say."

"Suit yourself." She turned and left.

Saadasi watched her go until the door clicked shut, and caught himself smiling. He decided there must be something about her he liked.

———

Syrina reflected on whether she was in over her head. She could fake her way through pretty much every situation she got herself into, but it took her almost half an hour just to figure out that FHASyL stood for Fetal Health and Safety Lab while still looking like she knew what she was doing. The act would get thin fast.

The FHASyL, once she found it, was a series of four large rooms, lined with bookshelves and wooden cabinets filled with small, unlabeled glass jars and vials, which were filled with sharp-scented liquids and powders. Test subjects were brought to an adjacent waiting room where they filled out questionnaires before a nurse escorted them to the first room, where doctors took various blood and fluid samples.

Syrina was sharp enough to mimic Stefaan—a portly, disgruntled man with a mop of thin, blond hair and a lazy eye—when he showed her how to draw the specific samples they needed from the women. Apparently, he made the opposite sex uncomfortable, so at least he was glad to have Faax there. He didn't make Syrina uncomfortable, but she had the urge kill him for no particular reason, so she thought maybe for her that was the same thing.

He watched her mix the blood of five different pregnant women with various chemicals and showed her how to look for whatever they were looking for. She had no idea what he was talking about and was relieved when he left her to go about his own business. She would need to spend all her free time studying if she was going to learn enough to lie her way to the bottom of the programs that the N'talisan-Kalis had told her about.

On the bright side, after her visit to Witt, she was pretty sure those programs existed. Unless, of course, the other Kalis had sent her on this mad personal quest with a few well-placed lies amid the truths. In which case, Syrina needed to admit she'd be impressed, professionally speaking.

———

In the meantime, she was just a liability at Witt, and she couldn't keep Ormo waiting any longer. So that night, she scraped up everything she could on the

Northern Resource Initiative. And just as Ormo said, it was one of those nebulous, omniscient collectives that only a few people had heard of. Among those who had, most were unable to say what NRI did or who they did it to. Nevertheless, their tendrils stretched all the way across Skalkaad.

She learned from dusty public records that NRI leased out hundreds of navaras farms as well as nickel, copper, and tin mines, all under different names, and owned hundreds of other locations where seed farms and mines might be leased in the future. In fact, they provided almost a quarter of the resources that fueled the wealth of Skalkaad without the liability of having their name on any of it. And that didn't even include the iron Ormo had told her about.

They were just as amorphous as far as leadership went. It should've been there with the other records, but Syrina couldn't find one name on the governing board, just general references to the *Directors Association*. They managed the conglomerate through either unanimous decision or majority vote, depending on which record she was looking at and when it was dated. It was frustrating but not surprising. The Syndicate kept terrible public records on all the big companies because they were the ones at the top of them.

NRI had several offices in Eheene, but their main building was in Aado, a town a few hours west, not much more than a fishing village until they'd built their complex along the water, where they could keep their own port without needing to deal with pesky bureaucratic things like Syndicate Customs forms. That explained how Lees had been able to ship stuff to Fom for so long before anyone got suspicious.

The conglomerate facilitated its habits by running

—once again, under different names—several shipping companies. Most of those kept their headquarters in Valez'Mui so they wouldn't be subject to Skalkaad taxes or trade regulations. Others didn't list any port at all. In the legal forms, they had just written *International* under the space allotted for the home harbor. None of them, at least on paper, ported in Skalkaad.

Syrina decided she'd head out to Aado early in the morning and try to get back to the city in time to put in a few hours at Witt. She didn't want Saadasi to think his new doctor was slacking before she'd even begun.

She let herself have a nap for an hour and spent the rest of the night in the shadows under the dome of the Syndicate Library, reading about biology so she might at least be able to pretend she knew what she was doing in the lab.

———

Aado was still just a fishing village. Homes of wood were built on a steep hill that drooped into the sea, which became an expanse of mud flats sixty spans wide during low tide. The NRI building was further west of town, but it was visible long before the little jumble of houses was. It crawled down the slope with arms of rough, speckled granite that reached across the mudflats, embracing its own private bay.

The building or wall—Syrina couldn't tell from outside if it was roofed or just a high rampart around a courtyard—was eight stories high and windowless except for a series of narrow slits along the top which extended all the way around. The front gate was wood, painted red, and wide enough to let two camel wagons through abreast if it ever opened, which it never did in the few hours Syrina watched it. A dozen mercenaries guarded the complex, along with four full-grown tundra hounds and a karakh.

Nothing labeled it as NRI, and the locals, all non-citizens anyway, had long ago learned to stop asking what went on inside. A trio of high stacks jutted from near the back of the compound. The air above two, which otherwise would have looked dormant, shimmered with heat from the naphtha generators. The last spewed white steam in a long, thin cloud that stretched off to the northeast in the light wind.

The karakh bothered Syrina a lot more than the hounds did. It lingered above the huge red doors most of the time, whistling and clicking to the shepherd perched on its back, making everyone nervous. Well, it made Syrina nervous, and she didn't imagine the mercenaries stationed below could ever get used to that thing wheezing and leering over them.

Its fur was reddish brown, shaggier than the ones in the Fom arena had been. She wondered if it had grown the thicker coat since coming to Skalkaad or if it was just a different breed. Its eyes were huge, luminous yellow, and reminded her of Triglav with a jolt of sadness she wasn't prepared for. It hung onto the roof with its giant six-fingered hands, and the tops of the walls were scuffed and cracked from its claws. Its tusks—at least nine hands long, unless the shepherd was tiny and she got her scale all wrong—were sheathed in leather, but Syrina could see the knobs blooming underneath where they'd been reinforced with sharpened brass bolts. The shepherd wore a woolen parka over his shoulders, against the bite of the wind, but the chains that connected to the brass rings in the karakh's cheeks were uninsulated. She wondered if his hands were cold.

She'd heard that the shepherds sometimes hired themselves out to organizations besides the Church, but she'd never seen it until now. That thing could smell her a mile away and probably see her, too. If Syrina ever had to break into the NRI compound, she was screwed.

That was as far as she got on her first trip to Aado, and her evening at Witt was just as uneventful. Everyone let her do her thing, and she was glad they were all kind enough not to ask her what that thing was because she still wouldn't have come up with much of an answer. She tried to look busy and soak in as much of what everyone else was doing as she could. She still didn't know what was going on, but she knew more than she did a week ago, and she supposed that was something.

———

Ormo sent for her before she'd come up with anything useful enough to bother him with. Even more surprising, it wasn't even noon yet, and the Fifteen almost never wore their masks during the day. That was when they were off living their unassuming, normal lives as regular, if wildly successful, citizens.

Syrina told him what she'd learned about NRI. When she misread his sigh, she got defensive.

"I wasn't going to come to you until I figured out a way in."

Ormo nodded. The motion was almost indiscernible, but his hood rustled with movement. "No,

173

no, my impatience isn't with you this time. It's with myself. I think I may have let things go too far. The karakh is new to me. It makes me think they know someone is nosing around, or at least they're worried someone might start."

"So you already knew NRI was involved?"

She sounded more annoyed than she'd meant to, but Ormo let it slide.

He sighed again. "The Northern Resource Initiative is a pet project of Ma'is Kavik. I've had my eye on them for years, suspected them of having dealings contrary to the greater good of Skalkaad. Kavik and I have never gotten along, even when they were their previous incarnation. The current Kavik is relatively new. They're as careful with facts as any Ma'is, though—and as you know, the Fifteen try to keep out of each other's business—as long as it's business and not the affairs of the nation. I've never found a reason to act against them, nor NRI. Not until now."

He looked at Syrina like he was waiting for her to add something.

"So you think Ma'is Kavik is the one at the top of this?" she said.

Ormo shifted under his robes. "Right now, it doesn't matter if they are or not. We still don't even know what *this* is. Not enough to bring to the other Thirteen. Even if I were willing to act on my own, choices are limited. I can't send you to deal with Kavik directly. It would be a civil war, taking down a full Member in their Hall like that, and you'd fail anyway. And I don't have any more idea who they are than you do. The old Kavik died of natural causes, and they were able to pick their own successor, taking what they knew of their replacement to sea on their pyre ship twelve years ago."

"You want me to drop it?"

"No. I can pull some favors. I don't have anyone in NRI, but it shouldn't be too hard to get you a job there. Give me a few weeks to see what I can work out."

"Sure." But Syrina grimaced.

The last thing she wanted was the stress of a second fake job.

14

THE NORTHERN RESOURCE
INITIATIVE

THE NORTHERN RESOURCE INITIATIVE WASN'T the kind of outfit that just hired off the street, but Ormo had done some legwork. Or rather, he had someone else do it, and he'd scraped up an alias Syrina could use.

Cairnsworth Menns had been a N'naradin engineer working under N'talisan back in Fom. He'd disappeared a few weeks after the death of his boss but had been, by all accounts, loyal to the Merchant's Syndicate to the brink of fanaticism. Ormo was certain Menns had never been to Skalkaad to meet anyone at NRI, nor they to Fom to meet him. He was positive Menns wouldn't show up now to prove Syrina a fraud. She didn't bother asking how he could be so sure.

The only person around who knew Menns was a fellow named Carlaas Storik, a former engineer, now current acting head of Research and Redevelopment, the branch of NRI most involved with the Tidal Works. Storik was in Fom, cleaning up after the messy disappearance of N'talisan and one of his assistants, and the accidental death of another. Syrina had

at least until his return to snoop around without resorting to crime or violence, both of which Ormo
seemed to be even more wary of than she was.

Since neither she nor Ormo knew what Menns
looked like, Syrina winged it. It was a bad idea for her
to try to look like someone specific anyway. There
was always someone around to notice one of the infinite little details lacking with something like that. It
was why she gave Rina such a vast array of different
styles and hairdos. Subtle differences were less likely
to stand out through the big intentional ones. Syrina
had always been modest enough to admit she wasn't
good enough to pull it off otherwise.

———

NRI's security was far stricter than just the hounds
outside and a karakh cruising their walls, and twenty
people must have asked for Menns' transfer papers
the first day. Syrina couldn't help but be amused at
the thought of how much trouble the real Menns
would have if he ever showed up.

Things were ideal for Syrina as long as Storik was
away in Fom. They'd put all research on hold. There
wasn't any work to speak of until Storik got back,
which meant there weren't many opportunities for
anyone to find out Menns didn't know what he was
doing. It put her in a good position to wander around
and ask a lot of questions, and it didn't bother anyone
if some days Menns didn't show up at all. She had a
good idea of the gist of things by the end of the first
week, and she was still able to squeeze in some time at
Witt.

Storik's theory, and therefore the theory that the

NRI research was based around, was that the Tidal Works stored and converted the tidal energy directly. Not the movement of the water, as almost everyone assumed, which was only used by the newer knot of machinery to channel power to the city, but the very forces of the Eye that tugged at the sea itself. No one knew how it worked, nor why the Ancestors required so much power in the first place.

By the end of the second week, most of the people at NRI knew Menns had been on N'talisan's team. They all had a slew of questions about what had happened to the archaeologist and what he'd found before he vanished. Syrina regurgitated all the theories and rumors she'd heard the previous week, tweaking them a little to make them sound like Menns' own.

She spent the next two months showing up at the NRI complex every other day to spew rumors back at those she'd heard them from, all to pick up one half-baked theory about the Tidal Works that no one had any solid facts on.

It might have been the closest thing to a real job she'd ever had.

15

CHOICES

Faax took her time filing Stefaan's findings in one of the minimum-security storage vaults on the upper floor. If anyone had asked her what was taking so long, she would've told them she was brushing up on some of the previous projects undertaken by Witt, which was true. No one else came in.

Over her weeks at Witt, she'd been able to finagle her way down to the position of mere errand girl, running files up and down stairs and transcribing dictated data. The other doctors thought she was insulted by such a demotion, and Faax acted indignant enough about it, but Syrina couldn't be happier. She never thought she'd have so much time to pursue her own goals. This was the ninth time she'd lingered here under the cracked plaster ceiling, among filing cabinets that smelled of old paper and polished pine, and no one had bothered her before, either. Not many people even knew she was working today. Just Stefaan and a couple others, and none had any reason to come up to Records. After all, they kept sending Faax so they wouldn't need to go.

She was lucky to have the place to herself this

time. If they caught Faax reading the hand-written note she'd stumbled across, there'd be questions.

In Reference to Report #AA-55.k:

We might as well stop forwarding our findings. Correspondence between Witt and all NRI subsidiaries will be terminated within the week, and there's no reason to think we'll start working with them again in the foreseeable future. Just letting you know so you can cut down on your paperwork now instead of next week. Storik is going to make it official in a day or two.

She'd come across the note lying loose and forgotten at the bottom of a cabinet filled with old Trade Commission filing forms. Beneath the message was the report number again, next to a black square with a circle in it—a timestamp for the secure archives. There were no names, but it was dated right around the time N'talisan disappeared. It didn't matter who wrote it or where they'd sent it. What mattered was that Syrina's two disparate investigations might be somehow related. That was either going to make things easier or a lot more complicated.

———

Doctor Stefaan's research consisted of examining women from pre-selected stock and determining the chances that their offspring would be resistant to illness, as well as looking for less defined but superior traits. Faax kept her growing suspicions about the nature of those other traits to herself.

That afternoon, she came up with a way to test her suspicions, and from what she'd seen of how things worked at Witt, to maybe worm her way into the maximum-security archives where she could look for the NRI connection while she was at it.

Test your own blood.

It was so obvious that she was annoyed it took a voice in her head to point it out to her.

A few hours later, Stefaan directed her to extract another sample and bring it to the lab for testing. Once she was alone, Faax pricked her finger, and with a subtle glance around to make sure no one was watching, added a single drop of her blood into the vial.

She hovered a while, peering at samples and shuffling through dusty data folders until it felt like a reasonable amount of time to make some sort of discovery. Then she rushed out to find Stefaan, who was in one of the board rooms, in the middle of a meeting with a group of other doctors.

"What is it?" Stefaan tuned to face Faax, with a scowl that further scarred his already-ugly face.

"I think I found something you should see."

"Can it wait." He turned back to the other doctors, making it clear it wasn't a question.

"You're going to want to see this. Now." Faax added a slight rise in her tone to help convince Stefaan of the urgency.

He sighed. "This better be important." He followed her back to the lab, with a mumbled apology to the others.

She led the way, aware that if the voice's hunch was wrong, Stefaan would be furious at her incompetence and she'd be fired on the spot. She'd also be reported to the Board that had supposedly employed her and exposed as a fraud.

He peered at the sample through an intricate se-

ries of copper tubes and crystal lenses that the researchers called a mirrorscope.

He raised his eyebrows. "Did you already add the
thyronine?" There was an edge of excitement to his
voice.

"No." Faax wondered which of the hundreds of
jars and vials contained thyronine. "I thought you
should see it first."

Stefaan hurried over to a cabinet and selected a
vial four-fifths empty, stained a raging magenta by the
remaining fluid within it. He added a few drops to the
sample with a thin glass dropper and peered at it
again through the series of tubes. Faax thought she
could see the blood glitter now in the bright naphtha
lights of the lab as if the magenta liquid had somehow
flecked it with silver.

"Water and sand!" he said.

And for the fiftieth time, Faax wondered where
that expression had come from, since Stefaan was as
much an Eheene native as she was, and she'd never
heard anyone say that until she met him.

"Take this to Saadasi." Stefaan jotted down some
notes onto a blank page, folded it, and handed it to
her, along with the tube containing the sample and
the rest of the paperwork already done for the mother.
"Congratulations."

"This is your research."

"Nonsense." Stefaan's voice was kinder than she'd
ever heard it. "It's your discovery. Again, congratulations."

Faax didn't bother concealing her smile as she
turned to go.

———

Doctor Saadasi was in his office, notes strewn about. He munched on an apple, eyes closed, ignoring the pile of documents for the duration of his meal. A half-chicken reduced to bones and a few knobby lumps of gristle lay pushed aside at the edge of his desk on a greasy wooden plate. The smell of it still filled the room.

The new doctor—Sailish or something—blundered through the door. She was short and plump enough that she probably blundered everywhere she went.

"Are you lost?" He tried to keep his tone even.

"Doctor Stefaan said you'd want to see this right away," she wheezed.

She waved a lab report around in front of her as she staggered to his desk. She clutched a test tube half-filled with blood in her other hand.

He snatched the report from her and scanned it, his eyes growing wide. "Is this accurate?"

She thought it was a stupid question, but she didn't say so. "Both Stefaan and I think it is."

Saadasi nodded, rang the little silver bell that summoned his secretary, and blurted at him when he arrived a moment later. "See this report? Sequester the mother. And find her family history. Don't let on what you're about."

The secretary nodded, glanced through the papers in Saadasi's hand, and scurried away. If Faax felt bad at the phrase *sequester the mother*, she didn't let it show.

"And you," Saadasi said. "You found this?"

Faax nodded.

"Come with me."

Saadasi's eyes burned holes into the back of Faax's head as he followed her down the stairs that led to the main archive facility, nestled in a separate building neighboring their main office, in the northern-most tendrils of Eheene. The stairs themselves were stone, but the walls and low ceiling were crumbling brick, and yellow light seeped from dingy naphtha lamps that dangled at every turn, fed by old brass pipes that ran along the center of the ceiling. The metallic stink of unrefined oil dribbled through cracks between the ancient blocks of mottled red clay.

Until she'd brought him one of the purest samples he'd seen in the past thirty years of looking, he'd thought Faax something of a dullard, not even capable of being the intern he'd demoted her to. She'd seemed incapable of keeping straight the simplest tasks, and the one report of hers he'd bothered reading made no sense at all. Spotting Ora in blood wasn't easy though, especially before adding thyronine. Everyone had their talents, he supposed.

They reached a cramped, arching oval chamber. A fat square door crouched in the opposite wall, flanked by two bored-looking security guards wearing blue and yellow Witt livery. They nodded at Saadasi and stepped aside a respectful distance before motioning for Faax to do the same. Saadasi produced a long, complicated key, and there was a clack of a bolt sliding back. He led Faax into the vault, where she paused to lean against the door frame, catching her breath and letting her eyes adjust to the thin, dusty light. It was cold. The walls and the center of the room were lined with high wooden filing cabinets and shelves packed with books. Everything was labeled with letters and numbers. To the immediate right of the door, one filing cabinet was tagged with dates.

"This is," Saadasi said, "the small collection of significant discoveries made since Witt's predecessor was formed three thousand years ago to assist the Syndicate in reclaiming biological knowledge lost since the Age." He took the file that Faax had been clutching, to a cabinet marked AV-BG, pulled out an empty drawer, and slipped it inside.

"This is all there is?" she asked.

"All worth keeping down here."

There were a couple things Syrina was counting on, but the biggest was that the guards wouldn't find the pin she'd slipped in the lock while Faax leaned against the door, gaping into the room. She couldn't always count on her luck, but this time, she could.

A few days later, during the Eye Night celebrations that coursed through most of Eheene, Faax appeared by herself at the bottom of the stairs that led to secure storage.

"Faax, is it?" one of the men said, cordially enough. "Working on Eye Night? Well, it's shit to be us. Seems like every damn holiday, one of you poor bastards shows up down here. Guess this time it's the new girl."

"It's always the new girl." She sighed as she fiddled with the lock, suppressing a smile.

Over two months at Witt and still everyone called her the new girl.

"Heh, yeah." The guard raised an eyebrow when Faax continued to jiggle the lock and tried to look over her shoulder to see if she had the key in right.

But just then, the bolt slid open with a *schlick* and Faax stepped away from him and into the room.

"Ah, well," she closed the door behind her, "the sooner I'm done, the sooner I can get out of here."

———

At least they were organized. Even in the fluttering yellow light of the lamp dangling from Faax's hand, AA-55.k was easy to find. Before she read it, though, she was curious about something else. Another hunch.

She went to the cabinet by the door, with different labels than the others. A list of dates was pinned on its side, with handwritten notations. She slid a drawer open and had a look at random. The file contained records of contributions received by the Witt Group Department of Research and Redevelopment. *What a mouthful.* She scanned down the fine print of the list, looking for names she recognized. Most were organizations, and most she'd heard of before in one context or another, but a couple stood out. For one, she learned that someone named Abethan Laak had been managing a couple of the Witt donation accounts up until a few years ago. Not very compelling by itself, but the fact that Laak worked at the same address as Ehrina Ka'id was an interesting bit of trivia. A lot of the other organizations listed were fronts belonging to Ormo.

She bit her lip but told herself it might not mean anything.

AA-55.k was thick—several hundred pages, at least. Syrina needed to get through it fast. Her presence was already enough to raise questions in the minds of the soldiers outside, however cordial they were to her face. Even if they weren't the suspicious sort, all it would take was one of them feeling chatty when he got off work, and word of Faax coming down here would reach more ears than would be helpful. Syrina had been dropping hints of Faax's imminent departure for a week now. She hoped the doctor wouldn't need to make another appearance at Witt after today.

Syrina relaxed her mind and scanned each page without reading it, absorbing the information so she could go over it later. The gist was interesting enough, even without the details. Tin—and lots of it—had been changing hands both ways between Witt and another redevelopment group, headed by none other than Carlaas Storik at NRI. Sure enough, the relationship between the two organizations had been dissolved just over a week after N'talisan's disappearance.

There was more. There was a growing body of evidence that pointed to a missing link between the blood research at Witt and the Tidal Works and other Artifacts. A respected group of researchers, Saadasi and Storik among them, thought there was a connection between certain Artifacts and the blood of a select few people, bred over hundreds of generations to achieve some sort of lost state of being.

The file didn't say as much. Even most of the major players probably didn't know as much, the way the Syndicate kept their pawns in the dark, but Syrina was sure she knew what lay at the end of those breeding programs.

Me, the voice in her head said. *They're talking about me.*

"You and me both," Syrina muttered.

And even that wasn't all of it.

———

Five hours later, she burst into Ormo's audience hall, not caring about protocol or that he was in the middle of a trade meeting with a dozen of the most powerful low merchants in Skalkaad, each a monarch in their own right.

There was only one thing Syrina cared about— killing her Ma'is.

16

JAIL

OUR PREDICTIONS, COMBINED WITH REDISCOVERED
records, hint that a Preas Prohm might be successfully
awakened with an intense emotional or physiological
reaction if there is a high enough concentration of Ora
in the blood of the subject. However, due to the unpredictable nature of Ora and our lack of understanding
of the Preas Prohm, which remains only theoretical,
more study is advised. The failure rate to awaken any
Preas Prohm to date remains at one hundred percent
through emotional and physical attempts.

Even so, experiments have conclusively shown
that high enough concentrations of Ora do replicate
once in the bloodstream [see data 1.14]. Furthermore,
it is drawn to itself when it exists within an outside
non-human organism (hereafter referred to as the simulacrum) via transfusion. This attraction manifests
itself in a range of ways as wide as the subjects sam-
pled. All, however, include signs of an intense chemical bond between the subject and the simulacrum,
similar to the state known in the vernacular as "love."

Though there is no room for a philosophical treaty
in this report, it must be added that further research is

also needed to understand why such loyalty cannot be induced between the subject and a human simulacrum, on which any blood transfusion seems to have no effect, thereby limiting useful application.

It should also be emphasized that this reaction occurs in both the subject and the simulacrum. Although sparse records suggest that the Ancients may have exerted control over their servants through a similar bond, it is not evident how the masters were able to keep from "loving" their slaves in return, if indeed they were able to do so.

There is as of yet still no connection found between the Preas Prohm, the Ora, and the device discovered at the center of the Tidal Works, nor in any similar Artifacts, despite the scattering of pre-Age records that imply the contrary. Our understanding of the nature of Ora after these tests also remains limited. Refer to studies AO-041 through AO-557 for further information.

Now that all NRI research on the subject has been halted indefinitely, please advise as to the continued status of our arrangement. It is this office's suggestion that all connections are dissolved until fieldwork in Fom is resumed.

The crowd of low merchants gathered around Ormo's dais scattered when Syrina's feet hummed on the floor behind them, and they noticed her for the first time. Even behind the paint that coated his fat face, Syrina saw red rage glowing under Ormo's hood.

This isn't a good idea.

She ignored the voice. "Out," she said to the merchants, who were still milling around.

They fled from the Hall. She waited until the doors banged closed behind them before she ascended the stairs.

"You have overstepped your bounds," Ormo growled. "This had better—"

"It was all a setup," she whispered.

Her face was just a hand from his, but she didn't touch him. Not yet.

"What was a setup?" His tone betrayed nothing, but fury and understanding bubbled through his gray eyes.

"Triglav. The other Kalis in Fom was one of yours."

"The other Kalis? I see you've been leaving out details from your reports." Ormo's voice was low, dangerous.

"You knew I left her out. You're the one who sent her. So fine. You want to see an intense emotional reaction?" She swung at him, aiming the rigid blade of her left hand at his neck where it would shatter his spine just above the shoulder.

Her hand hit what felt like an iron plate hidden under the collar of his robe, and her left arm went numb from the shoulder down. At the same moment, Ormo crashed his heavily-ringed fist into her face, impossibly fast for a fat old man. She felt her nose shatter, and her vision clouded red.

I told you. You should've listened. Or at least thought this through.

"Shut up." She lay crumpled where she'd fallen at the base of the dais.

Ormo stood now, his mass rolling under the wrinkles of his white and cobalt robes. She wondered what else he had hidden in its folds.

"It worked, didn't it?" He started down the stairs toward her.

Excitement had overcome the rage in his voice.

Syrina clambered to her feet, ready to take him on, but as soon as he was within reach, his own arm shot out, again faster than she thought possible. His rings crashed into her face again. This time, a tremendous jolt shot through her body, making her heart skip a beat and her limbs go rigid. She fell to the ground, unable to move beyond an involuntary quiver. She could see the patterned silk of the bottom of his robes out of the corner of her eye. The polished, onyx floor was cool and musty.

He leaned over her. "The Preas Prohm. Can I talk to her? Is she there now?"

No.

"No."

Ormo rolled Syrina over with his slippered foot, studied her eyes a few moments, sighed, and stood with a shrug.

"You are a fool, Kalis Syrina. But I suppose if it worked, it might still be worth it."

"Why?" she croaked, from the floor.

"Because theory suggests that the Preas Prohm can interact with certain Artifacts. Because there is so little we understand about who we are, where we came from, what we're entitled to. It was always the risk with you. In the entire history of the Merchant's Syndicate, you were the most promising one. If it was ever going to work, it was going to work on you. But it meant risking the shift of your loyalty from me to that damn bird."

Syrina thought of Triglav. "Fuck you."

"You are a fool because you mistake what you felt for an owl as love. It was chemical. Induced for the sole purpose of your own self-discovery. The love you felt, I hope you still feel, for your Ma'is, your caretaker, your provider, grew within you. It is as real as any love between father and daughter. You are my daughter, in spirit, if not in biology. Would you turn on something so natural? With your loss, you have aided the one you love. More than you can imagine. More importantly, you have found something within yourself. Something more ancient than humanity's entire tenure here on Eris. We believed we could never regain what was lost. You are proof we were wrong. Take solace in your sacrifice."

Syrina thought about it. About the bastardized love that still ached in her chest for Triglav, the jumble of confused feelings she still harbored for her Ma'is. The voice in her head that wasn't quite her own.

"Fuck you," she said again and tried to get up off the floor.

She thought that if he gave her enough time, she might be able to get to her feet and take him on. In a minute or two.

He sighed. "So much to do, still. I hope this isn't a permanent loss. There are so many unanswered questions, and I need you to answer most of them."

"I was going to say the same thing to you," she coughed.

"Then again," Ormo sighed, voice filled with regret, "I suppose many of those questions could be answered by way of your dissection. Or your vivisection." He bent down and brushed his rings against her face.

She gasped as the jolt flooded through her again, and then there was nothing.

———

The first thing that hit her was the stench.

A minute later, after it all tumbled back to her through the haze, she knew she was in one of the nameless holes where they threw naughty Kalis. She'd never been in one before, but Ormo had shown them to her back in her training years. At the time, she'd laughed at the idea that a Kalis could turn on someone as infallible as their Ma'is. She'd wondered if it had ever happened before now.

Apparently, it had. If she'd been the first to turn, they wouldn't have built such a specialized dungeon in the first place, and Ormo wouldn't have been so ready for her to attack him. Or maybe he would have. There was a lot she didn't know about the Syndicate she'd served her whole life. There was a lot she didn't know about everything.

It was pitch black, and the air was so permeated with the stench of rot it made the back of her throat burn. She knew from memory the space was round, about sixteen hands across, and cut from one seamless, polished hunk of granite, fifty or sixty hands deep. There would be a steel grate at the top, locked in place with a crossbar. The hatch led into another locked room in one of the Syndicate Palace sub-basements. There were a dozen identical holes, but when she'd visited here a lifetime ago, they were all empty. She listened for a while and decided that if there were any other imprisoned Kalis now, or anyone guarding the room above, they were being quiet about it.

You need to learn to listen. You should've waited.

"Yes. Yes, I should have," Syrina whispered.

She felt less uncomfortable talking to the voice now. At least she knew it wasn't just her imagination.

Did you ever think I was?

"But what *are* you? Besides something called a Preas Prohm, I mean."

Silence.

Syrina got the impression it still didn't know much more than she did.

She sat there for a while, avoiding what she knew she would need to do, but the only other option was to keep sitting where she was until she died.

She started groping around in the blackness. Her hand fell on something soft and cold and sticky and fuzzy. A rat. She was fully prepared to find a corpse down there with her. It was the sort of thing the Syndicate liked to throw at people they weren't happy with, but maybe there was a shortage of disposable bodies this week. Syrina didn't have any problems with being locked up with dead people over dead rats, except that people took up a lot more space as they lay around decomposing.

She found four other rats by the time she'd finished pawing around, all in a similar state as the first. Well, five dead rats were still better than one dead human. She pushed them all to one side of her circular prison and hunkered down against the opposite wall, then wiped her hands off on the granite floor, which was futile. Syrina could tell when she moved them that at least two had cleanly broken backs, confirming they didn't come in here and die on their own. She pictured Ormo up there somewhere, enjoying the sight of his favorite Kalis kicking dead rats around in a hole, even though she knew he had better things to do.

Her options were limited. She waited, slept, waited, slept, and waited more. No one came. No food, no water. Ormo knew she could survive a long time without either, and she was beginning to think he was going to see how long.

I don't think anyone is coming to let us out.

Syrina tried not to be bothered by the *us.* "Did you come up with that on your own or did you just start thinking that because I did?"

It occurred to me before now, but probably just because some part of your mind was already thinking about it. I don't know these people well enough to form opinions about them on my own.

Syrina tried to tell if the voice was being wry, but she couldn't.

"Any ideas?"

Maybe. What are we going to do if we get out of here, anyway?

The more she thought about it, the more she was glad she hadn't succeeded in killing Ormo. He was the only string she had to follow about what the voice was, what she was, what Kalis in general were, and now, how all of it was connected to the Tidal Works. As much as she pined for vengeance, what Ormo wanted to know, Syrina also wanted to know, and he was the only one with the wherewithal to guide her.

So you're not going to kill him?

"Oh, I'm going to kill him if it's the last thing I do," she whispered into the dark. "It's just not going to be the first. Why does it matter to you?"

Same reason it matters to you. He knows more

than he's letting on. You think you have questions?
Think about how I feel. You and I both want the same
thing—self-knowledge. So how do we get it? Go ask for
your job back?

Syrina considered that. Could she? By all rights,
she should be dead. Any other Kalis who tried to kill
their Ma'is would've been executed on the spot. Of
that, she had no doubt. None of the low merchants
she'd barged in on would be allowed to leave Syndicate grounds after seeing her. That would be a harsh
blow to Ormo even before considering the cover-up
job he had ahead of him when a dozen oligarchs never
returned home. And without Syrina to help with the
footwork.

Yet there she was, confined but alive. Ormo was
too smart to lock her up for a slow death as added
punishment. Too much time for something to go
wrong. He knew what she could do. He'd been the
one to make sure she was capable of it. He might be
waiting for her to get out so she could convince him
she saw things his way. Another experiment. The pits
were designed to contain Kalis, but maybe Ormo
wanted to see just how different from the others
she was.

All that crap about real and artificial love. From
everything Syrina had experienced in her lifetime of
willing slavery, she didn't think it mattered where love
came from. His *real* love could bite her ass. Still, if she
could pretend to be almost anyone, she might be able
to fake her way through believing what he'd said.
Even if she succeeded, though, he would never trust
her again. Not the way he had. Her second shot at the
bastard, whenever it came, would be all sorts of
difficult.

"I think so," she said to the voice.

But by the same logic that gave Ormo a reason not to kill her, it stood to reason that he might let her out. So she continued to sit and sleep and wait.

But days, then a week went by, and no one came to speak to her through the hatch or feed her or bring her water, let alone release her. She realized she really was going to die if she didn't try something.

You can get up there through the Door.

She almost asked, *what door,* until it occurred to her. "What happens when I pass out and fall back down?"

I think I can keep that from happening.

"You think?"

I haven't tried.

Well, it was better than sitting in there with a pile of decomposing rats, waiting to die.

Syrina tried to remember the setup of the hole and the chamber above from her visit two decades ago. A padlock was looped through the end of the crossbar that held the hatch in place. Or at least, it had been. If she could reach it through the bars, she could pick it open.

She hadn't eaten in a week. The Papsukkal Door would drain her. If she didn't die, she might only be able to have one go at it, and she was going to need at least two.

"Fine." She let her mind and body relax, and her heart grew still.

With one bound, she hit the wall six feet up, twisted, and launched across to the other side, then back again. On the fourth jump, she smacked her head into the hatch in the center of the ceiling, scrabbled until her fingers found purchase on the bars, and hung there a moment, getting her bearings.

Compared to the darkness at the bottom, it was bright. A trickle of light filtered through the bars from somewhere above. She pressed her eye up against the grate, her heart silent and still where it fluttered on the other side of the Door. She could make out the crossbar just inside her field of vision, but she couldn't see a padlock on either end of it. Damn. The keyhole in it was bound to be flipped away from the hatch, but maybe...

She swung back against the shaft wall and dropped down, sliding against the stone to slow her fall a little, broken further by the pile of decomposing rats.

Damn, you needed those.

She couldn't bring herself to care. She crawled across to the other side of her cell and fell asleep.

———

"Screw you," Syrina said when she woke up. She felt draped in heavy spiderwebs. "I thought you said you could keep me conscious."

There didn't seem to be any point. Now you can have another go.

The thought made her feel even worse, and she said so.

I didn't mean right away.

"Okay, then," Syrina mumbled and went back to sleep.

You don't need to talk out loud, you know. I'm in here.

She ignored it.

Syrina felt a little better when she came-to again, but the thought of trying the Door so soon still made her want to lie back down.

It's not going to get any easier.

"Shut up. I know."

She stood and steadied herself against the wall. "Eye take me. I don't think this will work."

Yes, it will. One more shot. Get ready.

She crawled over to the pile of rat carcasses and started sifting through them, picking out the long bones she hadn't smashed in her fall. They were big rats, and she ended up with a small handful of slimy, thin bones more or less the length of her middle finger. She hoped it would be enough, or she was out of ideas.

Something in the back of her mind cried when she tried to enter the Door again so soon on an empty stomach, but she went anyway. She'd already tried scaling up without it, but the walls were too smooth and far apart, and she was too weak.

Once at the top, it was a gamble of which side the lock was on, but she had a fifty-fifty shot. She slid her rat bones through one of the slits at the edge of the hatch, then picked one up between the two fingers she could squeeze out and wiggled it around. Bingo. The end of the bone poked something heavy and loose.

She spent the next twenty minutes hanging there, wiggling rat bones, prying at the lock until she'd flipped it over, so its keyhole faced her. It was still angled up, but it was as close as it was ever going to get.

The Door had long since shut, and she struggled

through waves of semi-consciousness while her body throbbed in agony, but she wasn't done. She could feel the voice busy in the back of her mind, keeping her awake.

As steady as her shaking hand would permit, she slid a long, thin rib into the lock, jiggled it, and slid it out again. Then she did it with three more and dropped back to the floor. The bones she cradled in her palm, hoping she wouldn't crush them when she hit the ground, but she was unconscious before she had a chance to find out.

———

They weren't crushed, but she was. Every part of her ached, and for the first time she could remember, she was cold. A deep, bone-gnawing cold that came from being naked and locked in a damp stone pit for over a week. Her tongue was swollen, and her stomach constricted with hunger.

In ideal conditions, Syrina could live over two months without food, and more than one without water. Ideal conditions meant she spent her time meditating, being still. Going through the Papsukkal Door twice in four hours would've done her in even if she'd eaten a whole goat in the time between, and now she was fading fast. If she didn't get out now, she wasn't going to. She didn't even know if she had enough in her to get through the Door one more time, but she needed to, or else concede her life to Ormo's pit.

She took the bones still cradled in her palm, closed her eyes—out of habit, since it was so dark at the bottom of the hole there was no change in her perception—and ran her fingers along their lengths, one at a time. It was a difficult task at the best of times, and almost impossible with the mound of distractions her fractured body was throwing at her.

She tried again. Slowly, slowly, the minute nicks and grooves scratched out by the workings of the lock formed a shape in her mind. She checked them twice and considered all the angles until she knew what she needed to do. The hard part would be getting up there one more time and doing it.

She sat back down against the wall. Even that small act made her body scream. She wished she'd choked down a few of the rats when she'd first woken up a week ago. Now they were too corpulent do anything but make her sicker than she already was.

The longer you wait, the weaker you get. It's now or not at all.

Syrina was looking forward to the day the voice in her head was wrong about something.

She stood, still clinging the bones, and let out an involuntary groan. Whatever else she did, she needed to eat something. The only thing harder on an empty stomach than going through the Papsukkal Door would be lying to Ormo's face. Not that she'd tried it yet, but she knew enough about her Ma'is to know it was true.

She fought down the protests of every muscle in her body, and let Papsukkal take her through the Door one last time.

17

TRUST

Syrina counted twenty of them, not including the dogs. She still hadn't eaten anything, and now she regretted it. She was beginning to think Ormo didn't want to see her, after all.

There'd been no resistance until now unless she counted that of her own broken body. No guards were in the upper chamber of the hole, nor did any come in on her where she'd passed out on the edge of the prison pit. The basement above was likewise guard-free, as was the small courtyard outside. Ormo must have had some warning of her escape though. He wasn't in his hall, but twenty Seneschal and their hounds were.

Syrina had intended to eat first, but she'd felt a rush of energy as soon as she'd awoken a free woman. It had pushed hunger to the back of her mind. So close to him, she'd thought. Better to just get it over with. The voice had rambled on about listening and being more careful, and Syrina had felt enormous satisfaction when she'd ignored it and went straight across the courtyard to Ormo's hall.

The voice continued to complain.

The Eye loomed over the black western wall of the palace, full, but its gaze was turned away. Its violet stripes were more red then blue tonight and turned the white flag raised on Ormo's tower a bloody purple.

The flag. Ormo was in his hall now. That clinched it. If she waited, he might be gone for a fortnight. Would he honor an appointment if she tried to make one? She didn't know. Anyway, she'd been trained to deal with little inconveniences like crippling hunger.

She settled for a long drink from one of the fountains in the courtyard and headed to the Hall, brimming with confidence. Ormo knew who she was. He knew she'd escape. It was all part of his plan. Now that she was out, she was sure he'd take her back, no questions asked.

Well, the Seneschal didn't look like they were going to ask any questions either.

Look at these people. They're afraid of you.

Under faces trained to be hard, were nervous men and women with eyes that darted between each other, waiting for someone else to make the first move. Syrina was the only one who knew she was in no condition for a fight. Seneschal, too, not just hired swords. The ones who wouldn't need to be killed after dealing with a Kalis. The ones who knew what they were doing.

Syrina didn't have enough energy for the fine movements that would let her go unnoticed, a fact she didn't think about until it was too late. Even so, none of them could see her well enough to make out how emaciated she was, and the group shifted as one, nervous. Only the dogs looked ready. They growled and whined and strained against their tethers, baring their fangs as Syrina's feet sang across the floor. The only thing she had enough energy to do was play the advantage she didn't have.

"You guys must've done something pretty bad to wind up here," she said.

More glances, but no one said anything.

She began walking toward the mob of guards and the empty dais, keeping one eye on the dogs, hoping none of the humans could hear her growling stomach over the growl of their hounds.

"Ormo," she said to the room in general, raising her voice.

It was a show for their benefit. She was sure he was listening, and he'd be able to hear her however loud she spoke.

"I'm sure you've spent enough tin training these people that you'd rather I not kill them."

The three men and one woman standing closest to Syrina edged backward. A hound off to her right snarled and lunged against the leather leash.

"I don't want to kill them, either," she said. "Or you. I'm here to talk. With you, if you let me. At you, if you keep hiding. If I still wanted to kill you, you think I would've just walked in here like this? You taught me better than that."

She waited. Still no answer. The Seneschal shuffled in place, but they didn't give any more ground.

"You can always tell when someone is lying, right? Are you getting old, or does it just not work through walls? Send your people away. I never got to tell you about NRI. Do you want them to hear all this?"

No answer, but there was still no doubt he was

listening. These Seneschal were here to deal with Syrina, and he'd want to know how it went.

By now, she was at the base of the dais, and she began to edge around it. She had a good guess of where he'd be. She didn't know how she'd get in, but she'd cross that bridge if she could get that far. The palace guards in front had backed away again as if Syrina had pushed them with an invisible wall twenty hands in front of her, but the others had closed into a ring behind her to block the only exit.

"He doesn't want us to kill you," a woman who'd backed away from the dais said.

Syrina was so surprised that anyone said anything she stopped walking. In all the years she'd spent hanging around the Syndicate complex, nobody but Ormo had said anything to her before. In their eyes, the Kalis were mystical beings lavished with privilege, while the Seneschal were mere servants. Funny, since the Kalis were the slaves. At least the Seneschal were getting paid.

Talking hadn't been a part of their plan, whatever their plan had been. The others eyed the woman who spoke with looks ranging from suspicion to horror, except for a man standing close to her, who eyed her with a mix of respect and lust. They were a thing, these two. Or at least, she wanted them to be.

Syrina took a step toward the speaker. This time, she didn't back away.

"Who are you?" Syrina asked.

"I don't think I'm going to tell you who I am."

That was probably prudent.

"Okay, fair enough. Since you're the one who spoke up, what are you doing here?"

"We're bodyguards."

"Ormo isn't here. Whose body are you supposed to be guarding?"

The woman shrugged. "He told us to wait in here, see if a Kalis came. See what she'd do if one showed up."

"You're bait, then. And fodder, depending."

"Basically." The woman shrugged again.

Syrina liked her.

It was coming together now. Ormo knew Syrina wouldn't hesitate to take out this lot if she was still burning for revenge. He was waiting for her to make a move. Then he could... what? Fill the Hall with fire? Gas? Neither would be hard for him to set up, and either was the sort of thing the Syndicate liked to put together. Perfect defenses against someone like a rogue Kalis, if she proved to be an investment not worth keeping around. Ormo was probably watching with one hand on the lever that would kill them all.

"So why are you telling me this?" Syrina asked the woman.

The woman, who kept her gaze turned away from Syrina to keep track of her in her peripheral vision, shrugged again and ignored the hisses for silence from the other Seneschal.

"No one said we couldn't talk to you," she said, more to her companions than to Syrina. "You're a Kalis. Maybe you find out he's not here and kill us because we weren't supposed to see you. But maybe you have a human heart under that mirage you wear, and if you know why we're here, you'll let us live. Even if Ma'is Ormo sends you after me in the morning for talking to you tonight, it's another ten hours I get to be alive. I'll take that over being dead right now."

Syrina couldn't help but be happy her reputation was being so helpful.

It's not just your reputation. Technically.

"My business is with Ormo," Syrina said, her own voice louder than it had been so the voice in her head would know she wasn't talking to it. "Your death would serve no purpose. If Ormo thinks you're ranked high enough to be here waiting for me, that's his business. I'd rather not kill you until he tells me to."

The woman nodded and shot a triumphant look to the others.

"So here I am," Syrina said. "Your job is done unless you lied about why you're here." It was Syrina's turn to shrug, though she couldn't be sure if anyone noticed it under the tattoos. "In which case, we might as well get this over with."

The Seneschal glanced at one another while Syrina gave them time to think about it. The woman was the first to shrug one last time, turn, and make the long walk toward the heavy doors at the end of the Hall. By the time she reached them, the rest had turned to follow her out, their feet singing on the stone floor like a flock of agitated mockingbirds. In a minute, Syrina was alone.

"Just you and me now, boss," she said to the empty room.

She went around to the back of the dais and stared at the white marble of Ormo's throne, the base of which rested on the gleaming block of obsidian that stood a few fingers higher than her head. She'd seen Ormo emerge from this place scores of times, but there was no trace of a door.

I know this place, the voice said. *Or a place like it.*

"Really?" She wondered what Ormo thought of

her talking to herself. "Is that information going to help me, or are you just talking to make sure I don't forget you're there?"

The voice refused to give Syrina an answer that would allow her the satisfaction of being able to argue.

Instead, it said, *Put your hand here.*

She pressed her right hand against the third polished slab from the floor without realizing what she was doing until she'd already done it. Her hand grew hot and tingled like a thousand needles were pressed against the skin of her fingers. There was a brief pressure, and the facade of the marble block to the right dropped open. Within was a teak and brass lever, polished with wear. She pulled it, and the entire low wall of the dais swung inward, revealing a steep, narrow stairway that descended into the bedrock beneath Ormo's Hall. The smells of oil and wet copper wafted from the opening on stale air.

The stairs jagged down through solid brown rock. She counted two hundred steps before they stopped at a white door with the texture and feel of porcelain, but much harder. A curved brass handle was latched into it as if jammed there long after the original construction. The door swung inward on silent hinges to reveal a low-ceilinged square chamber. Empty iron brackets were fixed to the inside of the door, and a heavy oak crossbar leaned against the wall. Ormo was at the opposite end of the room, standing in front of a plain wooden chair, watching her. On her right, rows of switches made from teak, ceramic, and bronze bristled, and valves marked with obscurely marked meters, all connected to a swarm of tangled bronze and brass piping and leather-wrapped wiring. In the center of the chaotic display, a lone panel rested—white like the walls and featureless except for a triangular-shaped hole in the middle, about twice as big around as a thumb. On her left, square glass portals lined the wall from floor to ceiling. Most were dark, but a few glowed a featureless soft white, and a couple flickered with images of landscapes from far above.

Ormo seemed relaxed, his hands hidden within the folds of his robes. Syrina stayed where she was in front of the door, trying to soak everything in without taking her eyes off her Ma'is. She wondered which of the levers he would've pulled to kill her and the Seneschal if she'd misbehaved upstairs, and what it would have done.

"Impasse?" He sounded jovial.

His tone annoyed her, but she raised her hands, making the motion as obvious as she could around the tattoos.

"Is it still called an impasse if I'm not trying to kill you?"

"I'm glad that time has come and gone, then."

For now.

Syrina didn't risk an answer to that.

"You were right," she said. "What you've done, what I am, they're a lot more important than my affection for a bird."

She didn't trust her skills enough to lie to him outright, but she thought she could work around the truth. They were more important, after all. To everyone in the world but her.

"Very few people can open that door, you know." Ormo nodded toward the stairway. "Not even all the High Merchants have the touch. Only a few of us have kept a steady line all the way back to the Ancients. I had every intention of ridding myself of you if you made any attempt to open the dais, right up to the point where you were able to do it." He raised his arms in an exaggerated shrug. "Curiosity won out, and so you live. Now prove to me I won't regret it."

"What is this place?" Syrina ignored the threat.

He was either going to kill her or not, and curiosity was winning out in her, too. She risked taking her eyes off him long enough to look around. The floor and ceiling were made of the same white, hard substance as the door.

"What it once was, who knows? Perhaps even a chamber from one of the great starships the Ancients used to get to Eris eons ago. Now it's my refuge. Passed down from generation to generation, Ma'is to Ma'is, Ormo to Ormo, since the Age of Ashes, or before. This room and a few others like it hold all we know about our Ancestors and their way of life before it was brought to ruin. Even after all these centuries, there is so much in here we don't understand."

"And yet you'd risk letting me down here after I tried to kill you?"

"You're unique, Kalis Syrina. We've tried for more generations than you can count to wake the blood in a Kalis. But you're the first time it worked. A little brash independence, unfortunate though it may be, must be tolerated."

"So you made me. What am I, then?"

Ormo laughed. "That's a question you'd be better off asking yourself. Stories—and that's all they are after all these thousands of years—say the Ancients carried the spirits of their own ancestors within them. Metaphysical blather with a grain of truth? Perhaps, but who now except you could say? A better question is, are you ready to resume your duties? Do you understand what you have now is far more important than your relationship with a stupid bird could ever be?"

"That's what I said." She wished he'd stop referring to Triglav as if he'd been just a bird.

Every time he did, she needed to swallow the urge to rush him, most likely to her own demise. That was probably why he was doing it.

"You have my answer," she said.

Ormo must've noticed how guarded her responses were, but he didn't let it show. Syrina tried not to worry about it.

"Then what did Cairnsworth Menns learn from NRI during his brief tenure there?" Ormo asked.

NRI. It seemed like an eternity ago, and Syrina realized almost all her activity leading up to her imprisonment was centered around her own personal goals. She tried not to think about how much Ormo might know about what she'd been up to.

"Not much." She hoped he wouldn't ask her anything about Witt. Hoped even more that he didn't already know everything. "The going theory is that the Tidal Works—or whatever the thing is that's running the Tidal Works—draws its energy from the Eye itself rather than from the ebb and flow of the water through it like everyone thinks. No one seems to know what it's actually doing."

"And their backers?"

She shrugged. "Tin is coming and going from a lot of different directions like you'd expect. I didn't find anything solid."

"That's not good enough." Ormo sighed.

"I'll go back to NRI, then. That's what you're asking, isn't it?"

She could try to learn some details about NRI's involvement in the Witt breeding programs while she was there.

He held her gaze for a long time. "Kalis Syrina, in the future, contact me in the traditional manner."

She left the way she came in.

18

BACK TO WORK

MARUS THAYN WAS THINKING ABOUT GOING home when he passed Menns slipping down the wide hall of Technical Development with his head down, unnoticed by everyone but himself. Thayn hid his surprise at seeing the other man again. He stepped in front of Menns and cleared his throat. Menns looked up from the patterned floor tiles, nodded an acknowledgment, and moved to step around. Thayn moved to block his path again.

Menns stopped, frowning. "Can I help you? I'm afraid I'm in a bit of hurry." He once again tried to get around.

"I was hoping to introduce myself." Thayn cleared his throat again. "We haven't officially met, and I try to get to know all the new staff. I won't keep you long. My name is Marus Thayn. NRI Security Head."

"Ah, yes. Hello. I'm—"

"Yes, I know. Cairnsworth Menns. I've seen you around, looked at your file. Just a cursory glance, mind you when I heard you were coming up here to join us. Mind if I walk with you?"

Without waiting for an answer, Thayn stepped aside and fell into pace alongside Menns, who gave a halfhearted smile and started down the hall, slower than he'd been walking before.

"After all I'd heard about you, I was beginning to think we wouldn't have a chance to meet. No one had seen you around the past few weeks. I thought maybe you'd already gone back to Fom."

"No, not yet."

They turned right and began to mount a smoky, windowless granite stairwell, lit by bright round naphtha lamps set into the ceiling on each landing.

Menns's voice was flat in the stale air. "Finalizing a few things first. Need to get some stuff out of the archives before I finish packing. The paperwork never ends. You know how it is."

"Ah, so you'll still be employed with NRI, then?"

"A subsidiary—Palisade Metals. But yes, I'll still be with NRI."

They reached the second floor and stopped in front of the Technical Development security check-in, where they lapsed into an awkward silence.

Thayn cleared his throat a third time. "Well, then, I won't keep you. I hope if your work brings you back here again, we'll be able to chat more."

"Likewise." Menns sounded like he wanted nothing of the sort, and vanished into the room.

Thayn could've followed Menns. He was head of security. He could've told Menns that Carlaas Storik had returned from Fom yesterday and would be over-joyed to see his old friend, but he didn't do that either.

Something about Menns had changed since the last time he was here when Thayn had seem him wandering around almost as if the man had no idea what he was doing. Something small and undefinable that no one else seemed to notice. Thayn wouldn't expect anyone else to notice, because as far as Thayn knew, he—she—was the only Kalis seeded at NRI.

———

Kalis Azhaa, in the skin of Marus Thayn, rounded a corner and fell into step behind a clamor of hired guards piling down the hallway toward the receiving offices that overlooked the harbor. With Storik back, security had erupted in activity. Their boots scuffed against the marble tiles as they walked, their curved leather scabbards slapped against their thighs. They ignored Thayn when he kept pace behind them and didn't notice when he slipped down another hallway and out of sight.

Azhaa was disturbed by the sudden return of both Menns and Storik. She hadn't given a report to Ma'is Kavik in months, and she hadn't planned to until she'd gotten to the bottom of the first suspicious disappearance of Menns, a few weeks after the archaeologist had vanished in Fom. Then he'd turned up in Eheene a few months later, disappeared just as suddenly, and now he was back yet again. That he could disappear and reappear so easily added to her suspicion, and no amount of combing Eheene had turned up anything. Now Storik was back, and he'd be talking to Kavik, and her Ma'is wouldn't be happy to learn anything from Storik that he had every right to know from her first.

It would take at least a half-hour for Menns to fill out the paperwork to get anything released from the archives, but as far as Azhaa knew, no one had bothered to purge his name from the employment rolls, so he'd still be cleared to withdraw.

Thayn ducked his head into an office and barked to a clerk who sat hunched over a stack of ledgers.

"Get word to Eheene that any sensitive material held at Ka'id's needs to be moved. All of it. By morning. Before that, if they can manage."

"*Sensitive material*, sir?" the clerk said, incredulous. "It will take until tomorrow afternoon just to file the request forms—"

"This is a security issue. I am holding you accountable for any losses resulting from delay." Without waiting for an answer, he turned and closed the door behind him.

A timid voice said, "Yes, sir," over the *thack* of the latch.

Storik's office hid behind a broad oak door, polished and carved in the relief of a vast, feminine face. Thayn entered without knocking. On the other side of the door, on the opposite wall, were other giant faces of women, surrounded by carved vines and flowers. They seemed to glare behind their slight smiles, and darkness pooled under their wooden brows. The other two walls were carved as gigantic faces of bearded men, and no little smiles hid their glowering contempt for whoever was in the room.

Azhaa had always wondered if the artwork was commissioned by Storik or by whoever had run the TDD annex before him, but it had never been Thayn's place to ask, so she needed to accept the fact that she'd probably never know.

Storik was there now, standing behind the polished desk of black wood that sprawled in the center of the office. The forgotten chair, stuffed and winged, was pushed back against the ivy-wreathed face behind him. His assistant, a thin weasel-faced man named Spaad, was there, too. But as Thayn entered, the wiry man gave a bow to Storik and a nod to Thayn before disappearing out the door and closing it behind him.

Storik was rifling through a leather satchel on the table. He was a broad-shouldered man, rippled with muscle under his dark blue silk shirt. His body didn't fit with the thinning hair and scruffy jowls that hovered over the maw of the bag.

He glanced up at Thayn as the door latched, gave the man a brief nod of greeting, and went back to his rummaging.

"Marus," he grumbled. "I was going to send for you, but I suppose word travels fast around here. Should've known you'd hear I was back before I even got through the door. I'm glad you came. So what's happened while I was cleaning up the mess in Fom?"

Azhaa cleared Thayn's throat, as if uncomfortable. She pitched the small sound just right, and Storik paused in his rummaging for the first time to look up at Thayn's face.

"Is there something I should know?"

"Not at all, sir. It's just that I thought you'd have been brought up to date by Menns."

"Menns? You mean Cairnsworth Menns?"

Azhaa made Marus's face perfectly surprised. "Of course. He came here to work with us a month or so after you left for Fom. He was just here. He said he was getting release papers to retrieve a few files from the archives at Ka'id's."

"What? Today?"

"Yes. Is there something wrong? I thought he said

he'd come here under your orders, but I didn't speak to him about it myself. I could be mistaken."

"No, it wasn't my order, but Fom was a mess. Still is. Everything's put on hold, people running scared. Menns disappeared a week or so after I got there, and I didn't blame him. So this is where he got off to. Well, if he's still in the building, I'd like to see him. I doubt he knows I'm back."

"Would you like me to bring him here?" Azhaa made Marus's voice casual, but she was bursting at the seams to track Menns down.

If he made off with anything important, Storik's wrath, as great as it might be, would be nothing compared to the inferno that would be coming at her from Ma'is Kavik.

"No, no. I'd hate to inconvenience him. I'll check with the door to see if he's left yet. If he hasn't, we can meet him on the way out."

"Good, sir. After you, then."

———

Syrina stepped out of the open bronze doors that led from the corporate offices, into the cavernous lobby of NRI. There was something wrong, and she could feel it tickling the back of her throat.

The lobby was high-ceilinged, fifty-feet wide and over a hundred long. The stairway she had emerged from rose from the back of the room on the right side. Sixty hands down, also on the right, the double wooden doors that led to receiving and the harbor stood closed. Opposite them were the broad iron doors leading to the mercenary barracks and armory. Between, a knee-high, broad-rimmed, reflecting pool rose from the blue and white mosaic of the floor tiles.

In front of each set of doors was a thick unadorned marble desk with a uniformed receptionist trying to look busy. A larger greeting desk stood in the center of the room, between the back wall and the reflecting pool, but the chair behind it was empty.

Security wore long, thin ceramic knives and blue and white NRI livery. Two soldiers flanked every doorway, and bored-looking crossbowmen stood on narrow balconies along the back of the lobby and along each wall. Thayn and a broad-shouldered, well-dressed old man stood at the front doors, heads close in private conversation.

Shit. There was no way she was going to get out of here without dealing with Thayn again. It had been careless to blow him off before, but something about him had seemed so... well, disarming. There were no other exits, though. At least none that wouldn't make Menns look even more suspicious if he tried to leave through them.

Syrina bit her tongue and began to walk toward Thayn in the same relaxed, hurried manor Menns had been scurrying around in all day. She made it to the empty reception desk before Thayn noticed Menns for the first time. By the look on the security chief's face, Syrina knew she was in trouble.

Thayn's features blossomed into a smile, betrayed by the angry triumph that flashed through his eyes. He said something to the old man, nodding in Menns' direction, who looked confused, then angry. Thayn barked a few incoherent words that echoed around the huge lobby, and a gong started wailing from some hidden room behind the huge landscape paintings that covered the east side of the receiving hall, beneath the crossbowmen's balcony.

Shit. It had been stupid to go back to NRI, but Ormo needed specifics on this circus. She couldn't even blame Ormo for this one. It had been her fault she hadn't done a proper job of it the first time.

Of course, she'd had her own reasons for returning to NRI, but obviously, today wasn't going to be a good day for side projects. She needed to get to the archives before someone moved them, and judging by the look Thayn was giving Menns, the order had already been given.

The surrounding guards moved forward, pale ceramic blades drawn. There were eight of them moving in from their posts flanking the doors, but if the wailing gong was any indication, there'd be more pouring in from the barracks any second. Syrina tried to make Menns look innocent, fidgeting and looking surprised in the center of the giant blue and white spiral mosaic that reached across the floor like a flattened octopus.

So they knew Menns was an impostor, but she didn't know what else they knew. Talking her way out may or may not be an option, but going full Kalis in here wasn't. There'd be no way Ormo could clean up a mess that big. Even if he didn't execute her outright for blowing it that bad, he'd never trust her competence again. However Syrina was getting out of this, she needed to do it as Cairnsworth Menns.

———

The guards approached the cowering form of Menns, weapons drawn but lowered. The soldiers with the crossbows watched from the balconies, heavy weapons dangling in their hands, un-cocked.

"You're sure it's not Menns?" Thayn whispered to Storik.

"Of course I'm sure." Storik didn't bother lowering his voice. "I worked with Menns for five years, and he looks nothing like this diminutive impostor."

Thayn nodded. "It's a good thing you came back when you did."

He walked forward to address the man who wasn't Menns, standing some thirty feet away on the other side of the reflecting pool.

Three guards surrounded the impostor, pressing the points of their long knives into his neck. The others looked on behind them, calm and menacing. The door to the barracks opened, and a dozen more mercenaries wandered in, chatting in whispers with the ones that had stayed back.

"Is there a problem? I have—" Menns began, his voice shrill enough to reverberate off the walls.

"Save it!" Thayn barked, drowning out the other man's whine. He spoke again when he was around the pool and no longer need to shout, making it a point to take his time, watching the Menns's impostor squirm in the silence. "We know you're not Menns. We'll learn who you are and why you're here soon enough. You can choose for yourself how much time and effort will be required before we get the answers we're looking for."

Menns swallowed. "What will happen to me?"

"That depends on what you tell us and how fast. Now, come. There's no reason we can't continue this conversation somewhere more comfortable."

Thayn made a vague gesture to the surrounding

guards, who spun Menns around and began to prod him in the back with the tips of their knives, toward the bronze doors that led upstairs.

Azhaa had just enough time to think, *why didn't any of these idiots tie his hands?*

A low, frightened moan emanated from deep within Menns' chest, and he stumbled away from the blades. One foot caught on his other heel, and he spilled with a grunt onto the glittering tiles in front of the empty reception desk. The fall pushed Menns over the brink of panic. He scrambled backward, crablike, until he pressed into the desk, arms flying up over his face as if protecting himself from blows, but the soldiers were only sheathing their knives to grapple him. The crossbowmen didn't look bored anymore, but they weren't aiming their weapons yet, either.

Menns snuffled and coughed and wiped the tears from his face, pressing harder back into the desk as he flinched away from the approaching guards. As soon as one of them reached for him, he screamed and jerked away from her.

"Oh, please don't kill me. Please don't kill me!" he shrieked, and lurched forward with unexpected strength, tearing his coat sleeve from the grip of the woman who'd made a grab at him, and bowling over another in a flailing, blind attempt to get away.

Menns made a stumbling, panicked sprint down the long lobby, toward the exit. Thayn stretched to tackle him as he shambled by, but Menns dodged wide, out of the security chief's reach.

"Alive!" Storik roared.

He still stood before the front doors and didn't look like he was going to move for anyone. Sweat beaded on the old man's forehead.

223

"Take him alive!"

The crossbowmen, who were finally aiming at the fleeing figure, hesitated. Menns tripped past the grip of another mercenary and fell against the obsidian rim of the reflecting pool. The guards that had only been watching swarmed him as he lay against the black stone. He looked helpless, but he had become a sobbing, crazed animal and he slithered between their legs, striking at knees and ankles and groins with his small knobby hands. He brought down three men as he struggled and broke free. No one managed to get a grip on anything but his jacket, which he slipped out of, leaving it dangling in the mercenary captain's hand.

As soon as Menns was clear of them, he charged toward the exit doors, right at Storik, whose sagging pale features had become blotchy with rage.

Menns tripped again and fell to one knee. Two more guards tried to grab him just as three of the crossbowmen fired, to the enraged protest of Storik. Two of the bolts clattered against the mosaic tiles of the floor. The other pierced through a soldier's hip, who'd been behind Menns before the impostor had fallen, dodging the shot. The mercenary screamed and toppled, and two others who might've been close enough to reach Menns instead spun to help their injured comrade. No one was able to grab the small, weeping figure of Menns as he bowled Storik over and ran into the courtyard.

———

Carlaas Storik surveyed the wide lobby. NRI's highly paid mercenaries were getting to their feet, lying on the floor, or disappearing out the door after the Menns impostor. Thayn was walking toward him, expression blank and stunned.

"These are the soldiers the Board of Directors has been paying so much for?" The words flooded out of Storik's mouth in a bubbly whisper.

"Yes, sir. I'll go now and—"

"Look at this. Look at this, Thayn! Your people blunder around and shoot each other at the first sign of a reason to have them here in the first place! Go. Don't come back until you've found this *Menns*."

———

Azhaa screamed inside her head, but she didn't let it show. Five years she'd built Thayn's place here. Five years. She could have stopped the impostor. She was a spy, not a fighter, but she could've stopped him. And given herself away and tossed five years of lies and insinuation into the harbor muck. And now, she might've thrown it all away, anyway.

Outside, the mid-morning sun was hot, and it wasn't much cooler under the dark green boughs of the gnarled cherry trees. The summer rains were still a few weeks away, and her feet kicked up little yellow dust clouds from the flagstones in the courtyard.

"There's no sign of him," a woman named Petsha panted, as she jogged up to Thayn from the outer gate. "Just disappeared. Might still be inside the wall somewhere. None of the gatemen saw him. Laas is checking with the shepherd, but he was on the other side of the building when it happened. I don't think he got back here in time to see anything."

"I know where he's going," Thayn said.

"Sir?"

"He's heading to the accountant's."

"But why?" Petsha asked.

She matched Thayn's trot to the carriage he'd summoned with a gesture to the gatemen.

"Corporate spy, most likely. Every company in Skalkaad wants a piece of one thing or another around here. We'll know more when we catch the bastard."

But that wasn't what he was after. True, there were a million things inside NRI headquarters that any company would pay a boatload of tin for. But he could've gotten anything he wanted when he was here a month ago. He was back now for... what?

She hoped he was only a spy. She'd watched Menns blunder out of their custody. No one was that lucky. Almost no one.

———

They were already carrying Ka'id's files from the Raymos building by the time Syrina got there. Four burly men loaded crates into an unmarked box wagon pulled by two shaggy brown and white camels. She could tell it was NRI's people because she recognized the driver and one of the goons from Aado.

It was afternoon. The high sun was warm on her back, but she couldn't enjoy it. In the southeast, low on the horizon, the rising crescent of the Eye blended into the firmament, almost imperceptible in the cloudless sky. The wind sighed now and then through the evergreens, which had been sculpted into abstract shapes and lined either side of the white flagstone street.

Just wait. See where they take it.

"Don't tell me how to do my job," Syrina said.

Thayn showed up a few minutes after she got there, looking worried and barking orders to the crew. Syrina wondered what he thought was going on. It had been quite the display back in Aado. Anybody who wasn't an idiot would question Menns' luck, blundering away like that. Kavik or whichever High Merchant was running the show at NRI would suspect, maybe even know the truth, but they wouldn't know who or why. Nothing concrete. They'd be forced to explain it away publicly as a lucky corporate spy that nobody could find again, but Syrina would need to watch her back for a while.

There were long periods where no one came out, probably sorting through what needed to go as they went. Four mercenaries stood around the door, and Syrina left her vantage long enough to find two more milling in the dusty narrow alley behind the bank. By the time they were done, they'd loaded five watertight shipping crates into the wagon.

The streets were narrow and crowded with people going home, so the camels needed to take their time through the press of silk-clad bodies, rickshaws, and palanquins vying for space between the rustling trees and white-pillared townhouses. The sun still glared across the tops of the marble buildings, making the shadowed streets glow. It was easy for Syrina to follow along on the rooftops. She hadn't paid attention to where the tides were when she'd arrived at Ramos, but Thayn led them straight toward the gate, to the District.

Syrina scuttled across a warehouse roof and over the wall to follow. The sun had set, and the horizon glowed orange. They pushed through the ever-present throngs toward the piers, where the tide was coming in and the hordes of foreigners mingled with landed crews and mercenaries.

Once into the slum, it was easy for Syrina to stay on the rooftops. But when she got to the water, she hesitated. People seethed around the docks, pushing on and off ships. There was no way she could get through to the piers unnoticed.

Swim, the voice said, matter-of-factly, like she hadn't already considered it.

"How?" Syrina whispered, into the air while on the edge of the roof, where she squatted like an unnoticed gargoyle.

She looked over the edge again. There was a wide, muddy street between her and the harbor, and a buoyant wooden pier, just as wide and at street level, bobbing as the tide neared its peak. It was a jump of at least sixty hands to the water, and the space between was packed with people.

The voice was silent for a moment.

She was just beginning to think it had gone away when it said, *What do you care? No one will believe anyone who says they saw a Kalis jump into the harbor. And even if they do, they won't know it was you.*

Syrina ground her teeth against a lifetime of training. It seemed like that was something she'd been doing a lot. Don't be seen by anyone who's going to stay alive. Don't work against the Syndicate. Honor your Ma'is. They were the only rules that existed for Kalis, and she couldn't kill everyone down there even if she wanted to.

The wagon turned down a pier, not quite out of sight, and stopped at the third ship in—something small with sails, wooden and fast-looking that couldn't quite be called a yacht, but couldn't be called anything else either.

Screw it. Might as well check off the last rule she hadn't broken.

Syrina took a running jump into the crowd and fell shoulder-first into a wiry black-haired woman, who grunted and stumbled into a fat man wearing a filthy captain's hat that looked like he'd looted it from a corpse. He lurched forward with an angry shout, but Syrina was off, staying low, darting through the mob, ignoring the screams of terror and confusion that followed in her wake, holding the image of the yacht in her mind's eye.

And then she was through. She hit the water with a small splash and dove down underneath the wood and metal hulls. The water was cloudy and frigid.

She came up for air once, two-thirds of the way there. The chaos of the harbor was intensifying as the tide started to ooze out and crews prepared for departure.

The NRI boat had the uninspired name of The Gull. It was drifting away from the dock with the rest of the traffic by the time Syrina reached it. She shimmied up the narrow ladder to the deck, hunkered behind a coil of reeking, dripping rope, and waited.

They'd cleared the harbor two hours ago, and The Gull was the fastest ship in NRI's fleet outside the steamships, but Azhaa still had a bad feeling. There'd been no sign of Menns. Anywhere. Not at Ka'id's bank, not at the docks, not in the streets between. She didn't understand it, and she liked it even less. No one would go to all that trouble and then just give up without a fight. Not someone as tenacious as the Menns impostor had been. He'd been after something from Ka'id's. Azhaa didn't intend to let the crates out of her sight, even if it was a five-day trip to the NRI storage facility, buried under the wild hills of eastern Skalkaad.

So while the navigator sat above, alone on the cramped bridge, and the rest of the crew slept in shifts in the two cramped cabins, Thayn huddled in the darkness of the cramped cargo hold, crouched on a crate, with his back to the wall. He'd refused to come up for food after they were clear of the port, and the others had left him alone to guard their cargo against ghosts.

Ghosts. If only Azhaa was worried about ghosts.

Six hours later, when the crescent of the Eye scythed the black sky high in the southwest, haloed by an ocean of silver stars and casting a wavering reflection in the sea, Azhaa was just beginning to think maybe she'd been wrong about Menns after all.

Then she heard a muffled thump followed by a soft splash, not quite in time with the waves against the hull. Her heart skipped a beat, and she held her breath, eyes closed, and focused on the sounds coming from outside the hold. Nothing. No shouts from the seamen, no stirring from the cabins, where there should be a shift change taking place any second.

Azhaa chewed her tongue a minute, thinking. If Menns was aboard, if he'd been aboard this whole time and taken out the crew with no more than a thump and a single splash, then her worst fears were true. No one could do that. Almost no one. Azhaa might be able to do it. Or someone like Azhaa, who might be even better at it.

If it was a Kalis, she would be an Arm, trained in Papsukkal, and she'd be able to kill Azhaa in a heartbeat. Less than a heartbeat, technically speaking. Azhaa was a Seed. She'd never learned how to use her tattoos to become unseen to the extent of the other Kalis. She'd never been taught how to find the Papsukkal Door with any real proficiency. Her training had involved mimicry and disguise that far surpassed what other Kalis could do, even most of her fellow Seeds. She knew how to inflect her voice to make people trust her, even tell her things they wouldn't tell anyone else. And she could lie so well not even Ma'is Kavik could tell when she wasn't being honest, Not that she would ever deceive him. She could make herself look like the head of NRI security and take his place for five years without even his mother noticing.

Her training had also taught her a few things about her own kind. They were everywhere, the Kalis, and she knew the one on The Gull would kill her.

She moved from her seat on the crate, deeper into the shadows of the hold, her gaze never leaving the gangway. Still no sound.

She considered. The documents were irreplaceable, but each piece of paper on board could be used against her Ma'is in one way or another. She could give a rat's ass if NRI suffered, but Kavik might be set back years if the crates were lost. On the other hand, if they fell into the hands of a seditious High Merchant, he could be ruined. Both thoughts made her sick to her stomach, but there was only one real choice, and she had to act now.

She thought about removing Thayn's face so she could at least try to slip by whoever was waiting above, but she discarded the idea as fast as she tossed aside any plan of trying to find the Papsukkal Door for the first time in twenty years. If there was another Kalis on board, neither would do any good. No reason to blow her cover and raise even more suspicions. Not if she was going to end up dead either way.

Azhaa padded up the low gangway, listened at the hatch, and slipped onto the deck.

———

Syrina waited for the thin slash of the Eye to start its downward slide to the west before she killed the first of the crew and tossed him overboard. Then she slipped down to the narrow mid-deck and killed the other four while they were sleeping, trying to suppress the unfamiliar guilt as she did so. *Just work, just work, just work, just work,* she repeated to herself, like a mantra, until the words became meaningless. She was prepared to jump overboard and drown herself if the voice said anything, but it left her alone.

Then she went back up to the deck to consider her next move. She was pretty sure only Thayn and the navigator were left on The Gull. She'd be able to pilot the little ship most of the way back to Eheene, scuttle it, and make off with the cargo so she could leave the crates hidden somewhere along the coast for Ormo to find. But she needed to be careful. Off the port side, the Barrier Cliffs of Skalkaad loomed three spans away, the current shifting to crash into them. If Syrina took out the navigator, she'd need to be ready. Or she, the documents, and the voice were going to end up pulped against the rocks.

Thayn popped out of the hold just then, looking grim and heading to the helm.

He's seen the bodies below, the voice said.

Syrina wanted to ask it how it could know that, but she didn't. She could see it was true. The look on his face said it all.

You could take them both now.

She could, but she didn't. She could kill them anytime, but then she wouldn't know what they were about to talk about. It wasn't like they could go anywhere.

Thayn opened the door to the little room that served as a bridge.

The navigator—Syrina still couldn't figure out if he was a real captain or just the guy steering— laughed. "So you decided to come up out of there, after all. I thought you were even going to shit down there. I didn't want to—"

Syrina didn't learn what the might-be-captain didn't want to do, because at that moment, Thayn, without a word, plunged a white ceramic blade into the man's neck, up through his jaw and into his head, all the way to the hilt. The sailor managed to look surprised before he fell where he stood.

Syrina was so startled she didn't do anything, and even the voice was shocked into silence.

Without hesitation, Thayn pushed the body out of the hatch with his foot and cranked the wheel hard to the port. The Gull lurched, and Syrina fell back against the rail. Thayn reached down and slid his knife out of the man's neck before opening the maintenance compartment under the wheel.

Too late, Syrina realized what he was doing. He slashed twice, and she heard the rope running to the rudder snap. The Gull lurched again and began to drift as the tide carried them toward the cliffs. Then he stepped out and reached up, slicing through the rope that tied the sail, which shuddered and collapsed with a hiss of fabric barely audible over the distant crash of surf.

Syrina got enough of a grip on herself to do something. She walked over to Thayn and punched him in the face. In the moment between when he saw her and when she knocked him out, the look on his face was even more unnerving than what he'd just done, even if it did explain quite a bit. There was no fear or shock at seeing a Kalis. Thayn had known she was there, and he was doing everything in his power, including sacrificing himself, to make sure Syrina would never get the cargo.

She looked north, now across the bow. The cliffs loomed closer.

There were five hundred questions Syrina wanted to wake Thayn up to ask, but she didn't have time, and she'd get answers to at least a few of them if she got the records to Ormo.

She looked again at the encroaching cliffs. Maybe a half-hour. More, if she got lucky again. She dragged Thayn's unconscious body over to the rail and heaved him overboard. Then she ran down to the hold and started dragging the archives up to the deck, one crate at a time.

By the time she had them lined up, she could hear the surf crashing into the rocks. The cliffs consumed a third of the sky to the north. The Eye hovered high, a thin purple and azure smile under the vast, feature-less black of its dark side, while the eastern sky was growing brackish red in a line along the horizon.

The crates were made from copper and oiled pine, rigged with thick copper rings on two sides so they could be carried by two people with poles. She ran a rope through the rings, alternating them with all the leather and wood life-preservers she could find and attached three hard air-filled leather boat fenders to either end. The boxes were tough and waterproof, but they were heavy. She wasn't sure the six fenders and the wooden rings would be enough to keep them afloat, but she was about to find out.

The cliffs were close now. It had only taken Syrina ten minutes to haul the crates out of the hold and rig everything together, but she could feel the spray of the surf as it blew off the rocks. Birds wheeled above in the predawn glow, launching themselves from hidden nests in the gray rock. The dark tideline was still thirty hands above the surging water, and the waves heaved foam, bloody red in the dim light, halfway up the cliff. She was down to five minutes, tops. So much for luck.

Syrina secured the last knot on the rigged crates, pushed the tangle of boxes into the rolling froth, and followed it over the rail. Instantly, she knew she was in trouble. Her head went under, and she lost track of where the crates were, where the ship was, where the cliffs were, where she was. This close to the rocks, the currents swirled and eddied. The water tugged her feet one direction and her head the other, flipping her over so fast she didn't have time to take a breath. She spun around, straightened herself out, and tried to thrust her face toward the red light, which was all around her, but pinker in the direction she hoped was up.

Her face broke the surface, and she tried to spend the moment inhaling instead of coughing, to limited success. She sunk down and bobbed back up, more stable this time, and rode up the wave from the trough. The first thing she saw was the string of crates, floundering half-afloat further on toward the rocks. She slid down the back of the wave into the next trough, and when she rode up the next one, she saw the hull of The Gull smashing into two pieces against a massive spear of stone that jutted from the water a few hundred hands from the cliffs. Each breaker tore more chunks off the boat and brought Syrina closer to the same fate. The white noise of the surf was so loud that the sound of the dying ship didn't reach her ears over it. There was no sign of Thayn.

She struggled toward the crates for a minute but gave up. They were headed into the rocks, too, anyway. There was no way she could get to them, and nothing she could do if she got there.

The cliffs were a less than quarter span away now, and they lurched closer with every wave. After everything she'd been through, dying like this was insulting.

You can't swim anywhere. We'll need to climb the rocks. Try to time the swells.

Her shoulder hit a rock so hard she felt her humerus snap. The pain blinded her for a second until she felt the voice ooze around it, dull it down to a throbbing numbness. She'd still been facing south when the surf threw her against the cliff, and she wasn't ready for the blow, which felt like she'd been shot with a cannon. Before she could recover, she slammed into it again. She sunk, tumbling, this time too weak to claw up toward the light, which was now a little more yellow than it had been a few minutes ago.

Fine.

No. Turn. Face the—

Syrina slammed into a rock a third time, this time with her face. There was roaring all around her, and she couldn't tell if it was coming from outside or somewhere in her head. The yellow light was fading, and she wondered how it could be getting dark again so early in the morning.

Snap out of it.

The light around the edges of her vision grew brighter.

Wait, wait. Grab it. One... two... three. Now!

Mindlessly following orders, Syrina reached up and out, toward the light. The water in front of her parted and turned to reddish gray stone as she smashed into it again. She scratched at it frantically with her good arm, hating the useless one that flopped broken in the surf, pulling her this way and that. The ocean was sucking her back down, away into darkness.

With the tips of her fingers, she found purchase on wet stone and the sea drained away beneath her. All she could do was dig in and brace herself for the next wave that slammed into her a few seconds later, somehow failing to sweep her off the rock, to her death.

You've got to climb.

"With one arm?"

Fine. You can try your other ideas first.
Shit.

She braced for the next impact, and as the water rushed down her legs, she pulled herself up to her chin, then snapped her arm up to scramble for another finger-hold before the next wave smashed into her. After five or six lunges, she was out of the fiercest of it. And after twenty more, she crossed the dark tideline, and the crashing surf dwindled to a heavy spray.

The sea coiled and writhed like a pit of snakes beneath her, reaching for her dangling legs. Looking up, the cliff went on, solid and eternal, to the zenith. The sun was up all the way now, a ball of flame resting on the southeastern horizon and hot on her back. The humid air smelled of brine and fish and birds. Her broken arm throbbed, and the fingers on her good hand were sore. There was no way she was going to make it.

Good thing you have another plan.
Shit.

———

After another twenty minutes of pained, one-armed climbing, Syrina reached a crack in the cliff that was big enough to squeeze into if she let her legs hang out the end and jammed her neck against a rock. She'd never been so grateful for anything.

She yanked at her broken arm, pinned the useless wrist down with her good hand, and maneuvered the bone back into place. She passed out not caring whether she fell from the crack while she slept.

When she woke up, it was dark. The reddish-purple crescent of the Eye loomed above, a little fatter than the night before. Her broken arm ached and itched so bad it brought tears to her eyes, but a little experimenting proved it had healed enough to hold her weight.

Before she began the climb, she poked her head out and scanned the roiling surf. The tide had gone down and was coming back in again. A few chunks of The Gull still lay among the rocks, now lifting with the rising water. A little way out, in the low purple light, she could make out a few other pieces of the ship. The tide had carried them out and was bringing them back. Below and off to the east, the crates, still tied to the rope and the boat fenders, hung entangled in a jagged stump of stone jutting from the sea, caught in a fissure six feet above the tideline.

The currents along the cliffs were circular, and sometimes it caught shipwrecks in them for years. Fragments serving as warnings for sailors of the Skalkaad Sea.

Syrina hoped that if the boxes dislodged and washed away, they would keep coming back again, at least until Ormo's people could find them. It needed to be that or nothing.

She began to climb.

That son of a bitch. Thayn might not have killed her, but he'd come damn close, and he'd screwed Ormo. It would take Syrina a month to hike back through the broken mountains and forests to Eheene. More, since there weren't any roads along this part of the coast. By then, the autumn storms would hit, and recovering the crates would be impossible until spring if they could even be found by then.

Son of a bitch. How did a glorified security guard like Thayn throw a shaft into the plans of a Kalis?

If the voice had any answers, it didn't say anything.

19

SMUGGLING

IT TOOK NINE MONTHS FROM THE SINKING OF THE Gull for Ormo's people to find the crates. They were close to where Syrina had last seen them, still caught in the loop currents, but it had been a harsh winter. Two of the five had been destroyed, and another two had leaked enough to ruin most of their contents. One had survived, beaten but intact. Ormo had kept Syrina busy in the meantime with irrelevant tasks. Busy enough to keep her from working on anything she cared about. Busy enough that she was sure that was what he intended.

It was spring by the time Ormo's people had finished sifting through what was salvageable—two years since Syrina had first departed to Fom on Ka'id's ship. It seemed more like twenty to her. Since Triglav, Syrina had been counting the days until she no longer needed Ormo, and each one dragged slower than the last.

She didn't know what to say after she'd read the condensed report. Most of the surviving documents were unrelated to anything that concerned her. NRI conducted shady businesses all over the place, but any other company that operated in Skalkaad did, too. Hood Manufacturing, though, that was interesting.

Syrina stood just inside the big double doors of Ormo's Hall. He'd glided up to her with the report, slippered feet chirping across the floor, and walked back to his dais to contemplate her from a distance. No invitation this time to approach his throne.

In the past two hundred years or so, a handful of companies had sprung up within Skalkaad that operated outside the Fifteen's realm of influence. The Syndicate tolerated them, as long as they paid their taxes and either kept a low profile or were unusually innovative. Hood Manufacturing was one of the latter. Without their contributions, the more refined naphtha engines that powered the Syndicate's ships wouldn't exist yet, and probably wouldn't for another decade or more. Rumor had it they were working on airships that could survive the harsh Skald winter, too.

Such contributions had earned Hood the Syndicate's grudging respect. But unlike other conglomerates that operated without Syndicate oversight, most of which could be traced back to some plutocrat or low merchant, Hood's hierarchy was even more obtuse than NRI's. Rumors persisted that it was a Ristro spy operation, throwing the Syndicate an occasional technological bone to keep the High Merchants off their back. There'd never been any proof of that, though, and not for lack of looking. Hood had survived an inquest and five tribunals. If there had been any evidence that they were linked to the Corsairs, they would've been put to the torch decades ago, innovative or not.

Carlaas Storik was an avid note-taker. The lone

crate that had survived the winter had contained detailed outlines, in Storik's own handwriting, of two separate meetings in Fom with a man named Asapalashvari. Storik noted him as an *unofficial contact* with Hood Manufacturing. Nothing suspicious in that by itself, nor anything in the notes that hinted at Hood being anything but a legitimate business. Hood and NRI had similar interests and did similar work, and both were licensed to do business in Skalkaad and in N'narad.

Where it got interesting was Ormo's note scrawled at the bottom of the page, in his small spidery script. A man named Asapalashvari was known to the Syndicate to be one of the chief advisors to the Astrologer running the Ristro prefecture of Chamælivishi. Since Ristro culture dictated that each given name be unique, it was almost certainly the same guy.

"Hood," Ormo grumbled. His voice rolled clear and deep across the chamber to Syrina from where he perched on his dais at his end of the Hall. "We have all the pieces. The Corsair Asapalashvari to Hood, from Hood to Storik, who runs NRI, which is run by Kavik."

"But as usual, we have nothing hard," Syrina said. "It might even be why they're funneling tin through Hood in the first place. Ma'is Kavik has got to know any investigation into them will die like all the others. Even Storik just calls this guy an *unofficial contact*, whatever the hell that's supposed to mean. There's nothing in here that will hold up."

Ormo rustled a nod. "But we have a name. Asapalashvari is a powerful man, at least according to what little information we have on the Ristro hierarchy. His connections to Hood are irrelevant. Although, if we could prove them, we might bring them down as well.

"Whether or not he's with Hood Manufacturing, he is in contact with Storik, which means it's likely that he's also been in contact with Kavik himself. Any High Merchant in a position to speak to someone that close to an Astrologer would rue passing up the opportunity. If such a meeting has taken place, there will be evidence of it somewhere.

"And if Kavik met with him, they didn't go as Kavik. Appearing in the guise of a High Merchant would be too dangerous for both parties."

Syrina frowned. "So how does that help us? They wouldn't even know it was..."

Ormo's not after Ma'is Kavik. He's after who Kavik really is.

A chill went down Syrina's spine. Ormo wanted to get rid of another High Merchant, and he needed her to do it.

Ormo shook his head, the movement barely discernible in the shadows that crowded his throne.

"To think, all this time I was concerned that Kavik could be working with the Church for his own profits, when it seems they've been working with the Corsairs, against Skalkaad."

"But what can you do about it?" Syrina knew the answer but wanted to make him say it. "You know Hood will be a dead end. All we have on Storik is some notes that cover legitimate meetings—whoever they're with, there's nothing illegal in them—and Ma'is Kavik isn't going to just confess to anything if you ask. In fact, they'll fight you every step, and in the end, they'll win because you don't have any proof solid enough to bring down another High Merchant. Even if Kavik does keep evidence lying around somewhere that proves they've been working with the Corsairs, they're not going to keep it anywhere where you or I can get at it. At this point, all you can do is tie the whole NRI project up in tribunals for a few years and toss a few low merchants like Lees to the dogs before it all fades away. There might even be another full investigation into Hood before a lack of evidence and a few friends in the right places gets the whole thing dropped yet again. A few of the other High Merchants will even help cover for them because they'll be afraid to lose their line on new technology Hood might come up with. After it's all over, Kavik can continue doing whatever he's doing, only more so. He might be set back, but he can be confident he won't be bothered about the same thing again."

"We have a name," Ormo grumbled again, "who may hold all the answers we need."

His words hung in the vast space of his hall.

"You want me to go to Ristro," Syrina said, with a defeated sigh.

Ormo slumped back into his throne with a grunt. "It's the only place where proof of these transgressions may exist. At least, the only place where, as you say, you might obtain such proof. This man, this Asapalashvari, has answers. The Astrologers are compulsive historians. If they, or one of their aides, are working with a traitor within the Merchant's Syndicate, it will be documented somewhere in Ristro, and the information pertaining to it will have spread throughout the hierarchy. Even if they don't know it's a High Merchant, the nature of the alliance will make it important enough for them to document, and it will contain all the clues we need."

"And there would be enough evidence there to hold up against one of the Fifteen?" Syrina asked.

"Enough to act on now and present as evidence later, if such a presentation were ever to become necessary."

Syrina hesitated. She hated Ormo, but she still didn't want him to think she might be afraid.

"And what about the fact that Kalis don't come back from Ristro? At least according to everything you taught me."

Ormo's silk robes whispered as he leaned forward in his throne. "That is true, Kalis Syrina. Your kind does not return from the Ristro Peninsula. In fact. few people do. Those who go willingly go to stay, and the natives who leave keep their secrets too well. If it were otherwise, we would have a better under-standing of our oldest enemies. You are, however, dif-ferent." He coughed a cynical laugh. "You've not been bound by my teachings for many months. Why start again now?"

"I don't speak Ristroan." Syrina's voice was soft.

"You learn fast, even for a Kalis." Ormo's voice grew harder. "I'm not asking for a favor, nor am I re-questing advice or debate, as lively as that would no doubt be. Prove to me you're different from the oth-ers. Prove once and for all you're still faithful to your Ma'is, by again doing what has never been done. Prove that you're worth all the extra trouble."

I don't like this. I think he's trying to get rid of us.

It was a win-win for Ormo. If she succeeded, he got everything he wanted. If she failed, he was rid of a liability.

"Of course, Ma'is Ormo." She tried and failed to suppress a smile at the voice's distress.

Ormo wouldn't be able to see it anyway.

He was still a moment, a dark shape hovering in the shadows atop the dais. "Good. I would suggest getting in touch with some of your old contacts in Valez'Mui. There may still be a few who can assist you with passage to—"

"I don't need to go all the way to the Yellow Desert. I think I might have another way there."

"Good, Kalis Syrina. Take your time. Do what you must."

That, we will do.

Syrina left the Hall without responding to either of them.

———

The journey to Fom was spiked with memories of Triglav, but Syrina forced herself to think about the job ahead. She traveled as a short, fat thin-haired smuggler named Darius N'uld, a Fom native who'd been living in Valez'Mui for the past ten years. Another wealthy unknown traveling to the Crescent City, with fingers where they didn't belong. One of a million.

N'uld checked into a sprawling inn that smelled of smoke and cedar. It was called The Milking Flats, and the sign depicted a painting of a busty woman holding high a glass of white fluid Syrina could only hope was supposed to be milk.

———

The little man entered the arched open doorway with the nervous hesitation of a man who knew he was in a place that was beneath him while trying to cover up how he felt because he was afraid of the people he found there. It was moldering single-floored wooden square a quarter span from the edge of the Lip, surrounded by brick and wood markets and filthy vendor stalls.

He stayed in his small room for two weeks, only coming out twice a day for food and when he needed to use the outhouse hunkered in the alley against the back wall. Rumors about him abounded among the staff. There were dares between a few to sneak into his room while he ate in the pub next door, but no one did. His tin was good, and he was paid up for the month. Curiosity wasn't worth getting fired over.

———

The pirate worked at night, so Syrina did, too. Every dusk, she slipped out the window of her room and crept up to the rooftops. Then she'd skip over the top of the Lip and down the cliff to Velnapasi's place, where she kept to the shadows and watched who came and went until she'd found someone suitable.

Then Syrina followed her for a week and introduced the woman to Darius N'uld.

———

Darius N'uld blinked and swallowed, but his expression remained hard. "I have a package, and I have tin. What's the problem?"

Marsa Marsan tapped her fingers across the top of

her yellow pine desk in a steady rhythm and glared at him with tiny black eyes set over a tiny pointed nose. Angry smashed grapes mounted above the crooked beak of a fighting cock. N'uld was a puny, grotesque man with a flat nose and piercing, watery green eyes.

"The problem is," Marsa Marsan said, "I don't deal with pirates, and I don't know who does. What's your problem?" She flipped a curly strand of salt-and-pepper hair from where it tickled the corner of her eye.

N'uld produced a ream of paper from his satchel and tossed it onto the desk. "Look, I know people who know people who know you. Know what I mean? I have a box that needs to go to Ristro, and you're at the end of the trail I followed to get it there. I'm not a spy, all right. I'm not some customs creep coming around to sniff you out. Just a businessman who needs to get something to Ristro so both you and I can make a lot of tin. And no, the *proper channels* won't do for this sort of thing. Too slow and too many questions."

Marsa Marsan thumbed through the folder, making a point of taking a long time to do it even though she could tell what was in it the moment N'uld dropped it on the table. Receipts, shipping manifests. A bunch of transactions she'd done with a bunch of different people that all looked fine on paper, but all of them had one thing or another to do with the goddamned pirate Velnapasi.

She studied N'uld, frowning. "So then, what are you shipping?"

"Are you going to do it, then?"

Marsa Marsan shrugged. "I doubt it. Not if I don't know what it is."

"So you're admitting you deal with Ristro?"

Marsa Marsan's expression froze, but N'uld just smiled and produced a small stack of papers from the folds of his baggy trousers. He dropped it on the desk, too, on top of the folder. She picked them up and examined them. Promissory notes from the Syndicate Bank of Skalkaad, each one worth a hundred Three-Sides.

She raised an eyebrow. "The Syndicate Bank?"

N'uld snorted. "Don't pretend you're too good for them."

Marsa Marsan frowned again, but she was thinking. A Church official wouldn't try to entrap her with Syndicate Bank Notes. They'd use cash. Tin was easier for them to get and harder for her to turn down. The fact that this guy had a whole pocket full of these was as close as she was going to get to proof that he had nothing to do with the Church.

"All right." She smiled and counted the notes—ten—before folding them up and tucking them into her blouse pocket.

Her gaze never left the little man's. N'uld smiled back at her, but there was no triumph or gloating in his glittering weepy eyes. More like relief.

"More after the package is away to Ristro," he said. "Ten thousand, total. I'll have left Fom by then, but you can be sure your payment won't be delayed. Do we have a deal?"

Marsa Marsan's smile drooped into a conflicted glare. She didn't like to take people at their word, but there was something about the squash-faced little man that made her think this time she could make an exception.

"Deal." She showed N'uld to the door.

He shook her hand, his eyes enthusiastic. "I'll

leave instructions on where to pick up the crate. It's a standard shipping box, eight hands a side. I trust that won't be a problem?"

Marsa Marsan patted the pocket that bulged with the bank notes. "No. No problem at all."

———

Syrina sneaked back into her hotel room long enough to dress as a temple boy before she headed over to a shipping depot to reserve a crate. Then she waited until dark and dropped instructions for Marsa Marsan into her mail slot and made up a package with the rest of the bank notes. That, she dropped off at a courier's office with instructions to deliver it to Marsa Marsan in one week. After that, she found a quiet alley to ditch the temple boy in and slipped back to the depot to wait.

She sat on the roof until the slate of the Fom sky began to grow brighter, eyes closed, breathing deep, calming her mind. As soon as the predawn light began to spread, she went down to the crate and slipped inside. It was a tight fit, even for her. She needed to sit with her knees drawn up against her breasts and her neck bent forward. She double-checked the lid for the safety release and eased it over her until it latched.

It was the same type of crate the NRI documents had been stored in. Copper and pine, waterproof, and airtight. A normal person would last maybe twenty minutes locked in there—a fact Syrina tried not to think of as she lapsed into the trance that would keep her alive long enough to reach the open sea.

Awareness was a fuzzy, far-away thing in the cramped black space. She'd timed the pickup well,

251

and she was aware of being jostled around as the crate was lifted and carted through Fom. Muffled sounds of voices and wheels lurching through ruts and crashing surf came to her like half-remembered dreams. After a while, she felt herself lowered down, down, until she came to rest close to the sound of the sea.

Then came ages of stillness and the constant white static of the ocean, peppered with bursts of human commotion, and then stillness again. She waited, mind far, far away but distantly aware that her body was dying, sinking in the blackness of stale air and the smell of herself.

And the voice would come. *You're fine. You've got ages. Stay focused.*

And for a little while, she'd imagine the air fresher, the box a less cramped. And she'd feel the cold stillness coming over her again, and again the voice would come and push it away. But each time, it lingered a little closer.

Another burst of activity. Her crate lurched, almost snapping her from the meditation. She sucked in a sharp breath of hot dead air. Her heart pounded against her ribs.

No, the voice said, tone calm. *Not yet. Everything is fine. You're fine.*

And Syrina thought she could feel a cool, fresh breeze from somewhere beyond the trance. Her chest calmed, breathing stopped. The stillness halted but remained this time, clammy and frigid, pooling in the bottom of the crate. Somewhere in her mind, past the meditation and the voice, another voice said it was taking too long. She should've been on the ship by now, in the air where she could breathe.

Don't think about it.

She tried not to think about it, but thoughts of air came again, unbidden as she was jostled a second time. Mumbled strings of Ristroan came to her through the walls of the crate, over the static hiss of the waves.

Finally! She could get out, take a deep breath, stretch her legs. She felt for the latch.

No!

Syrina froze, one hand still lingering on the catch.

A little while longer. You'll make it. Relax, relax. The voice was soft, soothing, a mother whispering her daughter to sleep. *Not long now. Just a little bit more.*

Syrina felt the coldness creeping up her legs. She felt sleepy. Strange to be so tired now. She'd been meditating for hours.

———

Yelling woke her up.

"Shut up," she mumbled. "I'm sleeping."

You're dying. Wake up. Wake up!

Syrina tried to brush away the tendrils of confusion that clung to her mind. Her neck hurt. Her back hurt, and she couldn't feel her legs.

Wake up and get out of the box!

Box? She remembered something about a box. A few more minutes of sleep and she'd be able to think. She felt herself slipping away again. It was a pleasant feeling. Just a few more minutes.

Get up!

Reality trickled back to her. She suddenly really, really wanted to breathe. She groped for the fastening on the inside of the crate, fighting down panic. Her fingers felt like sausages wrapped in leather.

Calm down. Calm. There.

She felt something metal. She fumbled once and flipped it with a clack.

The lid popped with a sucking sound, and cool salt-tinged air flooded over her. She sucked in a breath and felt the cobwebs drift away.

Syrina dragged herself out of the crate, into the small creaking hold of a wooden ship, suppressing her cough with the crook of her elbow. It was almost pitch black, but after her time in the utter dark of the crate, she could make out shapes in the shadows. She didn't care if anyone came down and found her or not, but she didn't have enough energy to argue with the voice, which demanded she hide. She dragged herself into a corner, behind a low stack of crates identical to hers, wincing at the pins and needles lancing through her legs, back, and neck, all of them still refusing to move the way she told them to.

She gasped again and went back to sleep. This time, the voice didn't stop her.

20

GHOST SHIP

THE NAMELESS SHIP SAT LOW IN THE WATER. IT was so small that Syrina had no idea how it would make it to the southern tip of Ristro. Two-thirds of it lay below the waterline, and it was painted metallic cobalt over the copper sheets that covered it. A single high mast topped by a red flag with a yellow horizontal stripe along one edge sprouted from the center of the deck.

Every nook was used for something, and the first night a crewman almost tripped over her while he was rummaging around in the hold. After that, she spent a few sleepless days watching the crew until she figured out the places she could be and when she could be there.

She wanted to not talk to the voice in her head, with as little interruption as possible, and the voice, besides a few snide pieces of advice, kept quiet.

The mystery of how the little boat would make it all the way to Ristro was solved on the third day when they dropped anchor near a sandbar humped just under the water at low tide. It was late afternoon. The sun sank in the west, while in the east, the gibbous Eye grew like a purple blister on the horizon. Far to the north, the sky was black with a roiling storm, the flashes of lightning a near-constant strobe, and the surf churned and spumed across the strip of exposed sand.

Syrina had found a place at the aft, away from the busy crew, and was beginning to wonder whether they would stop for the night when a shadow passed across the deck, and the little ship dipped into sudden darkness.

She looked up from where she crouched behind a tarp-covered pile of freight and watched the descent of a dirigible thrumming the air, with a propeller that jutted from the rear of a boat-shaped gondola dangling from the air bladder on brass chains. Its shadow grew over the sea around them like an obese bird of prey, and Syrina caught her breath despite herself. She'd heard of the Ristroan airships before, but this was the first time she'd seen one.

The enormous air bladder, ribbed in bronze, loomed, oblong and bulbous, tapered to points at either end and dwarfing the sea vessel she crouched on. A rumbling tarfuel engine that coughed smoke from four exhaust pipes dominated the gondola, which was about the same size as the boat. More bronze pipes, blackened with soot, led into the air bladder above, while others fed the pistons driving the lazily whirling propeller. Other pipes flared at the fore and aft on each side, bursting intermittent blasts of steam used for fine maneuvering. The front of the gondola was rounded and encased in brass-framed glass. The rest of it was built of copper-coated wood.

She needed to scurry out of the way when grapples and nets lowered from the airship, and half the small ship's crew began securing the freight she'd been hiding behind, while the rest began bringing more up from below.

You wondered how this little boat could get us all the way to Vormisæn, the voice said. *Now you know. You'd better find a way up there before we miss our ride and need to swim. Or end up back in Fom.*

She'd been thinking the same thing, and the voice must have known that, but she slipped up to the top of the freight without comment just as the ropes grew taut and the pile, now bound in netting, began to rise.

———

She spent the next day and a half alternating between studying the engine and gazing down at the whitecaps on the sheet of the sea below—from this height, no more than specks of snow against a blue sky.

The Syndicate had dabbled in airships, and there were the private ones that docked on the outskirts of Eheene and along the south coast of Skalkaad—luxury crafts for the low merchants wealthy enough to experiment. N'narad had a few, too, used as air ferries that shuttled dignitaries around on the Isle of N'narad.

The weather was the problem. The same force that pulled Eris's tides also pulled the air, and according to Ormo, created winds which became more unpredictable the further north one went. He had told her once that every High Merchant had detailed plans for naphtha-powered airships that far surpassed anything built by Ristro if only Skalkaad's northern climate wouldn't bring it down a few days or weeks after it first left the ground.

She had pointed out that the Syndicate had other lands, such as the quarries on the far side of the Yellow Desert, but he had just shook his head. The desert and the Black Wall presented their own problems. She had pressed him further, but he turned stern and changed the subject, and that had been that.

And now here she was.

The gondola she rode now was a hollow shell save the piloting deck and the rumbling hulk of bronze, brass, and ceramic that was the engine. Six crew manned the airship—two pilots and four mechanics who seemed to be ever-occupied with maintaining the machinery. All of them slept in shifts of two, when they slept at all, in two cramped bunks behind a curtain at the rear of the cabin, on either side of the door leading to the deck. The exterior was flat and empty except for some tool storage boxes along the low rail, so that was where she spent most of her time.

This high up the air was thin and icy cold, but neither of those things bothered her. The weather, though, wasn't just a problem in the Skalkaad.

———

The morning was cloudless. Even the storm that had roiled the northern sky for the past few days had either disappeared behind the horizon or blown itself out, so there was no warning when the gondola swung horizontal in a sudden blast of wind that sucked the thin air from Syrina's lungs. The chains snapped taut under the enormous air bladder, which began to bounce and twist with groans of strained metal, their complaints drowned out a second later by three short blasts of a klaxon, loud even over the scream of the wind.

Syrina skidded across the narrow deck and caught the guardrail just as it lurched back, shooting tingling pain from her grasping fingers to her shoulders.

On the downward swing, she lost her grip and tumbled back across the deck, this time managing to catch the rail with her legs. She pivoted, flailed, and grasped it with all four limbs like a baby karakh clinging to its mother's back, the wind so fierce it threatened to peel her off and cast her to the sea a span below.

The dirigible began to plummet, whether from damage or as an emergency measure, she couldn't be sure. The engine moaned. Black smoke twisted from the pipes and vanished in the wind.

The fall felt endless, their demise inevitable, until all at once the wind eased and the airship halted its plummet some fifty hands above the waves. A few seconds later, the klaxon ceased its blaring. The engine sputtered as Syrina unpeeled herself from the guardrail, heart still pounding.

We didn't die, so there's that, the voice said.

Indeed. We didn't die.

Curious about the crew, she made her way to the low hatch to the flight deck. After the fall, she was unsteady and leaned against the door as she peeked through the small, round portal into the pilot's compartment.

Their decent had scattered a few tools and instruments across the floor, but the damage was less than she'd expected. The levers, gauges, switches, and pedals that lined the walls and floor seemed intact. The four crew were busy at controls, while the two pilots stood at the curved front windows and argued. Syrina wished knew Ristroan enough to understand more of the muffled yelling she could hear through the door, but from their gestures, she gathered that one of them wanted to ascend again while the other was against it.

Before she could see the fight's conclusion, one of the crew turned toward the hatchway, forcing Syrina to scramble to the side, crouched low as he made his way across the deck to begin repairs on the engine. She decided that whatever either of the pilots wanted, the engine was in no condition to do much of anything, at least for now, and she let herself relax while she thought about what to do next.

———

They drifted for the rest of the day, always to the southeast, now only a hundred hands above the sea, which was much calmer than it had been when the storm was raging in the north.

As the sun lowered itself onto the western horizon, the klaxon sounded again, this time a long blast followed by two short ones, repeating over and over again. Syrina braced herself on instinct, knowing as she did that this was different. More urgent. Two more crew came out to help with engine repairs, their demeanor frantic. The airship altered its course and accelerated, but the engine whined and slowed again with a loud grinding noise that almost drowned out the panicked shouts of the crew. Another horn from behind them added to the cacophony—a bass vibration, so loud it made the metal and wood under her feet tremble.

We're screwed, the voice said.

Syrina didn't see any reason to argue as she scurried to the rear of the ship, past two crewmen too focused on the engine to notice her, and an enormous ship came into view. The Heaven's Compass. One of the three great naphtha ships of the N'naradin Navy.

Whatever complex trade laws dictated economic interactions between N'naradin and Ristro, Syrina knew a corsair airship would be shot down on sight, anywhere in this sea that the Church claimed as its territory.

The juggernaut cut through the water toward them at full speed, still only two hundred hands below them despite the airships abrupt panicked rise. Abrupt but ponderous, and even now the engine began to vibrate with a grinding, high-pitched wail.

Twin cannons on the Heaven's Compass burst gray smoke, the boom of the shots a second later almost drowned out by the blaring horns. The rear of the air bladder above Syrina erupted in a shower of flaming leather and twisted brass support beams, shattering the propeller and the deck under her and spilling her backward into the struggling engine. The dirigible began to fall.

Syrina clambered to her feet and bolted again to what was left of the aft deck, ignoring the shudder of the dying engine and the desperate cries of the crew. Above, black smoke rolled from the remains of the sagging balloon, and the remnants of the brass frame screamed as it tore itself apart in the wind of its collapse. The airship careened downward as the bow of the Heaven's Compass continued to charge toward them, not fast enough to catch the remains of the airship on the deck.

Without letting herself think about it, she jumped.

A moment too soon.

Instead of landing on the edge of the deck, she was barely able to grab the rim of it by her fingertips. Her body and face smashed into the green-streaked copper hull. She felt her nose crunch, followed by a rush of blood down her face and body, and she could only breathe in shallow, painful gasps. At the same moment, the dirigible died below her, exploding into the waterline of the warship with an anticlimactic crunch. The ruined remains of the airbag shattered around her in a hail of rigid burning leather and twisted copper and brass ribs.

A new blaze of pain erupted from her hip, hot and sharp. She was aware of shouting and the vibration in the hull as the enormous ship began to slow.

Up. The voice was firm.

Syrina could sense it getting a handle on the pain. *Don't think. Up.*

She clawed up. Something heavy and hot tugged her hip downward, and her mouth was metallic and salty. Blood streamed into her eyes from a gash on her forehead, and she still couldn't suck in more than light, desperate breaths of the humid air.

On the deck, she got to her knees, reached behind her, and yanked out the long curved copper pole that had harpooned her. With one hand, she tugged her nose back to where it belonged, while with the other, she wiped the blood from her eyes enough that she could look around. And she saw a young N'naradin seaman staring at her, frozen in terror.

Syrina took the deepest breath she could, intending to use the Papsukkal door the same time the sailor regained his wits and turned to flee toward a pair of men who were manning the still-smoking, dog-faced cannons looming in front of the forecastle. He shouted something about a Kalis on board, almost drowned out by the drone of the engines and the high-pitched scrape of the ruined airship against the hull.

To her shock, she felt resistance as she summoned the Door.

I wouldn't do that if I were you, which I am. Too much bleeding. It will kill you.

Syrina felt the Door fall away. Already, the cadet had gotten the attention of the cannoneers, who were squinting her way with looks first of disbelief, then shock. She was covered in blood. The only thing her tattoos were doing was telling everyone that she was a Kalis.

Don't panic. Run.

Syrina began a staggered run that arced as far away from the trio watching her as she could, while they began to follow with a lot more caution than was necessary. They seemed reluctant to confront her, battered as she was, and even in her broken state, she outpaced them and dodged around the edge of the forecastle. She coughed and spit a gob of blood over the rail.

Vent. Hurry.

Syrina thought that the voice was sounding further and further away, and was surprised to see a waist-high, round, brass air vent poking from the side of the forecastle, the grate covering it clipped but not screwed on. How could a Kalis not notice something like that?

A Kalis who's bleeding to death. Squeeze in. You need to find somewhere to be still so I can stop the bleeding.

Syrina felt too far away from the situation to bother arguing, so she pulled the grate off and slid in, amazed at how clumsy her fingers were.

"They'll see the grate. They'll find me."

There was a shout from outside, metallic and flat in the tight space.

"See?"

I know. Get lost in here. This boat is huge. None of those guys are small enough to follow you, and nobody who is will want to come in here after you. Probably.

Syrina obeyed, winding this way and that on her belly, climbing through the dark, down when she could and up when she had to. Every pull of her arms felt heavier. Dragging a sack of rocks across sand.

"I am the rocks," she said to herself. "I am rocks."

She became aware that she'd stopped moving, and the voice wasn't complaining about it.

It's fine. It'll have to be. I think the bleeding has stopped for now. You'll need to get cleaned up. But rest first.

"Okay."

She wasn't sure if the word had left her head or not. But it didn't matter. She was unconscious before she could worry about it.

———

Syrina knew it was hot. She wasn't used to being hot, or cold for that matter, and the sensation snapped her awake.

Hello, the voice said.

Syrina ached all over, and she still could only manage shallow, painful gasps.

Your side isn't bleeding anymore, but I think there's a rib in your lung. That's the sort of thing I can't fix without your help.

Syrina nodded. Even that slight gesture made her feel woozy. She squirmed but couldn't get into a position where she could reach into her chest in the confined space of the duct.

"How long have I been unconscious?"

Not long. My sense of time is strange when you're not awake, but I don't think it's been longer than fifteen minutes or so.

"They're looking for me."

I'm sure. You crawled a long way, though. They must not have any idea where you are. I think they're trying to flush you out. It started getting hotter a few minutes ago. A lot hotter.

"It might just be a coincidence."

Might be.

Whether or not it was coincidence didn't matter. She needed to get out. She began squirming along on her belly again. Each short gasp sent bright rays of pain from her chest to the rest of her body. She started to cough. Blood flecked the dusty metal and glinted in the trickle of light coming from somewhere ahead. Something black and lumpy splattered into the grime in front of her, and she grimaced as she dragged her body over it.

She found the source of the light after a nightmare two minutes—a square copper grate. Blueish light dribbled between the slats. She tried to see what was on the other side, but it was angled upward, so all she could tell was that she was close to a ceiling covered in pipes. A deep hum reverberated through the vent, louder than it had been. She spent another minute listening, willing herself to not cough, and somehow managing it. But she couldn't hear anything except the reverberation of machinery driving the ship. If anyone was down there waiting for her, they were doing a fantastic job being sneaky about it.

She pushed on the vent, but it was latched from the outside. Of course, there was no reason it would be latched from the inside, but that didn't stop her from cursing whoever built it for not being more considerate.

There was nothing to be done. She wouldn't find a better exit than this. She punched at the grate as hard as she could with the flat of her hand, wincing at the clash it made. The vent bent outward, but it didn't come off.

She dreaded making that noise again and paused a moment to listen again. Still no sound except the thrum of engines.

She struck again.

The grate dislodged with a second cymbal crash. She snapped her hand out to catch it before it could drop but missed. Instead, her fingers struck the falling square of metal, causing a second crash before it fell out of sight. A second later, a third metallic clatter echoed up to her, then silence.

Shit.

Still no other sounds from below, but she decided

she'd better hurry before someone came to see what all the noise was about.

She dropped down among huge drums of bronze freshwater condensers connected to the copper pipes along the ceiling with yet more pipes. Cogs and valves ran in an elbow-high line connecting each drum to the next. The heat was intense, and the drums gleamed with condensation. Crates of what looked like bottles of water were stacked by the open hatchway leading to the hall.

Perfect.

Syrina teetered over to the nearest drum and began scraping off the moisture to scrub at the drying blood coating her body and face. When she'd exposed her tattoos enough to do their job again, she squeezed between the condensers, relieved to see there was enough room for her to hunker down in the triangle of space between them and the wall. Then she bit her tongue and reached two fingers into her chest, tearing open the freshly healed skin. Another blizzard of pain radiated through her as her index and middle fingers felt something sharp and loose. A spasm of coughing exploded from her she couldn't suppress as they closed around it and pulled. Her throat filled with blood and she half-spat, half-vomited a stream of blackish-red ichor. It filled again, slower this time, and again she spat and managed to take a ragged breath.

"...back to N'narad," someone said, "just because some idiot deckhand thought he saw a Kalis."

Syrina froze at the voice at the door, her fingers still buried in her chest up to the second knuckle. Something inside her bubbled, wanted to force its way out, but she swallowed it and turned her face to the wall, biting her tongue, hoping the tattoos on the back of her head would conceal her.

"It wasn't a deckhand," another voice said. "It was two cannoneers and a petty officer. Anyway, the captain seems to think there's a—oh, shit!"

A few seconds later, Syrina heard the scrape of metal as one of the sailors picked up the grate she'd smashed her way out of.

"Look at this. It's bent from the inside."

Syrina could almost hear them look at each other.

More motion and tense silence as the two made a quick search of the room. She chewed on her tongue, her mind and every muscle focused on not coughing.

"We've got to report this," the first voice again, near the door.

Footfalls faded under the drawl of the engines.

Syrina allowed herself to hack a volcano of blood and phlegm onto the floor behind the water tank and took a deep, relieved breath. The air still burbled in her chest, but it was clearer for now.

You'll need need to kill them.

"Who?" Syrina's whisper was wet and harsh.

All of them. Everyone on the Heaven's Compass.

"Why?" Syrina asked, even as all the pieces fell together in her mind.

Because they've seen you. Even if you get off this boat and make it to Ristro, there's a thousand N'-naradin who've either seen you or know you exist. How's that going to go over with Ormo? Or anyone else? If anything gets back to Ristro and the Astrologers find out about this, they'll be looking for you before you even get there. Unless they're idiots, which they're not. You think they can't put together where you were headed when a Kalis ends up on a N'naradin naphtha ship right after it blows up one of their airships? And within a week of anyone in N'narad finding out about a Kalis, it'll be all over Eris, including Eheene. Kavik will put it together with all the other stuff you've been doing, and cover his tracks before you get back, making anything you learn in Ristro just more information that's useless.

"But if I can get to Ristro, I can still find something that'll help me. Us."

You're going to have to go back to Ormo if you ever want anything from him again, and he's still the only one that can tell you what we are. You don't think he'll notice that you allowed a ship of N'naradin sailors see you, and then go home to talk about it? You think you've lost his trust now? Talk about a liability. He'll kill you on the spot.

"The Astrologers might know something." She began squeezing out from behind the condenser, careful not to put any pressure on her chest, which still dribbled blood.

You don't know what the Astrologers know, much less what they're going to tell you. Do you want to burn the only bridge you've got to spare a few lives you've got no use for? You're a Kalis. Now isn't the time to stop thinking like one.

"It's more than just a few," she said, her tone defeated.

The voice didn't bother responding.

It was right. The problem was, Syrina didn't even know why she didn't want to kill everyone on board the Heaven's Compass. Not that she'd ever gotten any joy from killing. It was just something she did. Now, she couldn't get the idea of them as *people* out of her mind. Hugging their wives, playing with their kids, taking their mothers out to dinner. Why any of that should bother her now, after a lifetime of deception and murder, she hadn't a clue. A Kalis with a conscience. There was something grotesque about that.

Whether or not she was ready to admit out loud that the voice was right again, she needed to at least stall the ship long enough to get off it.

The engine room would be near the condensers. She slipped out from her hiding place and crept toward the open door, trying to ignore the burble that welled from her chest. There was no sign of the pair that had almost stumbled across her, but voices echoed down the humid hallway she found herself in. Copper pipes ran along both walls, but the floor was polished dark wood. She suppressed another cough and headed away from the voices. The ubiquitous hum of the engines grew louder as she passed another open hatchway. Stupid that they left all the hatchways open down here. It was no doubt because the passageway was cooler, but even she knew it was against protocol.

The next room was almost identical to the condenser room. Eight brass tanks lined the walls, four to either side, much bigger than the condensers. Each bore a plaque with an engraved flame. Brass pipes as big around as her little finger, each fixed with redundant pairs of valves, led from them across the floor to the aft wall. Dim, flickering glow globes hung from the ceiling, rather than the bright naphtha lamps everywhere else. The fuel room.

Syrina had a general idea of how N'naradin naphtha ships worked. These tanks fed naphtha to the burners in the boiler room, which would be on the other side of the wall from here. The burners heated saltwater from the bilge pumps, which then powered the engines. As much of the steam as possible was siphoned off to the condenser tanks, where it became freshwater for the crew. The rest went out the stacks.

She'd been required to learn all of that during her training, but none of it helped her know how to blow up the Heaven's Compass or even stall it for more than a minute or two. The naphtha was separated from the open flames of the engine room, for obvious reasons. That was the thing with real Skaald naphtha. It could be heated and still not catch fire. She could douse the tanks in fuel and ignite them, but unless any of that flame touched the goo inside, there was a pretty good chance they wouldn't explode. And even if they did, well, that didn't give her a lot of time to find her way off the ship.

She peeked around the next corner, into the engine room at the end of the hall. A lone engineer monitored gauges on twin rows of giant copper boilers. Piping fed off the top of them, into the low ceiling above and into the turbines. The finger-width pipes from the fuel room ran along the floor here, under copper grates thick with verdigris. Each pipe ended at a wide burner beneath a boiler. Four were lit, but as she watched, one flicked out, and a moment later there was an electric flash from beneath the one next to it and a soft pop as it ignited. With a whir of gears from somewhere beneath her feet, the sound of rushing water began to echo from the first tank. Its gauge, leaning toward empty, began to edge upwards.

Her breath was coming easier now despite the enormous heat, and the ceaseless driving need to cough had subsided to something she could ignore. She slid to a corner behind the nearest boiler. It was over thirty hands high and about the same across. Since she'd boarded the Compass, it was the first time she could pause and admire just how gigantic the ship was.

A man and woman entered and questioned the engineer. The din of the turbines above her, the rumble of the boilers, and the high hiss of the burners merged into a cacophony that she couldn't hear anything distinct over, but she could get the gist from their body language. They were looking for her, but no, the engineer hadn't seen anything. It must've occurred to the whole crew that a Kalis, if they existed, could hide anywhere and never be found.

They left, and the engineer went back to work.

Syrina had an idea. She returned to the condenser room, grabbed a bottle of water from one of the crates, and drank it down on the way back to the fuel room. It was hot and brackish, but she hadn't had a drink since the windstorm, and she only needed the bottle anyway. She trotted to the nearest aft fuel tank and froze. Voices again, and footsteps jogging down the hallway.

Shit.

Syrina slipped between the tanks, crouched down and watched the door from behind the maze of copper and bronze pipes.

"You three here," a woman's voice commanded, in N'naradin. "The rest of you follow me."

A second later, two men and a woman armed with crossbows and ceramic long-knives crowded into the doorway and stopped, sweating.

"It's goddamn hot down here," a ruddy man with a yellow beard and tired eyes said.

A dour gray-haired woman with a crooked nose

and wearing a blue officer's uniform appeared and set down a crate of water bottles.

"Here," she said. "If you need more, you can get it from the condensation tanks." She gestured vaguely toward the next room. "One of you can refill these and bring it back. *One* of you."

The three nodded without comment until their commander's footsteps had faded down the hallway.

"This is bullshit," Yellow Beard muttered.

A young nervous boy nodded, but the other one— a woman with short black hair and blue eyes shook her head.

"If there's a Kalis, an actual Kalis on board, you want her anywhere near the engine room?"

The bearded man guffawed. "If Kalis are real and there's one on board, you think us three are going to stop her? Like I said, bullshit."

"We're not the only ones down here," the woman said. "Anyway, you don't know anything more than the rest of us about Kalis. Rumors and stories. That's it. We have orders. You signed on to do what you're told, so do it."

The man grumbled something lost in the drone of turbines, and the group fell into silence.

Shit.

I wouldn't try the Door yet, either, the voice answered Syrina's unasked question.

Fine. There was nothing left to it, even as unfamiliar pangs of remorse welled up from somewhere she hadn't known existed. She had nothing against these people. She didn't have anything against anyone on the Heaven's Compass. Syrina looked down the narrow tunnel of her future and saw an ocean of regret pouring from a conscience that was going to get her killed.

You either need to do something about these people or hide behind this tank of naphtha all the way to N'-narad. I don't even know if you could live that long since they've got all the water. If you have a better idea, do it now. Otherwise, hurry up and decide whether or not you want to die back here.

Shit.

Syrina slid from her hiding place, biting her tongue against the sharp pain in her chest where her lung was trying to heal itself. Bad timing for a conscience. Bad timing for a lot of things.

She slammed her elbow against the back of the head of the woman, which snapped forward with a wet crunch that caused a swell of nausea Syrina wasn't prepared for. The woman crumpled.

That would be the only easy one without the Door, she realized as the others turned from where they had been focused on the doorway, panic rising in their eyes. Syrina sidestepped one ceramic blade but couldn't avoid the second, which sliced along her back just below her right shoulder blade. She grabbed the hand holding the first knife and twisted it free from yellow beard, then dropped and spun, still holding his wrist, and heard the arm pop as she jabbed the blade into the chest of the young, quiet boy who'd slashed her back. Really young, she realized with a pang of misery. Young and scared.

With her thoughts still on the boy staggering away from her, dimming eyes staring down at the knife in his chest, she rose again, carried by her own momentum, and brought her forehead into the bearded man's throat. He choked and fell backward.

Shouts from the hallway.

Shit.

A figure dashed by, headed for the gangway and the upper decks as Syrina picked up the fallen boy's dagger. She took a step out the door and hurled it into the woman's back. There was a tearing pain in Syrina's chest. She fought down the image of the boy staring at the knife hilt with dying eyes. The woman crumpled as the blade sank into the back of her neck.

Syrina coughed and gasped for air, spitting a fresh wad of blood into the snarl of pipes while running down the narrow hallway as another eight figures rushed from the boiler room. They hesitated when they saw her stalking toward them, drenched in blood.

Her breath bubbled—a sound she hoped they wouldn't be able to hear over the engines—and she coughed again, which shot pain across her abdomen, from her throat to her thighs. Sounds around her were growing distant and echoed in her ears. The soldiers in front of her were talking, but she couldn't make out the words. Somewhere in the back of her mind, the voice was taking over, and the pain in her chest and mind eased.

Crossbow.

Just as her brain grasped the word, it fired. She half-dove, half-collapsed and felt the edge of the bolt slice across her back in the same place the knife had slashed it a few moments ago, making an "X" with the first wound. Syrina hit the floor, rolled, and was up and running. She allowed her mounting panic to take over. She stepped around a knife point and slammed her shoulder into a body. Whether it was the one she'd just avoided or another, she didn't know. The world had shattered into darkness except for a narrow passage at the center of her vision. She was an animal. Nothing left but instinct and a voice in her head. She spun, twisted, lashed out and kicked, her mind underwater, her breath caught behind a flood of fluids foaming in her chest, unable to escape.

Motion ceased. Again, the only sound was that of the ubiquitous turbines. Bodies, unconscious or dead, scattered along the hallway. She had no memory of dealing with any of them. Even the engineer who'd been working on the engine. She didn't recall him leaving the engine room.

A boy's face staring down at his chest, wandered into her mind uninvited.

Don't worry about it. It's done.

Syrina knew she would worry about it, *needed* to worry about it, but she wasn't finished yet. She hurried into the boiler room, found a wrench that had been abandoned next to one of the bilge lines, and stumbled, still wheezing, into the gangway.

Back in the fuel room, she examined the pair of valves connected to a brass pipe leading from the tank to the wall. She used the wrench to unscrew the first one all the way, then unscrewed the safety bolt underneath it. A clear, blue ooze bubbled from the opening and dribbled on the floor. The smell of it, chemical and floral, filled Syrina's nostrils and made her cough again. She let it leak into the empty water bottle, trying not to get any on her shaking hand and failing. It felt slick, cold, and itchy.

Shit. She needed to be far away from the Compass before any fires started, or she was going to have more problems than a hole in her lung.

When the bottle was full, she poured a thin line

of it along the wall to the boiler room. It would keep oozing under the fuel tanks, but there wasn't anything she could do about that except hope nobody came along to find it. She poured the rest of the bottle out on top of one of the unlit burners.

The naphtha in the hallway and pooling in the fuel room was making the air pungent and oily, but she couldn't do anything about that either. She fled up the gangway, toward the deck. Two levels up, she needed to duck into a hatchway at the sound of footfalls coming down the stairs and found herself in an unlit cargo hold. She grimaced as they passed. Six people. They'd no doubt come across the carnage. She could only hope they'd be too distracted to find the pooling naphtha behind the tanks. She needed to hurry. By her best guess, she only had a few minutes before the clockwork system would light the burner where she'd emptied the bottle.

The top deck was quiet compared to when she'd first found herself aboard the Heaven's Compass. She supposed that most of the crew were below, looking for her. Still, she needed to avoid a handful of groups bustling about as she made her way to a lifeboat. There were only four—two on the fore and two on the aft, attached with a series of pullies that would swing them out and drop them into the water with the pull of a lever. They were large, but with a ship that size, most of the crew was left without a way off. The idea saddened her. She thought of the boy again and forced the image away.

Almost out of time. She sprinted across the deck, to the port lifeboat, and dove in, pulling the lever as she did so. Shouts erupted across the deck, footfalls charging toward her, but she was beyond caring as the pullies lifted the little boat up and out over the rail.

A blast of heat slammed into her, so intense she felt her eyelashes burn away as the force of the explosion tossed the raft away from the Heaven's Compass like a discarded toy. Blue and white flame, a low sky made of fire, rolled above her and she and the little boat were falling, falling, toward the sea below. Searing pain, infinitely more intense than that in her chest, roiled up from her hand.

"My hand is burning," she said to the voice in her head, her own voice distant and calm as she stared at the skeleton of light and heat her left hand had become.

A tremendous impact threw her from the boat. Fire rained down all around her. The water slowed the flames engulfing her hand but didn't extinguish them.

She swam back to the lifeboat and pulled herself half-aboard with her right arm when there was another explosion, and something heavy and dull struck her on the back of her head, and the fire and pain and water fell away.

21

THE BEACH

Syrina woke to heat and light and gentle bobbing that made her temples and hand pound in time with it. Her mouth was dry. She turned her head and squinted into the sky, looking for the sun. There it was, blazing high in the east. It was a few hours before noon. Her stomach lurched when she remembered, and she forced her gaze down to her hand. The flesh whirled and warped under the tattoos, which seemed to be trying to tie themselves back together again. Her middle and index finger were gone. The naphtha had reduced them to a charred lump of skin and bone. The knot in her stomach tightened and she dry-heaved, which shot new darts of agony through her chest.

Beneath the sun spread the shore—a strip of white sand, maybe a span away, burning just as bright. She must've rowed for hours to get to the coast, but she could remember none of it. She felt around the puncture wound in her chest. It was healing, but she was thinking about rowing for hours and not remembering, and the mangled stump that had been her left hand. Over all of it, lingered the frightened face of a boy with a knife in his chest.

We did what needed to be done. Just like always.

We.

She wondered whether it was her rowing, and what else the voice could do.

Whatever she was, she wasn't a Kalis anymore. She was fine with that. Or at least, she'd come to terms with it. What scared her now was the thought that the thing inside her head still was.

The sea ebbed low enough to wade, even as far out as she was, and she could feel the current tugging against her thighs as the tide followed the Eye west. She let it take the lifeboat away, and by the time she collapsed onto the beach, the raft had disappeared in the expanse of cobalt water and pale blue sky.

After a few minutes of lying in the sand, she dragged herself up the wide, steep, beach to the bushes lining the high tideline another span in. Then she slept again.

———

It was night, but other than that her surroundings were the same. However the voice had managed to row for countless spans while she'd been unconscious, it hadn't done anything like it again. Over the scrubby hills to the east, the waning Eye loomed.

She headed south, following the coast. She guessed she was somewhere near the middle of the barren northern half of the Ristro Peninsula, which meant she was about a year from the city of Chamælivishi if she needed to walk the whole way.

For nine days, she hiked south through the hills along the tideline, without another soul in sight. She devoured a few unfortunate rodents and birds along the way, which she caught with her hands and ate raw. There was no fresh water, even with all the humidity, so all she had to drink was their blood. It was feral and stomach churning. Nine days shouldn't be a big deal for her without resorting to raw squirrels, but after all the healing, she was ravenous, and as it was, small animals weren't enough. More than a week after the Heaven's Compass and she still couldn't catch her breath. She needed to stop and rest every few hours, and her ribs ached. The tattoos had knitted over her gnarled hand, but she couldn't bring herself to look at it. Absent fingers throbbed.

The tenth day was an Eye Night. The sun was only three hands above the eastern hills, which could almost be considered mountains this far south, when the black mound of the Eye caught up to it, a sharp circle of gloom twenty times its size. Everything went dark and the stars flared, but they, too, were devoured.

She thought about stopping, not so much because it was dark, but because Eye Night was a time for festivals or introspection or whatever, and she had no idea what sort of customs revolved around an eclipse in Ristro. Every culture on Eris had an Eye Night tradition except for Fom, where they were just civic holidays and barely even noticed through the perpetual clouds. If Syrina came across anyone today, she wouldn't know how to act, whatever disguise she might scrape up.

On the other hand, how much was she going to blend in on a normal day? She didn't even speak Ristroan beyond a few words and phrases she'd picked up on the Corsair ships.

There's no food out here. If you stop now, we're not getting up again. Every day you're weaker.

Part of Syrina wanted to just die and get it over with so she wouldn't give the voice the satisfaction. But instead, she dragged herself along in the dark and tried to think about something else.

As she trudged on, a gigantic fire flared somewhere to the southeast, just over the ridgeline. With it came the scent of roasted vegetables. Yellow light twinkled through the scrub and cast long wriggling shadows across the sea, which had chased the Eye up to lap at the rocky tideline.

With the tiniest modicum of caution left in her, Syrina scrambled up the hill. It was higher than it had looked from the beach, and it took an hour to get to the top since she needed to stop and catch her breath every few minutes. As she clambered through prickly, leafy bushes, she imagined what sort of rite to the Eye might be taking place. She wasn't naive enough to picture burning virgins, but anything with a fire that big was bound to be interesting.

It wasn't interesting. At least not in the sense she'd thought it would be. It was a shipyard, and a military one at that. The fire wasn't a bonfire, but an enormous open smelter they were using to forge the copper plates that covered Corsair airships.

The skeleton of a sleek dirigible a little bigger than the one she'd gotten halfway there on, sat at the end of worn bronze rails that glinted in the firelight. Her mind touched on the question of slavery or indentured servitude. The Corsairs had captured enough N'naradin and Skald crews to build a nation of slaves, but she discarded the idea. She couldn't understand much Ristroan, but the relationships she saw below weren't those of masters and serfs. They worked together, liked each other, probably went out drinking together. They were like everyone else on Eris, except they needed to work on Eye Night.

To be fair, so did she.

She scrabbled down the hill, using the thorny shrubs to slow her descent, wincing as they tore at her maimed hand. She hoped the rain of dirt and pebbles wouldn't draw undue attention, but she needn't have worried. The shipyard was well lit, but it was dark where she landed, and too noisy for anyone to hear her.

After finding the food stores and gorging herself on sweet dried fruit and some sort of pickled fish that tasted a lot better than it smelled, she decided there was no point in rushing into things, so she settled down to watch.

———

For three weeks, she observed and listened and healed, picking up a little of the language and culture so she wouldn't look like an idiot. Or if an idiot, at least a believable one. Her chest and hip mended, and the tattoos finished re-growing over the flesh of her hand, but they stopped at the charred roots of her two missing fingers, which still ached in their absence.

As usual, there was nothing to be done about it. She pilfered some wax and other supplies she could use to cover her face and what was left of her hands, wondering what she could do about hair.

The whole time, she hoped the voice would try to goad her into doing something rash so she could argue and resist whatever it suggested, but it let her do her job without saying a word.

22

RISTRO

TÆVARNAVASI BROUGHT HIS PAIR OF SPECKLED camels to a halt alongside the tiny frantic woman standing in the dust between the road and the scrub, but she continued to wave her arms at him like she thought he wasn't going to stop. She was tanned and sturdy-looking. Her baldness, which he'd first attributed to an inscrutable fashion choice, upon closer inspection looked like her hair had been burned off. Her scalp was red and tender, and her left hand was scorched deformed.

"You need help?" He looked down at her from the lopsided cart as she squinted up at him.

Her eyes were a penetrating green under the slits of the lids. A foreigner, he realized with a start. She stopped flapping her arms, but she still held them above her head. One shielded her eyes against the glare of the mid-morning sun, while the mangled one hovered off to the side as if she'd forgotten it was there.

"Fire shipyard at." Her Ristroan was almost unintelligible, and Tævarnavasi needed to think a second before he could sort out what she was saying.

"Where are you from?" He felt an itch of suspicion.

It wasn't unusual to hire foreigners in the domestic shipyards, but there were only airship yards this far north.

"Valez'Mui."

"Well, come on up here. You can tell me what happened, on the way to Vormisæn."

She took his hand with her good one and let him help her clamber into the empty seat beside him. Her hand was small and clammy, but her grip was iron. The grip of a laborer. He'd never met anyone from the desert before, but he'd heard they were strong. He supposed they'd have to be.

"Need go Chamælivishi." She settled beside him,

The camels lurched forward, grunting.

That gave him pause. "You'd better have some extra time on your hands, then. It's three months by land, at least. Depending on the weather and if you can find someone to give you a ride. I can get you as far as Vormisæn, anyway. From there, you can attach yourself to a caravan going south, or maybe find an airship to take you if you're lucky, rich, and in a hurry. What's your business down there, if I can ask?"

"Need Astrologer see about fire. Someone set."

Tævarnavasi frowned and lit a stick of yellow magarisi petals rolled in thin paper with a flint he pulled from the breast of his worn shirt.

"How long you been in Ristro?" he asked.

"Not long. Three weeks. Then fire set."

"Well." Tævarnavasi stifled a cough around the magarisi stick. "An Astrologer isn't going to see you, whichever prefecture you're in. As I said, I can get you to Vormisæn. From there, you can see for your-self." He paused. "The fire was *set*?"

"Astrologer in Vor-me-seyyn?"

"Aye, it's the seat of the northern prefectures."

She seemed to think about that for a while. "I know who burned it. Astrologer sees me."

Tævarnavasi shrugged, scratched his bulging belly, and took a long drag from the smoking herbs. He held it a moment and exhaled tangy gray smoke through his nose.

"Well," he said, "there are a lot of other people you need to tell first. He's got twenty people whose job it is to tell him things. He probably already knows about the fire, anyway. Someone tells someone else, who tells someone else, who tells him if they think he needs to know about it. Doesn't it work like that in Valez'Mui?"

It was her turn to shrug, and the only sound for a while was the wheezing of the camels and the crunch of their hooves on the gravel road, and the creaking of the cartwheels on their wooden axle. The sun grew higher, and the air was heavy and still. Sweat poured off Tævarnavasi's forehead and pooled in the small of his back. The woman didn't seem bothered by the denseness of the air or the growing heat. But then, she was from the desert.

He waited for her to offer more information or even her name, but she didn't seem to have the slimmest of manners. Foreigners weren't unpleasant. Just inscrutable.

"What's your name?" he finally asked, as he nodded a greeting to a passing camel driver heading north.

"Ser'ai. Mends. Father was ambassador from

Fom," she added when Tævarnavasi arched his eyebrows at the name.

"I see. So you're well-traveled?"

She shrugged again. "Not much. My father left. I was young. Trained as shipwright, after mother. Tired of desert. Petitioned to come here."

"You got the job young."

She chuckled. "Young to you. Years. Waiting in Valez'Mui."

They lapsed into another silence, not as uncomfortable as the first one. He wondered and *tsk'd* the camels and looked at her out of the corner of his eye, but she was looking off toward the hills on the horizon, cradling her injured hand, lost in thought.

———

They progressed from the scrubby humid hills into forested humid hills, alive with broad-leaved trees and small skittering creatures. Mountains loomed further to the east, where they could be glimpsed through breaks in the flora. Tævarnavasi was blind to his surroundings, like anyone who's seen the same thing for most of their lives. But Ser'ai gaped around, wide-eyed, then closed her mouth and tried to appear stoic every time she noticed him looking her way. Her awe made sense, he decided, if she'd come from the desert.

As they approached the first checkpoint, still an hour from any real view of the city, Ser'ai started to look nervous. Tævarnavasi *tsk'd* his spitting, grumbling camels up to the queue of other wagons in front of the stone and wicker guardhouse. When it was their turn, two guards, huge and swarthy, approached.

Each carried an obsidian and brass scalpel and small jars of alcohol.

Ser'ai shifted. "What going on?" She almost edged out the tremor in her voice.

"Nothing. Just a skin check. It hurts a little the first time, but if you travel around Ristro a lot, you get used to it."

He watched the approaching bordermen out of one corner of his eye, and her out of the other. She would've been subjected to more than one of these to work in an airship yard. Random checks were mandatory.

"Skin check?" She swallowed.

"Of course." He turned to her. "Just a little scraping. You must've had one before."

"What for?"

"To keep jungle-fly larvae away from the population centers. A little scrape from the back of the hand will tell them if you have parasites. If they find any, they'll keep you in quarantine until you're either disinfected or you die. Almost never happens, but better to be safe, I guess. No one wants an epidemic. Nothing to worry about. I'm sure you've been checked at least a couple times since you got here."

Ser'ai swallowed again and didn't answer him. She watched the bordermen approach. Her demeanor remained nervous, but her green eyes were calculating.

The guards smiled cordially, approaching on either side of the wagon. "Left hand, please," they said, at the same time in the bored monotone of people who've said the same words so many times they've lost all meaning.

Tævarnavasi caught a blur out of the corner of his

eye and the guard standing next to Ser'ai staggered backward, holding his face, blood squirting through his fingers. The scalpel clattered on the gravel somewhere out of sight beneath the wagon.

Before Tævarnavasi could soak in what was happening, there was a flurry of motion and Ser'ai was standing on the opposite side from where she'd been a moment ago, next to him, holding the other borderman by the throat. She was short enough that she'd needed to force the man to his knees to get a hold on his neck, all so fast that Tævarnavasi didn't see it happen. Her green eyes were still calm. Too calm.

She whispered a few irate words that sounded like Skald, to no one in particular, frowning, looking at nothing.

Then she addressed Tævarnavasi. "I don't want to kill anyone, but it's very important I see an Astrologer." She paused a second, and her expression grew angry. She muttered again in Skald, harsher this time.

The borderman with the broken nose stared at her a moment, then staggered back a few steps before turning and breaking into a run toward Vormisæn, but Tævarnavasi was only vaguely aware of his departure. He was staring at Ser'ai's left arm, wrapped around the borderman's neck. Her hostage's desperate fingers had clawed away long swaths of skin, revealing a swirl of tattoos he couldn't quite focus on, like oil rolling across water.

The girl muttered to herself in Skald again.

The tense moments of inaction that followed poured weight into the already heavy air. Tævarnavasi was aware of the ring of twenty crossbowmen that had emerged from their hiding places around the post, most of them probably not aware of what was going on beyond there being some sort of incident. He raised his hands in front of him, hoping they would see he wasn't a threat so he could explain what he was doing with this woman when they asked. He hoped they would bother asking.

"You have nowhere to go," a voice called, from somewhere behind him.

But he didn't turn around to see who it was. He kept his eyes on Ser'ai, who still looked much too calm. She shifted so she could get a better look at whoever was speaking, putting her back against the camel cart, still holding the squirming borderman close to her.

"I have to see an Astrologer. So, in fact, I have to go wherever there's one of those." She still spoke with a harsh, strange accent, but her Ristroan wasn't as broken as it had been a few minutes ago.

Tævarnavasi grimaced, but no one fired.

Instead, the voice behind him, dead-serious, said, "If you attempt to leave the spot on which you are standing, you will be killed, and apologies to your hostage's family will be issued."

The hostage guard made a whimpering sound.

"Wow." She laughed, a sound without humor. "You're as bad as the Syndicate."

The speaker didn't answer.

"Look." She sighed. "If you kill me, you'd be doing this gentleman," she wiggled the borderman's head, "me, and the Astrologers a grave disservice. If I wanted to kill someone, I would've done it and left again. Or more likely, just gotten killed trying. I'm here now because I want to talk an Astrologer, not kill one."

"There's no reason we should believe you, and no convincing argument you could produce."

"No. Probably, other Kalis have been through here, or somewhere, and they met with ends just like the one waiting for me. Or maybe different ones with the same ultimate result. They weren't trying to kill anyone either, probably. Just spy, which to you is almost certainly just as bad. Maybe even worse. By the same token, I could probably kill this unfortunate gentleman and disappear into the forest before any of you could even pull the trigger."

She paused, and her eyes sparkled at what must've been some private joke. "There's a... part of myself who wants to do just that, as would—probably did—any other Kalis you've caught poking around where she's not wanted, which I guess is anywhere you find one. As far as I know, you've either caught them all up to this point, or I've been lied to. Probably both. My point is, I didn't do that. I'm not going to. Don't you want to know why?"

As she went on, Tævarnavasi built up enough courage to look around. The man behind him who'd addressed Ser'ai—or rather, the woman who called herself Ser'ai—was bulky and dark. He had a shaved head set with three large pearls and a robust Corsair's beard with a clean upper lip. Around his waist, he wore the wide belt of a border captain, the iron buckle depicting the teardrop-shaped flame of Vormisæn. On either side of him, wrapping around Tævarnavasi's camel wagon in a misshapen circle, were the men and women of his guard. Outside of the circle, back the way they'd come, more wagons had lined up. Fifty or so gawkers watched in terrified fascination. The smell of fish oil wafted on the warm breeze from one of the carts.

Tævarnavasi looked back at the woman calling herself Ser'ai and wondered about her. In the stories, Kalis were always so sly and subtle, murderous and manipulative. This woman might've been comically obvious if he hadn't been stuck in the middle of an incident she'd started. He wondered whether this was some weird hoax, but then he looked at the shifting tattoos under the peeled strips of fake skin again and looked away.

The border captain didn't bother to respond, and Ser'ai answered her own question.

"I've decided to work for the Astrologers rather than my... current employer."

She sounded so unhappy it was hard not to believe her. The silence that followed was drawn out by the shifting, grunting camels. Tævarnavasi was looking forward to a stiff drink, but that luxury was looking further and further away.

"Your words are poison," the border captain said. "There is no evidence you should be believed."

The woman calling herself Ser'ai adjusted her grip on the kneeling border guard. "Nevertheless, if you kill me, you need to face the possibility that you're depriving your Astrologers of something they'd be interested in. I'm willing to be restrained in any manner that will make you comfortable. Let your leaders decide what to do with me."

23

THE ASTROLOGER

YOU KILLED US BOTH.

"Probably." Syrina was happy that all she could do was grunt around the thin metal bar pressed through her mouth.

She still preferred speaking out loud to the voice, despite its objections, but incessant muttering would have made her escort even more nervous.

She couldn't decide whether she regretted her new course of action. She'd made up her mind when she saw the borderman coming toward her with the scalpel, and she was still trying to sort out the consequences. Ever since she'd washed up on the beach in northern Ristro, she'd acknowledged that she would never make it to Chamælivishi. Then, in the long silence in front of the guard hut, she'd decided.

"Can you help me lie to Ormo?" She'd she stood in the road, surrounded, clinging to her hostage.

Maybe. The voice had sounded like it didn't like where Syrina was going with the question. *I doubt it.*

"Good enough," Syrina had said. "I'm going to get some answers. Even if they kill me afterward."

Even by her standards, it was a terrible plan, but she wasn't smart enough to come up with anything better. She was willing to admit as much to herself, but she wished the voice would shut up about it.

She'd expected the restraints to be thorough, but even so, she was surprised when they'd pulled out the bronze wheeled prison from the guardhouse that now suspended her.

The first thing they did was strip off Ser'ai until Syrina was naked. Then they ratcheted her ankles, knees, wrists, elbows, waist, and neck in place with brass vices, and pinched her head in place by a bit that crossed her mouth and eight blunt screws that dug into her skull. A leather strap squeezed across her forehead, just to be sure. She hung, suspended in a bronze frame the size of a coffin, only more open and less comfortable. They'd needed to adjust it at length to make it small enough to hold her. It had two leather-wrapped brass wheels at the head, while leather-gripped handles protruded from the bottom. They rolled her down the road, which went from gravel to flagstones just after the checkpoint, upside-down in this coffin-wheelbarrow. The border captain doused her with oily, fishy white paint someone found a half-span further on, just in case she somehow slipped free.

Syrina had every intention of seeing an Astrologer, and if suspended upside down in a metal coffin covered in stinking paint was the only way it was going to happen, so be it. She wondered if all the guard posts in Ristro had a few of these things lying around, just in case they ever found a Kalis.

Who was she kidding? More likely, they wheeled around all their criminals like that. And maybe the High Merchants sent Kalis to Ristro all the time.

That brought her thoughts around to why she'd come. One of the Astrologers was funding Kavik's research, and she wanted to know what they knew, whatever she ended up telling Ormo. They supposedly shared their information and documented everything, so in theory, it didn't matter which one she talked to. On the other hand, that was how the Syndicate was supposed to run Skalkaad, and Syrina knew how that worked out most of the time.

———

Her first experience of Vormisæn was limited to what was in front of her face—gray cobbles and the backs of the boots of the borderman in front of her, which were brown leather and caked in dried mud.

Passersby muttered in fear. Syrina didn't know enough Ristroan to understand much, but she got the gist. She imagined a mob following their procession at a safe distance, though she had no way of knowing if that's what was going on. Just cobbles and muddy boots and the hiss of incoherent whispering.

The building they wheeled her into late that afternoon was higher than those around it by three or four stories and constructed of massive rough-cut blocks of obsidian. The prefecture capitol seemed to be the only structure in the city that warranted the expense of shipping rock from the Black Wall. A veranda that traced its front formed arms that curved around in an oblong crescent reminiscent of the Syndicate Palace and the heavy awning of black stone was supported by smooth square pillars.

As they bounced her up the stairs to the main entrance, Syrina could feel the heat gathered in the rock hammering her face, but inside was dark and cool. A high-ceilinged hallway held aloft with jagged flying buttresses curved along the inside. The stone floor hummed and whistled as they traversed it the same way it did in Ormo's audience hall, and every other lamp was hooded with a weird, violet shade a deeper purple than the Eye. Their light was all but invisible until she noticed her legs at the edge of her vision. Her tattoos glowed blue in the strange luminescence where they weren't covered by the paint.

The voice remained silent.

They rolled Syrina through a pair of huge bronze doors, into a courtyard rich with the smell of flowers, and deposited her at the end of a causeway across a reflecting pool, which was ringed with immaculately kept gardens full of bright, exotic blossoms. At the center of the pool was a circular grassy island. A white marble gazebo perched there which would put the best Artisans of Valez'Mui to shame. Or maybe not, since it looked like it had been sculpted by the best Artisans in Valez'Mui. Its delicate roof balanced on pillars no bigger around than Syrina's thumb, and it cast wildflower shadows under its carved dome.

A lone man sat in a modest chair of wood and red velvet at the center of the gazebo, tall, thin, dark and old. He wore white linen, unadorned with anything but some flower embroidery along the seams of the front. He looked tired.

She hoped someone would let her out of the coffin so she could meet whoever it was with dignity intact, but she couldn't say it surprised her when the escort left her there the way she was and backed off somewhere out of sight.

The old man studied her for a while, and she studied him. His face was brown and hard. He looked like he smiled a lot, but he wasn't smiling now, and the creases around his dark eyes were as still as granite. His hair and beard were shaved down to a dusting of gray, like the first frost on a lump of rich soil.

He stood and sauntered down the causeway until he was five or six feet away, and then he studied her more.

"And who might you be?" he said, in Ristroan, but he had directed his gaze at someone behind her.

She dangled there and studied his ankles. He was barefoot, but his feet were immaculate.

"Um," an uncertain voice replied. "*Ahem*. Tævarnavasi. Of the Neevirisee family. A cartman."

Syrina winced. She hoped they'd let the poor driver go.

The old man made a non-committal noise in his throat and turned his attention back to her. "We don't know if your kind has names, so we will not ask you. And as to the reason you are here, we hope you will enlighten. Do you have a message?"

He took one step forward to lean over to slide the bit out of Syrina's mouth before stepping back again. She was taken aback that he spoke perfect Skald, even if it was in a roundabout way.

"I have no message to deliver beyond the one from myself. And I have a name. It's Syrina. Kalis Syrina, if you want to be formal, but you don't have to be."

As she answered him, she noticed how heavy her

face and lips felt, and it occurred to her she'd been hanging upside down for most of the day.

He arched a single, white eyebrow. "Well, then this is interesting. So you were not sent here by your master to deliver another message?"

"Another message? No. I was sent to Chamælivishi to find a man named Asapalashvari, by my master, but he's not the same High Merchant who controls the Northern Resource Initiative if that's who you're talking about. That one is called Ma'is Kavik if you didn't already know that. I was sent here to find out more about him. But I came here for my own reasons. I want to kill Ma'is Ormo, my master, but there are some things I need to know, and I need to find out if there's anywhere or anyone besides him I can learn them from. Like, maybe you."

A long silence followed. The Astrologer's face was unreadable, but there was a fair amount of surprise in there somewhere. Whether or not he was prepared to believe anything she said, he hadn't expected her to say that.

At length, he sighed, gave Syrina a quizzical look, and spoke past her in Ristroan. "Tævarnavasi the cartman, you are free to roam the Prefecture Building at your leisure. We're sure that Vesmalii will show you to the dining hall. We must humbly ask you, however, not to leave the premises, in case we require you later. A message will be sent to your family, so they will not worry."

"Yes. Thank you, Eminence."

Syrina could hear the bow from Tævarnavasi as he shuffled away, followed by the more certain footsteps of the man named Vesmalii.

"As for this one, store her."

She didn't like the sound of that.

———

You've killed us both, the voice said again, several hours later.

Syrina dangled, still upside down, staring into the pitch blackness of whatever closet they'd stuck her in.

She agreed but didn't say anything.

———

Syrina lapsed into meditation for a long while until they wheeled her again into the courtyard, to the gazebo and the Astrologer. It was night. The half-Eye loomed above them, washing everything in its polarized, ruddy light and making the shadows sharp and angular. Half-Eye. She'd been meditating upside down in the dark for the better part of a week. The scarlet hurricane of the pupil glared down on them, half-shadowed by its night side.

"Why do you call yourself, *we*?" Syrina asked, before the old man could say anything.

His voice was soft as he glided toward her, down the stone causeway. The white of his linen clothes glowed under the Eye like some malevolent ghost. Behind her, the door to the courtyard boomed shut.

"Why do you tell us you wish to betray your Merchant's Syndicate?" He halted three feet in front of her.

She could see his ankles but needed to peer up her nose to catch his face. From that angle, he was all chin and nostrils until he looked down at her.

Syrina told him all of it. About Triglav, the insanity, and the voice in her head that wasn't hers. Her failed attack on Ormo, her ensuing imprisonment, her driving need for revenge, and the even greater need to understand herself.

He nodded through it, watching her eyes, then sauntered back to his chair. The edge of the Eye kissed the roof of the Prefecture Building, and the shadows were longer but no less sharp.

"I see the things you say to be the truth, at least to yourself. But if that is so, why did you not attempt to kill your Ma'is when you first returned to him, before he suspected your rage?"

"I wasn't sure if it was him at first. He'd conditioned me to not believe it. And like I said, he's the only one I know who can help me figure out what I am. There was something else, too."

"Yes?"

"If I've earned your trust enough for you to hear me out, haven't I earned your trust enough to at least speak right-side up?"

There was the slightest hesitation before he nodded and made a small, vague gesture. Syrina heard the door open, and she was wheeled two-thirds of the way down the causeway and flipped unceremoniously over by a pair of guards, who then went to stand behind the Astrologer, under the gazebo. They settled their gazes on Syrina and kept them there.

The rush of being right-side up made her giddy, and it took a second or two to gain control of her senses.

"The Tidal Works," she said. "Everyone's got their fingers in it. It's at least ten thousand years old. By most accounts, more. And if it ever stopped doing whatever it's doing, it would reduce a fifth of the con-

tinent to ashes and steam. Including half of Ristro."
She paused. "This half."

The old man, his dusting of beard a violent purple
in the Eyelight, stared at her with an intense unreadable expression. The men standing behind him remained blasé. Syrina wondered if one of them was the
one called Vesmalii, which made her wonder about
Tævarnavasi, but she decided now wasn't a good time
to ask about the cart driver. She wanted a bath, too,
but she wasn't going to ask for that either.

"How much do you know of the Tidal Works?"
The old man's eyes glittered moist and blue.

She shrugged as well as she could still strapped in
the coffin. "That's pretty much it. I know it pumps
hot water for Fom and they use it for heating. And it
powers their glow globes and everything else in the
city that's attached to the ground. But that's not what
it's for. As far as I know, no one knows what it's doing,
except maybe you, judging by the way you're looking
at me."

The Astrologer stared at her for a long time,
shaking his head, but she didn't know enough about
Ristroan body language to understand what that
meant. Then he stood with a tired groan that surprised her and began to pace in front of his chair.

"About the Kalis, there are very few records that
remain from before the Age. Very few that we here in
Ristro know of. In one of them, however, it's mentioned that the servants of the Ancients, and also the
Ancient masters themselves, possessed a second soul,
so we agree with your Ma'is Ormo. This voice must
be real. These spirits existed to serve their vessels and
to grant them strength.

"The Ancients and their servants now are ten

thousand years gone, so who can know what your demon serves, or whom. Though it is safe to say that your Ma'is Ormo wishes it to serve him. That, perhaps, can serve us, even if the demon cannot. As to our interest in the so-called Tidal Works, you are correct in thinking we know a little. We might be willing to speak of it. On condition."

He stopped, so Syrina said, "I'm waiting."

"Just as the Fifteen wish to know about us, we wish to know about the Fifteen. You will serve this Ormo until it suits us otherwise, but now you will keep us in your thoughts as well. Whatever is left, you may keep for yourself."

Syrina spent a minute thinking about that. "So, you want me to serve you first, Ormo second, and my own goals third?"

"Inaccurately, yes. By helping us, you might further your own goals. They are not anyway unrelated."

"Might? As in, you might give me what I'm looking for, or you might not?"

"Just as your Ma'is Ormo may give you what you seek, or he may not. However, he will be less gracious toward the task of satisfying your revenge than we. He also has reason to deceive you, perhaps betray you. We do not, and we will greet your honesty with our own if you choose to trust us with it."

We don't have any way of knowing if he's lying or not.

Syrina laughed. "I've got quite the choice, don't I?"

"It's serving us or death. Or lying to us, which will lead to death, because we will know. Even the Kalis cannot deceive. But we think you'll take our offer and you will not lie to us. Otherwise, you would not have submitted as you did. Other Kalis have come here and told us stories, but you are one of the first to parlay with honesty."

If you think I can help you lie to Ormo, maybe I can help you lie to this guy instead. Let's give it a shot and try to get the hell out of here. It might not be too late to get what we came for.

Syrina was done with Ormo and the damn voice. "Take control, then, and do it yourself," she said under her breath.

The voice had the good grace not to answer, but Syrina could feel it sulking. The Astrologer raised an eyebrow at her but refrained from comment.

"Like I said, quite a choice," she said to the Astrologer. "Fine. It's as good an offer as I could've hoped for. Better, in fact."

He nodded and made an almost imperceptible gesture. The door opened. There was a clatter of locks and bolts and keys from the coffin. And just like that, Syrina was free, if still covered in paint, now stiff and flaking. She wondered how the old man could be so sure she was telling the truth, but since she was, she figured his methods must work well enough.

"You're welcome to explore the prefecture building at your leisure, but we ask you to remain within it. Your lack of restraints would upset the populace if it were to becom known."

"And then what?"

"When we're ready, we will tell you certain things."

"Um. Okay. And then?"

"That depends on what we tell you."

Syrina frowned.

That's a pretty shitty deal.

"Fair enough," she said.

"Please show our new guest to the Visitor's Wing," the Astrologer said to the guards at the door behind her. "And find her suitable quarters."

The soldiers were disciplined enough to not openly react, but they couldn't hide the glance they gave each other as they turned to lead Syrina from the courtyard.

She hoped that whatever closet they stuck her in this time, it would at least have a bath.

24

HISTORY

Syrina expected her *suitable quarters* to be another unlit closet, but it ended up being a suite of three large, square identically-sized windowless rooms. The walls were unadorned obsidian, so even with all the lamps burning, it seemed dark. She wondered why the astrologers seemed to have the same black-room fixation the High Merchants had, but she didn't mind. It was still brighter than the closet had been.

The chambers were furnished with overstuffed goat leather furniture, an enormous quilted feather bed, and a raised brass bath with an oil stove under it. There was a knob on the side of the tub to adjust the heat without getting out of the water. She was never a fan of sitting on gigantic furniture, and as always, she slept on the floor, but she made good use of the tub.

She was a good girl, mostly. Kept to herself and didn't pull anything, and she only left the prefecture building a handful of times, just to explore. She was sure they watched her go, even as careful as she was. She couldn't even get out a hall window without passing under at least a few of the hooded lamps which made her tattoos glow, though, no one was around to see her, as far as she could tell. She assumed it was a test. Even if they couldn't keep an eye on her after she left the prefecture building, they could keep their ears to the city, listening for anything to go down that they could blame on her. But they let her go and come back, and they never blamed her for anything.

Vormisæn was a small city, maybe a hundred thousand people, which included the sprawl of outlying farms, orchards, and forest reserves. The police force was modest but well respected. The streets were lit by gas lamps at night and bustled with people long after Syrina would expect a city of that size to sleep. The primary industries were pickling the fish carted in from the coastal towns and selling fruit from the surrounding orchards. Syrina noted all of it more out of habit than anything else. She couldn't discard the possibility that something might be useful to her later.

Most of the streets were wide enough to accommodate four camel wagons abreast, and down the center of the major boulevards, fruit trees and palms separated the lanes, creating a sense of peace and order amid the chaos. She was surprised that they only seemed to use camels here and not the steam cars she was used to seeing around Eheene. But there was a dirigible docking tower perched at the south edge of the city, and there was always an airship there when she went out.

Brown thick-walled stone buildings lined the avenues, one sometimes two stories, hunched behind low walls and sloping gardens. More often than not, the exterior wall of one house became the interior of the one next to it, making some streets meander for a span or more before coming to the next intersection. It made rooftop travel even easier than it was in the Foreigner's District, but Syrina dreaded the thought of needing to find her way through the city while confined to the maze of streets. Vormisæn grew out of a wide, low valley, spilling over the edges, into the adjacent hollows, like a bowl overflowing with chunks of brown curd.

She didn't get so much as a hello from the Astrologer for a fortnight, until one evening, a sweaty, nervous little government messenger arrived at her door and invited her to *join the conversation* in the courtyard.

It was an hour before midnight and clear. The Eye was new and not up anyway, and stars splattered across the sky. The Astrologer had taken his place in the spot under the gazebo. This time, he didn't approach her. He had a stack of papers in his hand, which he rested in his lap when he looked up at her. They hadn't subjected Syrina to the coffin-prison again, but a servant had painted her white, with a fine floral-scented powder before she entered the courtyard so the Astrologer could have something to look at. She was grateful it wasn't the fishy paint they'd used the first time. That stuff had been hell on the bathtub.

There was no light beyond the stars, which were bright enough to illuminate the old man's dusty face. He looked calm, considering he was being approached by an unrestrained Kalis, but it was stupid to think there wasn't at least thirty crossbows or their equivalent trained on her from the dark eves and windows.

"I hear you're going to tell me something about the world," she said after the silence had drawn on long enough to annoy her.

"Did you know the Ancients didn't name this world Eris?" he asked, in Skald.

She couldn't read his tone and wondered what his point could be.

She shrugged.

"It was not this world, but the orb known now as the Eye that was named Eris," he said as if he were reciting a lesson he'd taught many times. "Named after a goddess of discord that was ancient even to them. She is not our moon. We are hers. The Eye is a thousand times bigger than the nameless globe we ride, a fact that has been forgotten by most and brushed aside by the few who remember. They named it Eris because of the disharmony it caused the world on which they chose to live. When the Ancients came to this lonely moon, the tides that pulled at our seas were many, many times stronger than they are now. Those were the tides that heaved the Black Wall up from a turmoil of stone and water and molten rock, a million years before our ancestors first arrived. Eris's moon ever quaked in the beginning times, and waves ten thousand hands high shaped and reshaped the land. Only the meanest and most tenacious life had existed here when the starships landed. Who knows why humanity's Ancestors chose such a savage world? Perhaps they found something of value here that is now lost to us. Perhaps they had no choice. There is too little of the past left to guess."

The Astrologer stood with a long sigh and gazed

at the stars, brow furrowed as if he was trying to figure out which point of light the Ancients might've come from all those thousands of years ago.

His voice was quiet, but it carried well in the acoustics of the courtyard. He leveled his eyes at Syrina again. She brushed a few grains of white powder from her eye.

"The power and knowledge of the Ancients were vast," he said, voice stronger. "Even now, after ten thousand years of study, almost everything they accomplished is beyond our understanding. Over two thousand generations, yet the more we learn, the more we know is lost.

"They brought with them many creatures from their home, though once again, the reason why has faded to dust across the eons. Some died out, others thrived and went wild. The Ancestors, their servants, and their beasts were able to travel from another sun to settle here among the ferns and high trees and methra fish and karakh, and not just survive, but prosper. Though they couldn't diminish the energy of the tides, they constructed devices able to absorb and tame them, protecting their new home from the destructive pull of Eris."

"The Tidal Works."

"Yes." He glanced at the stars and sat again, in one graceful act, punctuated with a little grunt: the sound of an old man settling down to rest after a long day's labor. After a short pause, as if catching his breath, he continued. "Our Ancestors, no doubt, had more use for such relentless quantities of energy than heating and lighting cities and pumping hot water, but the principle was the same. When they turned the machines on, the seas stilled, the quakes calmed, and the mountains ceased their heaving, flaming belches."

"Wait a minute," Syrina said. "If that's what the Tidal Works is doing, isn't there a lot of energy that's not being used? It couldn't take that much power to heat Fom's water supply and light their glow lamps."

The Astrologer flashed a small, pleased smile. "Indeed, some of the energy stored in the Tidal Works is cast off as steam, shrouding Fom in its famous fog, but there must be much, much more we cannot account for. Neither do we know how many such devices there are. Some records say five, others hold the number to be as high as forty-one, but all the remaining histories that mention such things were written long after the Age of Ashes and are sourced from third- and fourth-hand records of much speculation, themselves. We are, however, sure that the failure of more than one of these tidal devices is what caused the Age of Ashes. Thus, you can see why the continued functioning of the remaining machines is in the interest of all living things."

"Oh," was all Syrina could think to say for a minute, her mind racing. "So that's why you've been funding NRI's research."

"In part."

"You mean it gets better?"

"The forerunners to the High Merchant's Syndicate were the first to rise out of the Age. Even children in N'narad are taught that, but no one ever asks why. No one ever asks how."

"How? Why?" Syrina was disappointed the sarcasm didn't seem to carry over in the translation, or else the Astrologer ignored it.

"The Age of Ashes did not begin as a gradual

thing. Within a day, perhaps an hour, the world was black with soot belched from the ground and all the cities reduced to ruin. All comfort and wisdom lost. Humanity itself almost extinct. When the clouds of ash lifted, a few thousand survivors, perhaps less, remained in tiny pockets scattered across the shattered world. Yet the Syndicate somehow held onto a portion of their knowledge. They were able to protect their secrets and maintain their position of power. Consider your tattoos. Only the Fifteen members of the High Merchant's Syndicate know the secrets necessary to create a Kalis, passed down for thousands of generations. Secrets kept even from you. Secrets held above the ashes, while around them all else burned."

"So the Syndicate's claim of existing before the Age of Ashes is true? They are direct descendants of the first rulers of Eris?"

"Certainly."

Syrina wondered. Ormo had taught her that the Syndicate could trace their history all the way back to the Ancients, and she'd believed it long before she'd started to doubt it out of principle. But now she was beginning to believe it again.

The Astrologer continued. "They were ready for the darkness. At least, more than others were. Even so, they would never regain all that vanished."

The Astrologer looked to the stars again. A daystar, catching light from the Eye somewhere beyond the horizon, glinted and faded back out.

"What pools of knowledge did they swim in when they first arrived on Eris's turbulent moon?" He asked.

His tone was rhetorical, and Syrina didn't respond.

He turned his gaze back toward her. The dusting of hair on his head and face glowed silver in the dim light.

"Whatever their reasons," he said, "coming here must have been an act born of desperation. Their journey from another star was a one-way trip. Any flight from the surface of this world is rendered nigh-impossible by the wind that tears across the highest parts of the sky, another invisible gift from Eris, and made even more difficult by the lack of iron beneath the soil. The N'naradin Church and the Syndicate squander what few flimsy dregs they can drag from their mines for war and ornament. Building machines that might once again take them to distant stars is beyond their primitive interests, just as it is beyond Ristro's. As to all our Ancestors lost, we can only guess at the fathomless knowledge that slid from their grasp. Whatever was forgotten, though, today's Merchant's Syndicate has nevertheless gained almost absolute power over a world washed in ignorance. Even the Church, whatever they claim, always, in the end, bows to the Syndicate's whims."

Syrina coughed. "An ignorant world? That's a dubious prize."

"Is it now? Even if it's the only world we know? Well, regardless of what they knew or did not, our Ancestors designed the tidal machines to last until the dying breath of the sun, but only as a whole. When one failed, another failed, and then another. When the chain reaction was over, Eris's moon had been plunged into an Age of Ash which stretched across countless hundreds of years."

Syrina nodded, understanding dawning in her glittering eyes. "And you're concerned about the additional strain on the remaining machines, however many there are, which is why you're willing to fund your enemies. In return, I'm guessing you get to see NRI's findings."

"The High Merchant Kavik has been unprecedented with his cordial interactions with Ristro. Perhaps through his own research of the Tidal Works, he has recognized the tip of the depths of the problem we face. Even so, NRI and most likely even High Merchant Kavik have only the inkling of the true significance of what they study, yet it would not serve us to inform them of more." The Astrologer sighed, equal parts sad and resigned. "Even if politics become the doom of us all, we are nevertheless slaves to its confines. But regardless of politics, at the very least we must know what signs the Tidal Works may give before it stops functioning if we're blessed enough to be given any sign at all. We believe the disaster some two thousand years ago which reduced the nation of Kamahush to a poisonous wasteland was another such machine giving out, adding yet more strain to the remainder. While the continued functioning of these Artifacts is more important than any nation's petty differences, ancient or new, we cannot trust the Fifteen to think so. Even with High Merchant Kavik, we can't know his true motives. Anyway, we have little to tell them that would be of any assistance and nothing that will add for them a sense of urgency. Perhaps the machines will last another hundred thousand years, and we worry and dread for naught. Perhaps the rest will fail tomorrow and the energy released will shatter Eris's only moon to bits, and humanity cast into the void."

"But why should I believe you know all this thousands of years later when no one else does?"

Syrina caught herself looking up the stars and lowered her gaze toward the Astrologer, who sat eyeing her, his expression unreadable.

"Before the Age of Ashes, when the eventual founders of the Syndicate realized there was a problem with their machines, a few of the ruling class wanted to give the world what little warning they could. The majority disagreed, thinking the truth would spread needless chaos and panic. They thought their efforts would be better spent preparing for the inevitable, preserving what they could of their wealth and knowledge. The minority split and fled when dissent wasn't tolerated. The majority declared the rebels a threat and hunted them, but then the Age was upon them all and the rebellion forgotten."

"The rebels became the Astrologers."

"Long, long, long after. The dissenters' priority was to shelter the truth about those that they saw as betrayers of humankind, and they did so, using it to fuel their rage against the Syndicate, who had turned a blind eye toward the deaths of billions. Through either the foresight of our ancestors or blind luck, the Age ravished what's now the Ristro Peninsula less than the rest of Eris's moon, and we lost less than most, besides the Syndicate itself, who had spent their time preparing for it."

Syrina was surprised by the illogical rage rising in her voice. "Then why didn't you rise up when you had the chance?" Syrina was surprised by the illogical rage rising in her voice. "Spread the truth while the Syndicate was still in turmoil right after the Age? Or better yet, take them out when they were in disarray?"

She realized the irony of asking the Astrologer that, but if he drew any comparisons between her question and her inaction against Ormo, he kept them to himself.

"Because our own Ancestors were not without their flaws. Their sole priority was to preserve the truth. They believed the Syndicate destroyed, wiped out by that which they prepared for but wouldn't endeavor to prevent. By the time the forefathers of the Fifteen had emerged, they were already too strong to be stopped with as something as gossamer as the truth. But not even the Syndicate is our greatest threat anymore."

"N'narad is the only player left."

"More than half of Eris's moon's population now belongs to the Church, which is a ponderous thing hindered by the inconveniences of history. Even if a few of the faithful were inclined to believe the truth, most would rather disregard it in the face of the promise of Heaven. The fear of their names being blotted from the Books or an increase in their Salvation Taxes is more immediate to them than some vague, ancient doom. Doubly so, since when that ancient doom comes, their place in the afterlife is secure. The Syndicate has been our enemy since before the onset of the Age of Ashes, but the Church is the greater threat. And so we study in secret, through our erstwhile greatest enemy."

"All that, and you know nothing else of the Kalis?" Anger shadowed Syrina's voice.

"Any insight about you and the demon within wasn't one of the secrets taken with us when we fled the Syndicate ten thousand years ago. Any knowledge of the Kalis was lost in the Age of Ashes, except what the Fifteen members of the Merchant's Syndicate know."

————

It was almost dawn when Syrina went to bed, but she lay awake a long time on the cool stone floor. She asked the voice what it thought of everything, but this time, it was the one who had nothing to say.

25

TRAVELING

THEY SENT SYRINA BACK TO FOM ON A
smuggler's ship. She'd given them a list of materials,
and they'd complied, giving her everything she
needed to do a proper job on a disguise. She only hesitated a second before giving up that little secret. Why
stop breaking the rules when she was on such a roll?
This time, she even got the skin tone right.

Syrina got the bad end of the deal, and on the way
back she had a lot of time to think about it. On one
hand, the Astrologer probably already regretted
trusting her, but at least he got a Kalis spy out of the
bargain, even if it was one he couldn't trust. On the
other hand, she got nothing. Nothing she wanted. Just
a story about the Tidal Works that she would've been
happier not knowing because now she felt obligated
to do something about it, even if she didn't know what
she could do. No one could tell her who Kavik was,
and she wouldn't have believed them if they had.

The only thing the Astrologer could do was give
her a few documents that would back up the story she
planned to tell Ormo. She supposed that was something. It still wasn't going to be easy to lie to him, but

at least she'd be telling him what he wanted to hear, with evidence in hand to back up her words.

The papers, which the Astrologer claimed were accurate copies of original records, proved Ristroan tin was channeled through NRI and signed off on by Storik—a simple engineer who, for some reason, was also on the board of directors and head researcher of one of the most influential conglomerates in Skalkaad. In return, Storik gave periodic reports to Asapalash-vari, under the guise of business meetings with a rep from Hood Manufacturing.

Storik had been involved in the Tidal Works project from the beginning, and he wielded unlikely influence at one of the most powerful corporations on Eris, not to mention he had had at least one Kalis working under him as N'talisan. He then reported everything he learned to the leaders of Ristro. If Syrina was going to accuse Ma'is Kavik of being a traitor and Storik of being Kavik, she wouldn't be able to find much more evidence than that. There were a few meetings with others, too, infrequent and trivial-seeming, but every sign except one pointed to Kavik being the obvious choice. She hoped her suspicions were right.

She'd asked the Astrologer how he felt about losing the most influential contact they'd ever had with Skalkaad. To which he replied that now they had their very own Kalis instead.

———

If it surprised Ormo to see Syrina again, a half-year after she'd left, he didn't let it show. She told him her theory about Storik and showed him the documents the Astrologer had given her, which Ormo translated that same night. The voice guided her, kept her calm, kept the lie from touching her voice. She was afraid of going into details, but Ormo didn't inquire about her methods, or even where she'd gotten the paperwork from. Not that he ever had, but this time it made her nervous.

One of Ormo's other spies had tracked down Xereks Lees while she was in Ristro. Or rather, they'd found Orvaan in Valez'Mui and watched him board a ship to Maresg. They'd sent a hawk to Eheene with the news. Ormo was expecting word any day from someone in Maresg to back up the report. He had a new request for the job—however she did it, he wanted it public. Lees had gotten away from him, at least for a while. Ormo wanted to remind the world that accidents happened to those that crossed the Syndicate. Especially to those that got away.

Syrina ended up being in Eheene less than a week before she was on another ship, this one bound for the Upper Peninsula, on her way to finish what ended up being the easiest part of the job.

———

Xereks Lees glowered over the edge of the veranda, eyes pinched. He placed a finger against his sharp nose and snorted, then spat down into the latticework of bridges and support beams that wound their way through the massive, umber trunks of the mangrove trees and the crooked, whitish, vertical beams of the ruins. He watched it fall, glittering in the smoky after-noon light like a clot of blood, passing between walkways and kiosks, pedestrians and prostitutes, before vanishing into the glint of the incoming tide.

"Damn," he said.

"Stop worrying all the time," Nazaa said, from the open doorway. "I don't know why you still worry. It's been months now. Anyway, they already said it was an accident."

Lees grunted at his wife but continued to peer down into the lower levels of Maresg. A cloud passed in front of the sun and the sea far below became lost in rust-tinged shadows.

Nazaa looked at his back a moment longer and then vanished into the house.

The cloud passed, but the recent storm still painted the sun bloody where it hovered two hands above the tops of the tallest ruins. The white non-metal beams and plates glowed pink in the dying light.

Lees tugged at the high collar of his bleached linen shirt, damp with perspiration, and absentmindedly wiped his hands on the baggy black silk of his pants. It was too hot here. His silver ponytail had become dull gray and matted with sweat. It would be spring in Eheene now. Cherry blossoms would carpet the streets and cling to the gnarled branches, wafting onto the marble lanes like pink perfumed snow. He could imagine the canals brimming with the winter runoff, the faint scent of naphtha. The chaotic ballet of the harbor. All of it coming together to make the music of power and money.

Here in Maresg, it was already summer, but the only difference between now and six months ago was less rain to wash the stench of brine from the air, wafting up from the tidal pools at the base of the mangroves.

Lees hated this place, but he could never go back to Eheene, whatever his wife said. First, the incident at his warehouse. Then the alarm at the vault. Nazaa kept telling him not to worry, but she didn't take these things seriously enough. Never had. He'd rather spend his life hiding in Maresg for no reason than go back to Eheene and find out he'd been right the instant before they killed him.

He turned to the open door and called, "I'm going to Calveeni's."

If Nazaa heard him, she didn't bother answering, and he only waited long enough for his bodyguards to join him. There were five of them, including Orvaan, all dressed in the gaudy silks and linens popular on the Upper Peninsula. Back in Eheene, Lees had made it a point to stand out from the crowd. Now the idea terrified him.

They wound their way down to the gate at the bottom of the polished spiral stairs that connected Lees's balcony to the Westbridge Thoroughfare like a giant corkscrew supporting the top floor of his home.

His house was a slender six stories and crooked, like a guard tower smashed between the trunk of a mangrove tree and a bent white pillar of the ruins. The whole disjointed mess of it was slathered in primary colors that made his head hurt.

The Thoroughfare led from Lees's neighborhood of Mourner's Lookout in the north, through the heart of Top Market. Along the way, smaller walkways and stairs of wood led down into the lower, darker parts of the city. Parts of the city Lees didn't spend any time in.

Westbridge, though, was the finest strip of real estate in Maresg until it hit the southern edge of the city and sank into the Malak Ravine, where fugitives maintained the immense wooden chain that stretched across the canal, holding the passage for ransom. Plenty of captains would rather pay two-thousand Three-Sides to common criminals than take an extra three or four weeks to sail around the Upper Peninsula. As a merchant, he loathed them. As a citizen of Maresg, he found that he hated them no less, but he'd come to appreciate their business acumen.

The Thoroughfare itself was a haphazard smattering of wood and sheets of the white nonmetal hauled from the surrounding ruins eons ago, when Maresg had first grown above the ebb and flow of the tides, up the mangroves and through the ruins like cancer. Shops, homes, brothels, tanneries, and tattoo parlors ran above and below the wide, wobbling bridge, clinging to it with ramps, ladders, and stairs, with no sense of pattern or design. Every hovel and hut, tower and mansion were unique, splashed with red, blue, orange, and yellow, wedged wherever they fit among the filthy white bones of the ruins and the giant trees. All they'd ever had in Maresg was fish and fruit and whatever they could embezzle from the desperate or steal from the foolish, and they'd prospered. The pigs.

Nazaa was right. Certainly right. They'd only taken the tin from his warehouse office. The investigator had found the ledger ignored and ditched in the harbor the next evening after the tide had gone out. And nothing had gone missing from Ka'id's vault. The inventory had been triple-checked. Something had dislodged from one of the ventilation shafts and

tripped the alarm. Lees hoped the idiots in maintenance had been fired for that. Every damn one of
them.

So maybe he was overreacting, but he hadn't
learned the details from Ka'id until he was already
settled in Maresg, and for some reason, finding out it
had been a false alarm didn't make him feel any
better.

So they stayed, and Nazaa complained, and Lees
couldn't blame her. The bottom line was that he was
just too much of a coward to go back to Eheene.

Instead, he'd taken to spending time at Calveeni's
where he could drink in peace and gaze from the balcony. Like a little boy, he would imagine himself
leaping off, soaring away above treetops and over the
sea, back to Eheene where he would take back the life
that was stolen from him. A childish dream, of course,
and one he kept to himself. Not even Nazaa knew of
such fantasies.

In the end, only part of it came true.

26

THE FARM

When Syrina got back to Eheene, she watched Storik for a while, trying to decide what to do about him. He wouldn't be easy. According to Ormo, the man had barely left the NRI compound since Syrina had first encountered him, and she couldn't just take him out, in any case. It needed to look like an accident. Even more so than usual. On top of that, she couldn't be sure if any other Kalis might be keeping an eye on him, not to mention the karakh.

Storik left just twice in the two months she watched the compound. The first time, he went into Eheene to meet with a lawyer. She didn't bother finding out why, but no opportunity for an accident presented itself in the day he was there.

The second time, he went up into the taiga, three days northeast, to meet with the manager of a naphtha company about the navaras harvest, which hadn't started yet but was going to be too small. Syrina followed his carriage at a distance, hoping for a chance at an accident, but nothing came up that wouldn't have raised at least a couple eyebrows. With

Storik, even one eyebrow raised was too many. It hadn't helped that the karakh had come along as part of his personal escort. All things considered, she might wait years for him to make himself available to be killed.

And then she had an idea.

———

The creation of naphtha involved the mining of certain minerals and the extraction and refinement of tarfuel, but the whole process started with the harvesting of navaras seeds, which could only be grown in the taiga of Skalkaad. Tarfuel was produced and refined in N'narad and Ristro, but it was far inferior, the same amount burning a sixth as long as it did when made with navaras. True naphtha only came from Skalkaad, and every High Merchant, whatever their other differences, wanted to keep it that way.

Well, they could have it. She wasn't out to break anyone's monopoly on flammable goo.

A navaras farm during the harvest was a swarm of activity, and the unharvested seed pods were closely guarded. The navaras plants were low, scraggly, and miserable-looking—benign, considering they were the core ingredient of one of the most feared and useful substances on Eris. The farms were sprawling, rocky, and difficult to work. The people that did were either indentured prisoners or paid very, very well. It was the paid ones Syrina needed to worry about.

The farm below, where she hunkered at the top of a broken ridge, lay one week north of Eheene, but she'd taken two to get there so she could set up a few things on the way. It sprawled to the hills slouching on the horizon, where cultivated land met taiga.

She knew the place from a job she'd done ages ago, before Lees, Triglav, and the rest. The company that managed it was called Nathco, but they were a subsidiary of NRI.

The buildings that concerned Syrina were scattered on the south end. There was a barn that housed the hounds and shaggy camels that helped with the harvest, and a huge dormitory for the workers. Next to that was a squat administration building, and a little apart from everything else loomed a trio of silos where seeds were stored and ground to a powder before getting hauled by cart or steam truck to one of the refineries along the coast.

The silo closest to Syrina was attached to a warehouse where camels hauled carts laden with sacks of seed in and empty sacks out. Everything was covered in sloppy white paint, so it looked like the buildings were covered in dirty snow. The green mountain and tree symbol of Nathco was stenciled on every building.

She was banking on the fact that the Northern Resource Initiative conglomerate was the biggest producer of naphtha on Eris, and Storik was at the top of it all. However important the Tidal Works was to him, the naphtha needed to come first. It wasn't called the Northern Resource Initiative for nothing, and judging by Storik's actions in the past, he was going to take care of any big problems himself.

Guards and their hounds patrolled the perimeter. She'd need to watch out for the dogs. She hoped she wouldn't need to hurt any of them. These days, she wasn't too thrilled about hurting the guards either.

Syrina considered herself lucky that everything was coming to the edge now, during the harvest. In the summer, there wouldn't be a lot she could do to cause problems, short of a full-blown forest fire, and that could interrupt a lot of interests beyond Kavik's. In the winter, now just two or three weeks away, the place would be all but deserted, and anything she messed with would be buried and unnoticed until spring, if it hadn't washed away by then.

She picked her way down the shallow slope until she was in the edge of the field. The plants around her had already been harvested, their rough leafless branches bare of the cerulean seed pods she could see further afield.

If anyone noticed her, she'd need to kill everyone at the farm and set it all up as some sort of calamity. The voice didn't need to tell her that for her to know it was true. If word got out that a Kalis was screwing around with the harvest, nothing Syrina did to Storik would be called an accident.

She slunk over to the silos. She was eighty hands away when a patrol and their tundra hounds came around the nearest one, talking with each other in low voices, and headed toward her across the field. Syrina dropped onto her chest and tried to press herself further into the dirt, but the ground was already frozen solid under a thin layer of topsoil. Her hand ached where her fingers had been, and she bit her lip against the pain. She shimmied backward, hoping it was enough to get out of the path of the dogs. They'd already smelled her, but she hoped they couldn't tell her scent from any of the hundreds of temporary migrant workers.

She kept her head low and listened to the dog's

panting and the crunch of feet on the cold uneven ground. The guards weren't talking anymore, so she couldn't tell their mood, other than it was silent, which might not be good. Then the panting turned into sniffing. She froze. The footsteps stopped. There was more crunching, but no one seemed to be moving so much as shifting around, thirty hands from where she cowered.

Take them now before they loose the dogs on you.

She bit her tongue against the *shut up* that was blooming to her lips and didn't move. The sniffing intensified and moved a few feet closer. She felt her limbs coil, ready to spring. Three seconds and they'd be close enough that she could take the dogs, followed by the men, even if the thought made her miserable. At least she could probably rig it up as an accident and spare everyone else.

Three... two...

"Come on." A loud voice in the vast quiet interrupted the furious sniffing. "We've been out here long enough. Let's go eat."

There was a disgruntled growl, and the footsteps crunched away.

Syrina lay there a while, breathing in the cold jagged clay of the frozen ground until she decided she should get up before the next shift wandered by. She sprinted the rest of the way to the warehouse, hunkered against the rear wall, and waited for the evening whistle.

———

The blank gray sky dimmed to something between afternoon and evening, and a bell rang off in the direction of the administration building, but most of the camel drivers and pickers had already started off toward the smells of camel porridge and roasted apples. Syrina edged to the front of the warehouse to snatch the lamp and flint from the hook inside the door, then crept around the back to shimmy up the silo.

The silo and the warehouse were made from a conglomeration of wood and stone, reinforced at random with white-washed rectangular plates of copper. The tower's rough construction made it easy to climb, even with an unlit oil lantern and flint gripped in the remains of her left hand, but Syrina began to worry about the next step.

You'll be fine. Just don't hesitate.

No, hesitation wouldn't do at all.

Syrina flipped open the little ventilation hatch in the roof of the silo, sighed and closed her eyes.

Unprocessed navaras seeds burned with a little fizzle, and the silos were full this time of year. The hard part wasn't going to be blowing the place up. She couldn't risk a fuse. It would leave evidence for an astute observer, of which there would be plenty around in a week or two. The lamp was risky enough, but if she demolished the silos and surrounding buildings, she didn't think anyone would be able to tell where it had come from.

Trust me.

"Shut up."

The bright side was that it might be the last time she'd need to say that to herself.

She lit the wick and felt her heart slow and stop as she stepped through the Papsukkal Door and dropped the lamp. Then she jumped.

On the other side of the Door, she floated more

than fell away from the silo. She began to think she'd miscalculated, that maybe the navaras wasn't churned up enough to ignite, when a flash of blueish-white and yellow light bathed the twilight across the farm. She twisted to face the fireball blooming behind her and hoped the impact of landing on her back wouldn't kill her. Then again, she wouldn't need to worry about that until she'd survived long enough to hit the ground. The wall of light spread toward her, fast even from the other side of the Papsukkal Door.

Syrina spun, ducked, and somersaulted away from the molten chunks of copper and flaming bits of wood. The sound of the explosion came to her as a low steady rush that drowned out all other sounds except the roar in her own head. Even through the Door, she wasn't fast enough. A smoldering rock grazed her cheek, drawing blood, and as she contorted away from it, she threw her leg in front of a burning spear of wood that impaled through her thigh. The shockwave hit her with a wall of heat, like standing on the lip of an erupting volcano. It launched her faster, further, and she was just another piece of shrapnel waiting to get embedded into the first thing she hit. She turned back toward the rushing ground and attempted to twist away from the oncoming trees. Somewhere, someone told her that her leg hurt.

The ground approached at an angle that a duck landing on a pond might be comfortable with. She curled into a ball, tucked her head beneath her shoulder, and hit the ground like a wheel. Syrina rolled up a shallow slope and launched off the top, bracing for some sort of horrible impact, but none came. She hit the ground again, felt something sharp slice into her back, rolled twenty more times, and came to a stop against a rain-smoothed boulder.

It wasn't so much that she stepped out of the Papsukkal Door as fell from it, and she lay there for a while, watching the sky growing dark in the quiet of the evening. Dark, except for the orange glow to the north which lit up the low clouds and turned the damp smell of the forest acrid. Quiet, except for the shouts drifting from the other side of the ridge. It wasn't just the farm burning, but the forest around her, too, as the gentle rain of fire set the underbrush alight. Syrina couldn't pass out here.

Her back and cheek itched, and she needed to bite on a piece of wood to yank the spear of timber from her thigh. Then she staggered away, trying to stay pointed more or less south, fighting the sleep that crawled out of the cold ground, inviting her to lie down and rest a while. She could feel the entity in her mind occupying itself with keeping her focused enough to drag one foot in front of the other.

When both fire and shouts were lost in the darkness, she lay down for an hour. However she felt, she couldn't take more time than that, and the voice did a commendable job of making sure she didn't.

Syrina had to get back to NRI before anyone else did.

27

THE TRAP

Words poured from the woman's mouth, and it was a moment or two before Adan Spaad, Storik's head receptionist and personal valet, could put together what she was talking about. She was short, filthy, and breathless, with matted brown hair cropped short. What was left of one of her hands was knotted with old burns. She'd burst into the vast lobby of NRI's headquarters with a flare of dust and sunlight, already in mid-rant, and had focused her attention on Spaad. It was only a few minutes before the management offices in Aado closed for tomorrow's Eye Night, and he wanted to go home.

There'd been a silo explosion at one of the farms. A bad one, too, she said over and over again, as if there was another kind. Spaad forced himself to accept that he wasn't going home just yet. He was reluctant to give into a migrant's hysterics, but an explosion up north had the potential to sink their numbers for a year or more. Storik needed to know about it.

He fetched her some water and told her to sit still and collect herself so that when his boss came down, the old man would be able to understand even half of what she was rambling about.

Storik was busy, of course, even this late in the day, and it was almost an hour before he appeared in the lobby, disheveled and frowning. The woman had cleaned her face and reduced her sobs to a quiver in her voice, which rose and fell when she spoke like she was asking random questions. Her breathing was quick and exaggerated, but at least she was coherent.

"What's this about?" Storik's frown edged downward.

She took a deep, shuddering breath. "The silo? The grind silo at Nathco three-thirty-nine. I saw a flash. I think the grinder sparked? Then..."

He shook his head, and his eyes narrowed. "Why didn't you go to the Nathco office?"

She shook her head back at him. "It's another day into Eheene, and they won't be open for Eye Night, so that's another day. I don't think anyone was hurt? But I thought it was important enough to stop here? I ran the whole way."

"And you knew to come here?" Storik's brown eyes were piercing.

The woman shifted in her chair and looked at the floor. "I heard a manager talking the other day? To someone about the head office in Aado. Was I not supposed to come here? I didn't know..." She looked like she might start crying again.

Storik sighed. "I see. No, it's fine. I suppose you were right to come here. Whatever you saw, though, it wasn't the grinder. They've all been updated. It's been ten years since one jammed bad enough to cause an explosion."

The woman shook her head again. "I heard it catch. Right before the flash. I'm sure."

"Pah. Well, I'd better have a look at it."

Spaad's small black eyes looked nervous. "Sir, it's winter already up there, that far north and away from the coast. Anyway, your wife is waiting. I'm sure there's someone else who can—"

"If there's a problem with the grinders, it's better to know about it now and not after there's another accident. And my wife can continue to wait."

Spaad drew his eyebrows together. "But after an explosion, there won't be any trace of what might've caused—"

"Nonsense. I'm the one who designed the new grinders, and I know what to look for. I'm not going to trust anyone else to find the problem, and I'm not going to wait until the spring thaw when everything is rusted or washed away. An airship this time of year is out of the question, I suppose?"

Spaad shook his head, looking terrified that his boss would ask for one anyway.

Storik only sighed and nodded. "Fine. We'll leave first thing in the morning. Make the proper security arrangements."

Spaad wagged his head and slid off. Storik turned his attention to the weeping woman. The injury to her hand looked like an old one. He always marveled at what the non-citizens had to endure.

"You. You're coming with me. Show me what you saw and where you saw it. Now go get yourself cleaned up. I'll see to it that someone finds room for you in the barracks tonight."

"Of course." She smiled a little, through her tears.

Storik scowled at her, spun, and disappeared back

into the NRI complex, leaving her to find her own way to the barracks, under the watchful eyes of security.

———

They packed extra fuel for Storik's carriage lanterns and left early the next morning, giving them a few hours of thin light before the Eye Night. Syrina followed in the skin of the woman she'd decided to call Myna, though no one had bothered to ask her what her name was yet.

They first traveled up a winding road, then a straight trail. The forest was thick on either side. There was no conversation, and their procession was silent except for the steady *creak, creak* of a carriage wheel turning on an under-greased axle, and the gentle clatter of the camel's hooves on the frozen ground. She watched the karakh travel alongside, surging in and out of the darkness. It leaped from tree to tree when the trunks were thick enough to support its massive body, tearing huge rents into the bark and smashing through limbs. Through glades and saplings, it scuttled at an angle like a shaggy, saucer-eyed crab, whistling, clicking and warbling at its shepherd. Watching it in its natural environment for the first time, Syrina realized just how unsubtle the thing was. Almost cute in its ungainliness.

They moved north until what would've been dusk if the Eye hadn't hidden the sun, but the going was slow, with no light except the swinging beams of the lanterns. Clouds had rolled in from the west, and after the Eye set, there were no stars.

The air was sharp with cold. The six guards and

Myna huddled around the little fire they'd built with Spaad, who doubled as Storik's carriage driver. No one said anything, and Syrina was too hung up on her own thoughts to strike up a conversation. She couldn't see where the karakh had gone off to, but every once in a while, she heard something clicking and crashing in the bushes around the campsite. Storik never emerged from the heated carriage except to relieve himself.

———

Day returned, but the sun didn't. The girl who brought the news of the explosion, Myna—one of the bodyguards had finally asked her what her name was —sometimes muttered to herself. Spaad couldn't blame her. He'd heard stories of silo explosions. He wouldn't have handled it any better.

They began to pass a trickle of people coming from the other direction. A few were driving caravans from other farms, hauling navaras, but most were empty-handed, returning from the Nathco farm. A few suffered from minor burns, and one man had a broken arm, but most were just in the after-effects of shock.

Storik interrogated the first dozen from the cracked open window of the carriage, but no one had many details beyond what Myna had already told him. It had happened right after the evening bell, and so far, she was the only one who had seen it.

Myna greeted a few of the migrants as friends, relieved they had survived, but they just looked at her with dull, tired eyes and responded with confused looks or weary nods. After a while, they passed each other in silence.

The returning workers warned them that one of the bridges was out ahead. Probably the wind. The weather was strange this far north, one had babbled. Especially in the fall and spring. Isolated storms, like miniature hurricanes, could blow through an area with no warning, covering everything in hands of snow or ice in a few hours, before evaporating into a gentle breeze as fast as it had come. Storik had only grunted at him and closed the carriage window.

A few days later, they reached the broken bridge. It had been rope and wood, spanning over a narrow forested canyon. At one time, it had been sturdy enough to hold two teams of camels at a time, pulling carts loaded with navaras. Now the remnants of it hung down into the gorge. Chunks of wood and long tangles of rope gnarled in the giant trees around the creek below like the web of some giant, drunken spider.

For the first time, Storik left the confines of the carriage for something besides relieving himself along the road, which at this point was little more than two wheel ruts cut through the hard ground of the forest. He frowned over the edge of the broken bridge and spat into the canyon.

"I know this place." He walked back to the waiting door of his carriage, held open by Spaad. "This bridge was only six or seven years old. Cut five, maybe six hours off the trip. I hope no one was on it when it went down. I suppose we'll find out."

"The weather can be like that up here," Myna said.

Storik ignored her. "An hour behind us, maybe

less, the old trail leads down into the ravine. Probably too overgrown now to take the camel and the damn wagon." He shot a triumphant look at his bodyguards and climbed back into the carriage.

———

What began as cliffs some three hundred feet above the creek tapered down to steep wooded slopes. The grassy land around the stream was level, wide enough for an overgrown trail that crisscrossed every two hundred hands or so. The brook was a little too wide to jump and painfully cold. Remnants of the old road could be seen through the dead summer weeds, littered with saplings and clogged with fallen rocks.

They had left the carriage where the road forked toward the broken bridge with one of the bodyguards. Storik seemed to enjoy walking. He selected a long walking stick from the side the path and plodded along between his men, humming to himself. The bodyguards tensed and complained that they needed to keep track of their ward while he was exposed outside of the carriage. Storik conceded that there were occasional robberies during the harvest, but the idea didn't seem to bother him much.

The karakh went on ahead, leaping from tree to shuddering, creaking tree, back and forth across the brook when the trunks were big enough to support it, which was most of them along the stream bed. Storik and his guards followed while Myna and Spaad took the rear, hiking together in silence. Myna seemed nervous and fidgety. Spaad left her alone.

Evening was growing somewhere behind the clouds when they got to the first remnants of the bridge scattered along the bottom of the canyon. First, a copper bolt. Then a few shattered boards that had fallen all the way to the path. Wooden support rods and broken planks dangled in the twilight, and a huge snarl of rope wove through the trees above. The limbs were bare except for a smattering of dry leaves, and a thick blanket of the ones that had already fallen coated the path.

There was a waterfall nearby, a little further up. They could hear it rumble somewhere beyond the bend in the canyon. The constant mist from the falling water made the ground icy, and gray moss clung to the immense trunks of the ancient trees and hung from their branches like wisps of dirty snow.

As they approached the bulk of the ruined bridge, Myna slipped on a wet stone and fell to the side of the brook, yelping in pain. Spaad paused, torn between helping her and following his boss, who had continued on after a glance back. The karakh bounded on ahead, taking advantage of the massive trees that grew near the waterfall.

Spaad decided on chivalry and turned to Myna, who was curled on the ground, holding her ankle and muttering curses under her breath. Storik stopped to yell back something about needing to hurry and the sun going down, his words drowned out by the rush of water.

There was a tremendous crack, like a strike of lightning. One of the biggest trees, rotten on the inside and gouged by a falling boulder, had splintered under the weight of the karakh. The snap was the old fir's death knell as it made its final tumble onto the steep hillside.

The karakh, off balance, leaped across the creek,

toward another huge trunk, reaching back and tossing the shepherd in the same direction, intent on catching him after it landed to protect him from the impact of the landing. They had done the same move hundreds of times in the past few days. This time, though, the shepherd's right arm snared in the web of rope from the fallen bridge as he flailed through the air. The karakh, focused on the landing, reached back to catch him, and its strength and weight turned the gesture to a yank. The shepherd screamed as his arm ripped off at the shoulder.

There was a convulsion of blood. The karakh placed the shepherd back in his place behind its head, but the man didn't grab onto the chains. He balanced there for a few seconds, then keeled forward into the fur of his mount, pressing his face into it, letting go of the tattered flesh of his hemorrhaging shoulder to run his fingers through the coarse hair. Then he slid off and landed with a thud and a splash, face down and half submerged in the stream.

Myna began to cry in low, peeling sobs.

The karakh, for all its brutal ugliness, looked down on the body of its shepherd with human-like shock and unleashed a long warbling, clicking scream. Then the glaze in its owl-like eyes turned from grief to rage, and it focused on the people closest to it—Storik and his personal guard.

A few of the bodyguards had the wherewithal to draw their weapons and move between the karakh and Storik, who was staring up at the beast with detached horror. None of them had any real way of dealing with a karakh.

There was a brief pause before the creature took a short hop to get within arm's length. Its first swipe tore two bodyguards into slabs of meat that splashed into the stream like flabby red stones tumbled from the cliffs. Their blood swirled with the shepherd's and turned the brook crimson as it bubbled past Myna and Spaad.

Entrails and strings of blood still hung from the karakh's right hand as it lurched forward another step and impaled Storik on its bronze-bolted tusks. It shook its head like a dog shaking off water, and uttered more whines and clicks until the Chief Engineer and Chairman of NRI tumbled in two pieces among the corpses of his bodyguards. Spaad screamed and tried to run, but Myna grabbed him and pulled him down to her, holding him in a grip strong for such a small woman.

"Please don't leave," she whispered.

He stopped fighting her grip. It wasn't like he'd be able to outrun the thing. He might as well not die alone.

The remaining guards had come to no such conclusion and fled, two going up the path, one back the way they'd come. The karakh whistled a long squealing cry and bounded after the pair that had fled toward the waterfall, away and out of sight. A few seconds later, there was a man's scream, choked off, and another long low whistle, followed by the fading sound of snapping branches. Then silence.

Spaad and Myna lay cradling each other until long after it grew too dark to see anything but a few stars through the naked branches and wispy clouds, but the karakh didn't make any more noise and didn't come back.

Spaad, misinterpreting Myna's need for comfort as something more, began to nuzzle her neck, mumbling that she smelled like candles. She gently pushed him away and wiped the tears from her eyes.

Predawn light silhouetted the trees on the eastern ridge above them.

"Let's go back," she said, in a small voice.

And they did.

28

THE TRUTH

SYRINA HAD PLANNED TO HURT THE SHEPHERD enough that he and the karakh couldn't go on. She figured she had one clean shot at the karakh where she'd woven the snare out of the remains of the bridge she'd hacked down on the way north. After that, she was going to wing it and rub Storik among the charred ruins of the silos, whether the monster was still breathing down her neck or not. She decided there'd be plenty of opportunities for accidents among the broken machines of a navaras farm.

Now the voice was droning on about how lucky she was that it had panned out so much better than she'd expected. She even had Storik's personal secretary telling the story to anyone who'd listen, and nothing pointed to a Kalis. Accident achieved.

It didn't matter how lucky she was. She felt awful. She couldn't stop thinking that it hadn't worked out for the shepherd, or for that matter, the karakh, which had probably lay down to die somewhere and would spend its last days lonely and cold and filled with grief. The bodyguards, she could get over. They knew the risks going into that profession. But the mournful glitter in the karakh's eyes as it had looked at its dying shepherd haunted her, and behind them lurked memories of Triglav. The tears that Myna had wept that long night had been Syrina's own. The voice chided her and congratulated her and annoyed her, but it kept her focused enough to finish what she'd started. Still, her dreams grew darker and more haunted, full of fear she never knew when she was awake, and she was glad she couldn't remember them when she woke up. She was even more glad that she didn't need much sleep.

Ormo took the news cautiously. After all, no one could be sure Carlaas Storik had been Ma'is Kavik, and only time would tell if the other High Merchant would turn up again.

Syrina had her own ideas, and she was going to confirm them herself.

———

Storik. He'd had at least one Kalis working under him. All his unlikely power and connections. The contacts in Ristro. Every sign but one had pointed to Storik being Ma'is Kavik. And that sign was, if all signs pointed to someone being a High Merchant, then it was probably someone else.

There was only one other person involved on more points than Storik had been, and if nothing else pointed to the woman being a High Merchant, it made Syrina all the more sure she was.

She arrived at Ehrina Ka'id's a little after dark, but the days were still getting shorter, and the accountant's office was open for business. The woman was with a client—a businessman from Fom, which Syrina found ironic, and Syrina let them finish their conversation without eavesdropping. She went as herself. No need for disguises this time.

After a while, the N'naradin left, smiling to himself. Syrina hoped that meant Ka'id would be in a good mood, too.

Ka'id didn't look up from her desk until Syrina closed the door behind her. The accountant looked blank for a minute, until her gaze found the Kalis's, tried to focus, failed, and it dawned on her what she was looking at. She sat up straight and put her pen down, but her expression was calm as she found Syrina's eyes.

"I assume you're not here to kill me, or you wouldn't just be standing there."

"I just thought I'd let you know, I know who you are. Who you really are. Ma'is Kavik."

Syrina was prepared to look for a reaction under all the denial, but the accountant didn't argue. Ka'id was silent for a full minute, shifting in her seat, and laid her hands on the desk like she was showing Syrina that she wouldn't try anything. Her expression wasn't so much concerned as considering.

Then she said, "All right. Where does that leave us?"

Syrina decided that if Ka'id was buying time until a couple Kalis showed up to deal with her, they would've made an appearence by now.

"Ma'is Ormo is behind the recent... ugliness. At the moment, he thinks Kavik is dead. Use that however you want, but I thought you should know before you show up at the Equinox meeting in a few weeks. In case it's something you can use."

Ka'id was quiet another minute. Syrina could see the pieces falling into place behind her eyes.

The accountant nodded. "Storik."

Syrina nodded back, exaggerating the gesture so Ka'id could see it around the tattoos.

"Well, thank you." Ka'id paused, smiling at the answer she knew she would get before she asked the question. "I don't suppose you can tell me how you fit into all this."

Syrina grinned, knowing the other woman couldn't see it. "I don't think I could explain that if I wanted to."

EPILOGUE

"You have heard of Albertus Mann?" Ormo asked Syrina, three months after the death of Carlaas Storik.

She nodded where she stood at the base of his dais, an imperceptible gesture. "The General?" Sarcasm was clear in her voice.

Mann was an army general in a naval nation. An orphan boy from the Lip, taken in by the Grace herself. A figurehead the Church of N'narad could point to when they wanted a public example of how anyone might find glory in the quest for Heaven, and someone they could blame for all the things they screwed up. A reviled national hero.

"Yeah, I've heard of him."

"The Archbishop has entrusted him to collect some items of extreme interest to the Merchant's Syndicate, from a place in the Black Wall they believe they have discovered."

"Mann?" She couldn't hide her surprise. "Why him?"

Ormo didn't answer.

Syrina bit her tongue. "You want him rubbed?"

"No. Just watched. I will give you a list of contacts around Valez'Mui. New ones. I'm sure a few of your old ones are still around, too. They'll have hawks, or at least know the nests of some that are homed to Eheene. Contact me when you get there, and I'll send you further instructions. Mann is bringing an army, so I suspect you'll be able to arrive at the Yellow Desert well before he does."

"An army?" Syrina snorted.

Ormo rustled. "According to sources."

"What the hell does he need an army for?"

"That, my dear Kalis, you shall tell me."

"Ah, I see. Is that all?"

"For now."

Ormo watched the shadow of Kalis Syrina leave, his face clouded under the shapeless dark of his hood. He wondered what she was up to and whether it would've been better to have just finished her back when she'd escaped from his prison. Back when it would have been easy.

Her report about Storik hadn't added up, and however he thought about it, he came to the same conclusion. Kavik would always have at least one Kalis keeping an eye on him, just like any of the Fifteen. Maybe two or three on a trip north at harvest time. Even so, no Kalis had tried to save Storik from the karakh, and yet Ma'is Kavik hadn't been seen since.

The other Thirteen were already seeking a replacement, pleased they could gain a modicum of control over one of their most powerful members by picking his successor. But Ormo knew better. Kavik had either put everything together on his own, or Syrina had figured out who the High Merchant was and warned him, joining the traitor and turning on Ormo completely.

That Kavik could've figured it all out, down to which High Merchant was working against him, was impossible. Unless he'd just happened to have a complex operation going on against Ormo at precisely the right time. Syrina, on the other hand... Ormo thought of her, how she'd changed, and knew it was true. The thought of Syrina's betrayal made Ormo's heart hurt. She'd lost Triglav, but he'd lost her.

No. Not yet. He hardened himself. Told himself a rabid hound could still be useful if he was careful to point it in the right direction. The cold distance of the comparison eased him a little, almost burying the smoldering ember of loss in the pit of his stomach.

Ormo swallowed the despair and smiled, changing the black and white geometry painted on his face. He knew what Kalis Syrina wanted—to know herself. And with the Church's discovery in the Black Wall, maybe he could give that to her.

Until then, he wouldn't give up.

Dear reader,

We hope you enjoyed reading *The Kalis Experiments*. Please take a moment to leave a review, even if it's a short one. Your opinion is important to us.

Discover more books by R. A. Fisher at

https://www.nextchapter.pub/authors/ra-fisher

Want to know when one of our books is free or discounted? Join the newsletter at

http://eepurl.com/bqqB3H.

Best regards,

R. A. Fisher and the Next Chapter Team

———

You could also like:
The Fargoer by Petteri Hannila

To read the first chapter for free, head to:

https://www.nextchapter.pub/books/the-fargoer-
fantasy-set-in-historical-finland